A Gentleman's Reckoning

Jennie Goutet

Copyright

Copyright © 2025 by Jennie Goutet

All rights reserved.

No part of this book may be reproduced, stored in a retrieval system, or transmitted in any form or by any means — electronic, mechanical, photocopying, recording, or otherwise — without the prior written permission of the author, except for brief quotations used in reviews or scholarly works.

This is a work of fiction. Names, characters, places, and incidents are either the product of the author's imagination or used fictitiously. Any resemblance to actual persons, living or dead, events, or locales is entirely coincidental.

ISBN: 9782494930421

Human Authored™ Reg #: 5162340

This book is dedicated to my brother, Jeff Lawlis. I listened to the Rachmaninoff piano concertos while writing it and thought of you.

Prologue

November, 1816
Haymarket, London

"Aubin! Your toast?"

John Aubin turned to face his three friends who sat sprawled in their chairs with easy insouciance. Lord Stuart had a cigar balanced between two fingers, Sir Theodore paused in his act of taking snuff, and Fanning set down his cup of brandy in anticipation. John turned back and caressed the chin of the newly arrived lady of easy virtue, who was particularly easy on the eyes.

"Later," he mouthed with a lift of his eyebrows, and she offered a dimpled smile in return. He faced his friends with a broad grin. Putting a booted foot on his abandoned chair and leaning his elbow on one knee, he reached his other hand up and snapped his fingers. "A bottle of your finest champagne."

A servant hurried to do his bidding and, after opening the bottle with a muted *pop*, he poured the champagne into flutes, setting one in front of each of them. John lifted his glass, then, remembering the importance of the occasion, stood on both feet and waited for his friends to clamber to theirs. None of them were particularly steady.

"Gentlemen, when a man has the misfortune to lose four thousand pounds in a single night…" He paused and pointed at each of them in turn, laughter bubbling up in his chest. "And let that be a lesson to you to keep your head whilst playing cards, lest you fall into the same trap."

"We hear you, and we heed you," Fanning replied, with what soberness he could find within him.

"The toast?" Stuart prompted, his lazy eyebrow lifted.

"The toast," John repeated, clearing his throat. "And when another gentleman has the fortune to win those four thousand pounds in a single night through fair, honest play, then 'tis only *fair*…that the gentleman act bountifully toward the friends who have supported him throughout the evening, bringing sustenance and encouragement—"

"Aye, that be us," Theo said gravely.

"And so I lift this toast," John went on with an admonitory look at his friend who had just interrupted. "And with it a promise to share my fortune with all those in need—"

"That be us," Fanning said with an inebriated bout of delirium, and this time it was Stuart who silenced him with a look.

"Let us now drink to our good health, to the poor fellow who was foolhardy in his play, to the horses next week who will carry our luck further on the racetrack, and to this very fine bottle of champagne. I shall not consider the price but will only salute poor Barnsby in thanks and hope his descendants do not judge him too harshly. I certainly do not." A cackle of female laughter came from behind him, and he sent the two straw damsels a wink.

"I raise this toast to my excellent friends and declare, 'May Fortune favor us yet. To Fortune!'"

"To Fortune," came the cry.

"To us!" He lifted his glass as the others repeated, "To us!"

John's eyes smarted as he drank, and the bubbles came back up, causing him to cover his mouth with his sleeve. When he blinked and opened his eyes, the room seemed to grow obscure and the voices and sounds to blend into an unintelligible din. He blinked again and brought his eyes to the window, whose burgundy velvet curtains were open. The pinkish light of dawn appeared between the two houses on the opposite side of Haymarket Street.

Could it be dawn already? Granted, they had begun their game at five o'clock the afternoon before, but he had formed the vague idea that they had only just arrived at Mrs. Woodstone's establishment an hour ago. A thin vertical ray of yellow light pierced the dark space between the buildings, and he blinked against the sudden glare. A woman on the far side of youth went over and untied the curtains, drawing them closed. How could it be daybreak?

He brought his bleary regard back to his friends, who were now involved in their own pursuits of pleasure, having appeared to forget all about him. The sight of discarded glasses and melted lumps of wax on the table, another bout of raucous laughter from somewhere in the corner of the room, and his brief spell of victory so soon forgotten depressed him beyond measure. Ah, perhaps he was growing too old for such things. But no—twenty-eight was far from old. He was in the prime of youth!

John shook his head. It was the drink that was causing this maudlin attitude. He needed to sleep and perhaps eat something sustaining. He opened his mouth to inform his friends that he was leaving, but one glance at them told him they would not care. As he accepted his hat and cane from a servant, the lovely straw damsel came and linked her arm through his, peering up into his eyes. He smiled down at her, but it fell as he studied her unlined face. She looked too innocent for such a life.

"What is the matter, milord?" she asked him, though he was no lord.

He fixed his gaze on her for another moment before shaking his head. "There is nothing the matter with you. It is only I. Good day." He bowed and walked out into the street.

Haymarket was quieter at dawn than it was in the middle of the night, but it was never entirely still. Some, like him, were heading home after a night's debauchery. Other, more honest folk were setting up their wares to begin selling, one offering breads and rolls, another hot drinks, and still another meat pies. John began walking in the direction of Hanover Street and crossed a vendor selling both ale and gin from two barrels on his cart. The smell turned his stomach, and he hurried on.

It was a short walk to his rented lodgings, and before he reached it, he had already decided to leave for his brother's estate in Surrey—the estate that would soon be his. Perhaps the change would help him to be more worthy of the gift Gregory wished to bestow upon him. Lately, he had been unable to resist acts of folly and found himself burrowing more deeply into a troubled, wastrel existence. A sort of restlessness had seized him that he could not shake off, at least not while he was in London. The time to take a break from his current life was now. He would likely suffer for the journey after a night out, but perhaps he deserved any misery he brought upon himself. He could not say. The fresh air of the ride could only do him good, and even if he stopped at an inn to break his fast, he could accomplish the rest of the journey by noon.

An hour later, John had collected some basic necessities in a traveling portmanteau, had his horse saddled, and gave word to his servant to bring the rest to Westerly. He rode southward, and by the time he had navigated his way past the throng of people, carts, and livestock on the London Bridge, he had decided to stop at The George Inn in Southwark for a meal. He had always been well satisfied with his fare there. It was but a few streets more, and he was indeed feeling the effects of his intemperance by the time he reached it.

He swung down and handed the reins to an ostler, then went inside in search of a free table. Sinking down into an empty wooden bench by the window, he resisted the urge to put his head on his arms and fall asleep right there. Why had he not had the wisdom to simply stay in London and recover for a day or two there?

The inn was active, but not bustling. It was too early for it, he assumed. A servant came and took his order, which included strong coffee, bread, eggs, and fried ham. He tucked into the fare, his spirits lifting as the scent of delicious food teased his nostrils, and the hot, bitter brew revived him. Each bite seemed to restore him to health. The room brightened as the morning advanced in increments, and at last, he leaned back and tucked his hands into his waistcoat, satisfied.

"...discuss it here where it's quieter."

John looked through the window on his left where the voice came from, but he could not see anyone. The glazed window-panes were thin enough, but it was more likely the cracks along the window frame that carried the sound of voices as well as a stream of frigid air. The man outside took a step back, and John saw his fine-cut coat through the edge of the window.

"I have more invested in the steam-powered machinery than I would care to lose." The man speaking had the refined accent of a gentleman, and his words were easily distinguishable. "Although Perkins invested twenty-five percent, I invested forty. Therefore, I must cover my assets."

Perkins. Unless the man was referring to some lesser-known gentleman, Perkins was Lord Perkins, the earl. And this man spoke as though they were on intimate terms. John looked through the window again and now made out the shoulder and sleeve of a man's coat but it was not enough to identify him. He and his companion were standing along a stretch of wall between John's window and the one behind him and must not have imagined their words would carry. Or the gentleman thought that no one of consequence would be here to overhear the conversation at this hour.

"I need you to sell off my shares quietly," the voice continued. "Not everything at once, for that would look suspicious. Sell off thirty percent so that I only lose ten. Or thirty-five, if you can. My source in the Commons tells me the tax they plan to vote in will ruin all potential for gains."

"And should Parliament not levy the tax in the end? You will lose out on the shares you sold," the other man observed, his accent less refined, though educated.

"It doesn't matter that four years have passed; people still fear Luddite retaliation and will bow to their demands. There is no doubt those fools will vote for the tax," the first gentleman retorted, his tone revealing his tension. After a moment, he must have regretted the lapse, for he added in a more conciliatory voice, "But if by some miracle they don't, then I will still have benefitted from my more moderate investment."

"I hope so, my lord."

"We are agreed then. Look for someone to purchase the thirty percent minimum. He should be a businessman, not a gentleman. Someone who will not be able to harm my reputation once the money is lost. Do your best to make me appear innocent. You've done it before."

"Yes, my lord," the man repeated.

"Send written word to my Brighton address that Mr. Such-and-Such has requested to purchase my shares, so that it appears I did not seek the transaction. And move quickly. I was able to get a lead on the information before the other investors, but it will soon be common knowledge. I need to remove myself from London before it is."

"Yes, my lord."

John wondered who this *lord* might be. Despite his own questionable night, he was unimpressed with the man's way of throwing his peers under the wheels of their collective loss while seeking to minimize his own. He frowned as he fiddled with the knife on the table in front of him. That was the behavior of a scoundrel.

Just as he was debating whether he should lumber to his weary feet and head outdoors to try to catch sight of the peer, the man stepped backwards in front of the multi-paned glass, temporarily blocking the light. He was facing away, but his carved cane and signet ring were distinctive and identifiable this close to the glass. It was none other than Lord Goodwin, the earl who was known for his consistent attendance at church, curating investors to build a foundling asylum, and for his character upon which there was no smear. Well—almost no smear. There had been unfounded rumors that he had pocketed some of those investments, leaving the asylum in a state of disrepair, but those had been widely rejected as false. Now...

Lord Goodwin! Blast! Was there truly no righteous man in all of London?

John sat poised as he contemplated this development, wondering what he should do with the information. On one hand, he could not allow the earl to get away with such a scheme. But how was he to inform Lord Perkins or the other investors in these promissory notes without solid proof, other than what he had witnessed? John was a member of White's and Boodle's because his deceased stepfather had been one. He was generally well-liked but he was not a peer and was hardly a man they would listen to over an earl. If Lord Goodwin knew *he* was the one informing on him, John's own reputation would be in tatters.

Despite the dilemma this posed, and despite his own deplorable state, John knew he had only one option before him.

He must warn the other investors through the only one whose name he now knew. Perhaps he could request a private audience with Lord Perkins and tell him what he had learned, asking that he remain nameless. Of one thing he was sure: if he merely sent an anonymous letter, it would not be taken seriously, and they would all lose out. He would have to go and see the lord in person. Then, once the bill to impose the steam duty passed into law, the truth would back his claims. He would have Lord Perkins's gratitude with none the wiser.

These thoughts raced through his mind, and just as he came to the conclusion that he should not be sitting in plain sight in case the earl thought to look through the window, Lord Goodwin turned.

John froze in place, skewered by the earl's piercing regard, perfectly aware of the implications. He may have been young and of little consequence, but he spent half his time in the clubs, and the earl could not fail to recognize his face. It would be a simple matter to find out who he was. The face of Lord Goodwin that John had always thought benevolent now wore an icy expression of disdain as he glared at him. He touched his hat and turned away.

John leaned back in the hard booth, his head pounding in earnest. Why had he not simply stayed in London? Now, he was honor bound to inform Lord Perkins and everyone else what Lord Goodwin was planning. But he would not have the cloak of anonymity, for Lord Goodwin would know who had been the source.

His hope of a discreet word in Lord Perkins's ear was out. Instead, he was more likely to be stripped bare before the *beau monde*. Still—he had no choice but to go through with it.

Chapter One

April, 1817
Mayfair, London

"My lady, you wished to be woken at ten." Charity, maid to Lady Eugenia Stanich, hesitated, the curtain only partially open. "However, you'd be excused for staying abed, you would."

Geny shook her head, which sent a small throb of pain through it from fatigue. "No, for if I do not go, who will read to the orphans? I cannot allow society's amusements to keep me from doing what is most important."

Her maid opened the curtains wide and allowed the sun to stream into Geny's room of gold, white, and yellow. Normally the brilliance and the colors cheered her, but this morning they seemed almost an affront. She tossed the covers to one side and put her legs over the edge of the bed, refusing to give in to her exhaustion. After all, it was not often her father insisted she attend a ball that would last until the wee hours. She would like to attribute such delicacy to his abiding affection for her, but she feared it was more due to his distraction—that he had forgotten he had a daughter at all. That was, until he had a potential match he wished her to consider.

But perhaps that was unkind.

"I've brought you chocolate," her maid said as she went over to the wardrobe and began to sift through the gowns there.

Geny allowed her to choose one. After all, her maid had good taste in clothing, and she did not particularly care. She went over and sat in the chair in front of the dressing table where the chocolate was placed. Rarely did she take hers in bed. With each sip, thoughts of all there was to do flew through her mind, and it made her feel restless, as though she were wasting time even pausing to dress. The poor did not have a choice of whether they wished to take chocolate in bed or wake at the crack of dawn to begin work.

"I will lay out the blue cotton dimity." The maid performed the action as she spoke, then came over to brush her hair.

Geny took another sip of the sweet chocolate and wished it were tea. Charity separated the strands of her hair and pinned them in the modest, plain style Geny favored.

"Miss Buxton's maid has gone sweet on Jimmy what works in the Buxton stable."

"Is that so?" Geny was not particularly interested in gossip, but her maid's was never unkind, and it soothed her to listen to someone prattle. Goodness knew the house was quiet enough in the years since her mother had died.

"'Tis. He wants to offer for her, she says, but Mr. Buxton doesn't take kindly to his maids finding husbands."

"Not many employers are in favor of their servants marrying." She glanced up at Charity in the mirror, a smile hovering on her lips. "And you? Have you found a sweetheart?"

The maid returned an inelegant snort. "My lady knows I'm not likely to attract a husband."

It was true that with her bulbous nose and thick features, Charity would easily be overlooked as a candidate for marriage, even though her spirit was beautiful. Fortunately, her maid had told her she was perfectly happy remaining single. And Geny had no desire to lose her.

Charity made quick work of her hair and helped Geny into her stays and gown. It was early enough in the spring that she put on her velvet-lined bonnet and warmer pelisse. The ride to Bloomsbury was sometimes as long as an hour when the roads were congested, and as they went, the chilly air tended to seep into the carriage. Once they were on their way, her maid fell silent, allowing Geny to entertain her own thoughts. She needed this time of solitude, for once she arrived at the foundling asylum, there would be little rest. Each week, she taught her own class and on other days assisted in others; she gently admonished younger orphans who disobeyed the rules and welcomed visitors interested in seeing how the asylum worked—or those desiring to see how their donations had been put to use.

Geny wished her father had continued his interest in the asylum, for that might have brought them closer. She believed the earl had begun it with a good heart. He staffed his house with those who had been trained in the asylum, Charity being a perfect example of this. But even before Geny's mother died five years ago, the earl had already begun to show less interest in the orphans. After her mother was gone, he showed none whatsoever. Not only did he never step foot in it, he gave full control to his agent, Mr. Peyton, to oversee its running. Until last week, Jacob Biggs had served as steward, and when the orphanage had grown large enough, Mr. Dowling was retained as headmaster. It was he who placed the orphans who had completed their training, hiring them out to various London establishments. Everything had run smoothly until Mr. Biggs announced it was time he retired from his position as steward. Now, change was inevitable.

The carriage pulled into the covered opening of the

foundling asylum—a large, brick building with windows in every room. The structure formed a square with a courtyard in the middle, spacious enough for a stable and small garden for those being trained in the outdoor professions. Behind them, the iron gates clanged shut, and when the carriage came to a halt, Geny opened the door rather than waiting to be assisted.

The cold air assaulted her cheeks and brought with it a barely discernible smell of earth and spring. At the moment, only two boys were visible in the plot of land, crouched down in the thawing mud to weed around the shoots. Other boys were training as stable hands or as caretaker of the asylum's small number of livestock. Charity crossed the courtyard to go to the kitchen where she would visit with old friends and assist where she could.

From inside the asylum came sounds of life as children of different ages carried on the responsibilities they were being trained for. Older girls watched over the small children and babies, learning to care for them and feed them. Others were engaged in spinning wool or needlework. Children of both sexes were employed in the kitchens and would rise to positions according to their ability. Geny's friend Margery Buxton had told her it was all quite progressive, and she had to agree.

Simply walking through the asylum's orderly rooms brought her satisfaction. It also consoled her, both in her ongoing grief at having lost her mother and her sorrow at bidding farewell to her ten-year-old brother, Matthew, who had returned to Eton. Or—if she were being precise—Lord Caldwell, Viscount Fernsby and heir to the Earl of Goodwin. The father Geny rarely saw these days.

She stepped into the entrance and strode toward the corridor where a group of girls in pinafores hurried forward, stifling their laughter. They nearly ran into her and stopped short, throwing their hands over their mouths to cover their exuberance.

"I'm sorry, my lady," the girls murmured, dipping into curtsies.

"Have a care, girls," Geny said, hiding her own amusement with a stern expression. They saw right through it, however, and she heard the escape of hushed giggles as they continued past her.

She delighted in their youthful spirit and joy, knowing they were well looked after in the asylum. They would have found little to laugh over had they been left on the streets. However, it was important to train them to be discreet if they were to be employable. The asylum must be known for the quality of its trained help so it might continue to attract donors.

Geny went into the office she shared with the head matron and set down the wicker basket she had brought with her. The head matron came from an adjoining room and dipped into a curtsy.

"Good day, my lady." Mrs. Hastings dressed soberly, with no frills or color. Geny suspected she would have done so no matter what her station was in life, for she did not possess a ready sense of humor. The earl had approved her position, and there was no need to change it, of course. But Geny would have preferred for the children to receive more warmth from a head matron.

"Good day, Mrs. Hastings. I have brought the new stockings for the children that Miss Buxton and I made."

"They are fortunate to have you dote on them, my lady." She arranged the books on her desk in a neat stack. "Mr. Rowles, who has come to take over the steward's role, is waiting to speak with Mr. Dowling." Mrs. Hastings indicated the meeting room with a dip of her chin. "I told him he was early, and that Mr. Dowling wasn't expected for another hour."

Geny's first thought was that she would regret Mr. Biggs's departure. At the very beginning, there had been a nasty rumor spread about that the investments her father had solicited from his peers had not been wisely put to use. After the initial pledges, the donations had trickled down to nothing. If it had not been for Mr. Biggs's work to disprove the rumor—and a large donation from Mrs. Buxton, the wealthy wife of a ceramics merchant—the asylum might not still be functioning. Geny had trusted Mr. Biggs with the smooth running of the asylum, and it was important to find someone equally as trustworthy.

She also wondered why Mr. Dowling was late. It had happened more than once, and she was beginning to think she should speak to him about it. Although she was a woman, and therefore stripped of the power to make decisions, she *was* the daughter of an earl. Not only that—it was her father's asylum. That meant she could meet this Mr. Rowles and assess his qualifications for herself before Mr. Dowling made his own determination.

"I will meet Mr. Rowles." Geny had not yet removed her bonnet or pelisse and did so now before retrieving her basket.

"You, my lady?" Mrs. Hastings sounded disapproving. "If you wish, I can accompany you."

"Nonsense," Geny said cheerfully. "I am not fresh out of the schoolroom. I have been accustomed to volunteering in all aspects of the asylum for the past three years, and in a limited capacity for the three years before that. Who better to meet this new hire than I, if Mr. Dowling is not here to do it?"

She walked into the next room, which was used as an informal parlor, then continued on to the larger room nestled at the end of the offices. This served as a board room or meeting place for anyone visiting on official business. Her breath had quickened from the pace she'd set, but she was also aware that the change in personnel was making her nervous. The asylum was the one place she found peace and order—where she had a part in bringing goodness and light into a shadowed, tumultuous world. Her mother had made the orphanage the bright place it was, and it was all she had left of her mother.

Geny opened the door and turned to close it behind her, hearing the chair scrape as the visitor came to his feet. She turned back just as he stood upright, and her breath left her at once.

This...this specimen of masculine attractiveness standing before her was nothing less than a gentleman of the *ton*. Surely he must be! There was nothing flashy about his appearance—on the contrary, it could only be described as understated. Yet, it was evident in his bearing, his attire, even the jaunty expression that lurked underneath his serious demeanor. If the close fit of his coat was any indication, he was a Corinthian to boot. Surely his life must consist of clubs and...well, whatever other less savory pastimes such gentlemen engaged in, not that she would know. Thank goodness her father was above such things. And yet, if he was a gentleman, why was he *here*? He would have had a formal education, but no gentleman of birth would apply for a steward's position in a foundling asylum.

Mr. Rowles bowed. "Good day, Miss...?"

He paused, and she realized she was staring. Her manners had fled.

"Lady Eugenia," she corrected. "Good day, Mr. Rowles. Please, resume your seat." She gestured to his chair and took the one across the table. Not directly across, for that seemed too intimate. The table was not wide.

"My lady," he murmured before sitting again. His brow had wrinkled, and he seemed as much at a loss as she was.

Mr. Rowles was likely not accustomed to dealing with women in such a capacity, but he would soon learn that she cared too much for the children to give up her active interest in the asylum. As for her, she was struggling to make sense of who he was. Not once had she imagined a gentleman applying for the role of steward—and such a distinguished one at that. It was as though a member of the *ton* had come calling here in the orphanage. It was out of place.

"I understand you are here to serve in the capacity of steward for the asylum's financial and daily operations," she began in a brisk tone. It would be better to direct them to the matter at hand without delay. "What experience do you have to recommend you in assuming this role?"

He looked at her oddly, and she could easily guess why. He wondered what she, an earl's daughter, was doing taking a hand in the inner workings of the orphanage. It was one thing to volunteer. Many gently bred women did that. But to interview him as though he—a man—were her inferior? It was not as though Mr. Peyton had not already interviewed him for the position. But she would not back down. This was her orphanage. Or, more accurately, it was her father's, and it had been a project close to her mother's heart. She would not let it be run into the ground because some gentleman had decided to take over the operations for a lark. It would not surprise her in the least if that was what this was.

"I have served as steward to a gentleman's estate," he answered at last.

So, he was *not* a gentleman. How was it then that he looked so much like one? His gaze remained unwaveringly upon hers as he replied, and she had to fight the urge to lower her eyes.

"If you held such an honorable position, why have you sought and accepted this one?" she asked. She did not mean to sound accusatory, but it was a curious thing to give up the running of a gentleman's estate to work in a foundling asylum, unless it was because...

"Was the estate solvent?"

A hint of a smile—a scant turning up of the lips—appeared on his face. It was so brief she almost missed it, but it made Mr. Rowles more attractive—dangerously so, she admitted to herself, if she were to be in his presence on a regular basis. It should not even be a consideration for she was so far above him in station, but she *was* a woman.

"I assure you, Lady Eugenia, I left the estate entirely solvent and in the capable hands of the next steward. I have not come from ruining one gentleman's estate with the intention of repeating the blunder with your asylum. I hope that reassures you of my capacity—*and* my intentions."

She did not trust him.

Geny allowed her gaze to drop, resisting the urge to fidget, then brought it steadily back to his. She would ask the question that was foremost in her mind. "May I ask why you wish to take on the position of steward here if you had an estate to run, which must surely be a more satisfactory—and better-paid—position? It hardly seems logical."

He spread his hands briefly, then interlaced his fingers on the table. "Let us just say that I wish to take on this position for personal reasons. When I spoke with Mr. Peyton, I was under the impression that my skills would be welcome." He left the rest unsaid. That he had not expected to be grilled as soon as he entered the premises.

"You must understand, Mr. Rowles. My father began the foundling asylum"—she paused briefly when she saw the flash of surprise on his face—"and it was of particular interest to my late mother. I am intimately involved in every aspect of the orphanage."

"Your father, then, is…"

"The Earl of Goodwin." He had not known her father was Lord Goodwin, she realized. This relieved her mind of one thing at least. He had not come in hopes of worming his way into her father's good graces by taking a position in the orphanage. That would make for a nice change.

"I see."

He dropped his own gaze and appeared to be reflecting upon her revelation. She had the odd impression that this point was not in her favor. But surely he had taken the time to discover who had founded the asylum? It was well-known, and it was natural that the man's daughter would volunteer her time here.

A new worry assailed her. Mr. Rowles had nothing against the earl, she hoped. Her father had not been the same since her mother died. He had never been a particularly doting husband or father, but he was a good man, and had been a faithful husband. However, she saw so little of him now, she did not know what occupied his time.

"My lady, I wish to set your mind at ease regarding my presence here. My intention is to continue the regular functioning of the asylum and ensure that not a shilling is wasted. I am here to improve it, if it can be improved."

That was a reassuring statement to make, even if there was something odd about mentioning wasted shillings which disconcerted her, considering the early rumors. She hoped Mr. Rowles did not know more on the matter than he was letting on.

"Very well." When she realized there was nothing more for her to say, she stood. "Mr. Dowling will wish to meet you as soon as he arrives. You will find your office by entering the corridor through this door. It is the one on the far end. The other one is for Mr. Dowling. In the meantime, if you require anything, you need only ask Mrs. Hastings."

"Thank you." The visitor bowed, and she allowed herself one last glance at his handsome face. He was an enigma, but that need not be a bad thing. If only he would be good at his duties, that was all that was needed.

Geny left through the same door she had indicated then turned in the direction of the stairwell and went to the classroom that held the five children learning to read. She should not own to having favorites, but she did feel the happiest on Mondays when she taught this class.

"Lady Geny," Samantha cried out as soon as she saw her. She

curtsied with clumsy grace, her face split in a smile that revealed four missing teeth in front. Only the bottom ones had begun to grow back in. The four other children, three girls and one boy, also greeted her with curtsies, a bow, and obvious signs of pleasure.

"Good morning, Samantha," she said, smiling back at her before turning to greet Anne, Lacy, Martha, and Jack in turn.

She set her basket down on the small table in front of the modern blackboard that had been set up. The six chairs had already been pulled into a circle, and they eagerly sat, each darting their eyes to the basket, knowing that sometimes treats would be hidden inside. Today was one of those days.

After taking a seat, she announced that they would begin by reciting the poem they had learned last week. After that, they would have a chance to write on the blackboard to practice their letters.

"I have a piece of chalk for each of you to use today," she announced, and the children looked at each other with shy smiles of awe. This was why she loved them so much. Six was such a sweet age, and every day she delighted in the fact that they were safe in the orphanage and would hopefully never know hunger or want again.

They began.

> *Tyger! Tyger! burning bright.*
> *In the forest of the night,*
> *What immortal hand or eye*
> *Could frame thy fearful symmetry?*

THEY FALTERED OFTEN, BUT SHE SMILED HER ENCOURAGEMENT and urged them on. Mrs. Hastings did not approve of her teaching them poetry, and it was true that they needed nothing more than the simple ability to read and write, and to learn a trade. But it was much easier to entice them to learn a string of words if they realized that the string revealed something interesting. And if she had thought Jack to be the only one interested in Mr. Blake's poem, she was proven wrong. Even Samantha pronounced all the *S's* and *th's* with gusto, ignoring her lisp.

They went from reciting to writing their letters, and Geny lost track of the time. She was only brought back to it by the appearance of Mr. Dowling in the doorway.

"Lady Eugenia," he greeted, before stepping into the room and bowing. He turned to the children. "You will find that there is soup for you in the dining hall. You may go and eat it now." The children scrambled to their feet, preparing to leave, but he put up a hand. "Do not forget to take leave of Lady Eugenia."

At their looks of chagrin, she sent them a reassuring smile and reached for the basket. "You must not go off without taking the warm stockings Miss Buxton and I have knitted for you."

"Lor', miss." Samantha's eyes grew wide as she looked at the stockings Geny held in her hands. She corrected herself hastily. "Lor', my lady."

"Do not say, 'lor'," Samantha. You must simply say, 'thank you, my lady.' Here is your pair of stockings. And here are yours." She handed one to each of them, including a gray pair for Jack. "Put them in your boxes with your other articles. Mrs. Hastings knows I am to give them to you, so your house maid and master will not be surprised to see them there."

With enthusiastic expressions of thanks, they ran off cradling their treasures, and she turned to Mr. Dowling. "I could not let them continue in the ripped and dirty stockings they have on now."

"Of course you could not. You are much too kind, my lady." He looked at her fondly, which always caused her to grow tense. She knew he harbored feelings for her, although he never went above his station and gave them voice. She was grateful for this reserve, for she did not return those feelings. She had long suspected he had merely taken the role in the asylum because of the earl's connection to it rather than any charitable instincts.

He turned to walk beside her. "The new steward has arrived."

"Yes, we have met." She glanced at Mr. Dowling. "What do you think of him?"

He went silent for a moment as he knit his brows. "I find him to be a puzzle. Why would he leave such a distinguished position only to accept one here? It is unusual."

"I agree," she said. Then, out of a strange reluctance to alienate Mr. Rowles without giving him a chance—or to align herself too closely with Mr. Dowling—she went on. "However, it is not unusual for a man to wish to serve in some capacity for a benevolent organization. He said he has personal reasons for doing so, and I will give him the benefit of the doubt."

"You are very gracious, my lady," Mr. Dowling said, attempting to catch her eye. She kept hers trained forward. "You need not fear, however. If there is anything out of the ordinary, I will surely discover it and bring it to your attention."

"Thank you." Geny's reply was clipped. It was just this sort of thing that made her keep Mr. Dowling at arm's length, despite their acquaintance that was above two years. In him was a mix of condescension and obsequiousness that bothered her—such as hinting that she required his assistance on any matter concerning the asylum workers. She did not.

They climbed the stairs to the cluster of offices where she would retrieve her pelisse before returning to her home on Upper Brook Street, and he would go on for his midday meal. Perhaps it was to put Mr. Dowling in his place that she did so, but Geny stopped in front of the doorway to the steward's office. Mr. Rowles looked up from the ledger he was reading, and when he saw her, quickly stood.

"I am leaving, Mr. Rowles," she said. "I hope you find your

first day to your liking." The beat of silence that followed was one of surprise, evident in his eyes. She had surprised herself.

"Thank you." He bowed. "I am certain I will. Good day, my lady."

She smiled and turned away, acknowledging Mr. Dowling with a nod from where he had paused at the entrance to his own office. "Good day, Mr. Dowling."

She moved at a sedate pace, retrieving her pelisse and bonnet and going down to the courtyard, although there was something in her that wanted to run. She rarely had that urge now that she was a woman grown, but there it was, urging her in her breast the entire way down the steps. *Hurry! Leave! Before even you know what it is you are feeling.*

Chapter Two

John stared after the departing figure of Lady Eugenia and then at the empty doorway once she had gone. It had been a shock to discover that she volunteered at the earl's charity. After having raised the capital to begin the foundling asylum, Lord Goodwin had tapered off his involvement. Following the death of Lady Goodwin, it had dwindled to nothing. The light digging John had done into the institution had been enough to tell him that. But no one had thought to mention that the earl's daughter spent her time assisting at the orphanage, and apparently did so on a regular basis.

That had been his first shock. His second had been the cordial way in which she had taken leave of him. She had not been so during their brief interview, and the last thing he expected was for her to return and bid him farewell. John had taken her for the frigid sort, especially after having learned she was Lord Goodwin's daughter. He should have known her parentage from the moment he had first set eyes on her. She had an air of her father, particularly in her bearing. And although she had still appeared cold when she bid him farewell, the action was not of one who had no finer feelings.

He brought his eyes back to the ledgers in front of him. At last, he had achieved his ambition to secure a place in the orphanage the Earl of Goodwin had established seven years hence. It was a start toward repairing his reputation with the *ton* and had only taken five months to bring into effect. After having witnessed the earl's meeting with the courier that ill-fated morning, he had correctly read the expression in Lord Goodwin's eyes: *If you indeed overheard what I think you did, then you had best keep it to yourself, or there will be consequences.* Well, John had been foolish enough *not* to keep it to himself. No, what had he done? He abandoned his idea of driving to his brother's estate and instead returned to London. The very next day, he had gone straight to Lord Perkins's house to disclose what he had seen.

Lord Perkins believed the assurances of his friend the peer, of course, not some young upstart who was nothing but a commoner. The rejection had not been immediate, but John felt the frost of it even before the invitations began to drop off. And then, not only did Parliament shoot down the proposed bill to raise steam duty taxes, there was a post-war boom in trade that led to high profit margins for those who invested in steam-powered machines. So Lord Goodwin's evil intentions of pawning off bad investments were never exposed. Instead, he loudly regretted having sold off thirty percent of his investment and looked upon others with a saintly expression of regret—and had John shunned from society. White's was the first to inform him that he would not be welcome there. Boodle's was next. And then two of his friends gave him the cut direct on Bond Street. Lord Stuart had already left for his estate, and John hadn't dared to seek him out to see what reception he might receive from him. Stuart was the highest-ranking of his friends and the biggest stickler for good *ton*.

That had been over three months ago; his life had since changed, and not for the better. After having spent the holidays and early winter on his brother's estate, he resolved to find out if Lord Goodwin could be charged with bad dealings in other areas. Since John was closed out of every social circle that might allow him to obtain this information, the asylum was quite literally the only area left to him. Any twinge of conscience that he should not be looking for revenge in an orphanage he covered with the consolation that if Lord Goodwin had kept any of the investment money for himself, John would be bringing good to the orphans rather than harm by exposing it. If he could take down Lord Goodwin at the same time, all the better. He was not entirely comfortable with his decision to use his unknown birth father's name instead of his stepfather's who had adopted him. But he could not see that he had any choice in the matter.

Mr. Dowling entered his office without knocking. "How are you getting on, Rowles? Are you finding everything?"

John lifted his eyes. The question had been politely worded, except for the familiar nature in which Mr. Dowling left off the honorific of "mister." He had already taken Mr. Dowling's measure. This was a lower-status gentleman who wished to show his superiority to anyone he thought beneath him. Besides despising such things, John was not accustomed to having to report to anyone. The agent who hired him had told him that the position would largely be an independent one. He would report back to Mr. Peyton's office and not to a senior officer. Certainly not to Lord Goodwin, which had been his fear.

"Thus far I am. I have only just begun, however." He offered a polite smile that made it clear he was not interested in building a relationship, especially with one he would be forced to see every day and was not sure he liked.

Taking the hint, Mr. Dowling replied, "Of course," before leaving to enter his own office.

It was not like John to be unamiable, but his misfortune had changed that. Besides, he suspected Dowling was a mushroom. He did not need any social climbers in his entourage, even though it would not be apparent to anyone that he was someone worth seeking an acquaintance with. For another thing—and this had been hard to bear—it would be better not to make any friends in the asylum at all. He was not ready to have anyone else shun him once his reputation came to light. He hoped it would not in this smaller sphere, but one never knew.

And then there was Lady Eugenia.

John focused his eyes on the numbers, refusing to think of her and what her presence in the asylum might mean. Perhaps her father was not quite as hands-off as he had thought and would soon appear at the orphanage. After all, how could he let his daughter go to the asylum unattended? Leaning back in his chair, John lifted his eyes to the walls, which were bare. In the corner was a door to a closet that would need straightening from what his quick look had informed him. And there was a narrow table on the other wall to his right, next to the window. From what he had seen of this and the other rooms thus far, the interior of the orphanage was shabbier than what one might expect for a charitable institution that bore Lord Goodwin's name. The window overlooked the courtyard, and he stood and went over to it.

Some of the older orphans were grooming the horses in front of the stable under the watchful eye of the groom. In the plot of earth beyond the cobblestones, other boys worked the soil in preparation for planting. This plot of land sat in front of another section of the building where he could see benches and tables through the stretch of windows. Then, from a room on the far corner, sounds of clanging and smoke issuing from a pipe in the brick wall indicated the kitchen, and the smell of bread that reached him even from across the courtyard confirmed it. Surprisingly, there was something in the sight of such activity that soothed the pressure he had been carrying—even from before his disastrous run-in with Lord Goodwin. He didn't know why that was.

Perhaps it was the safe, orderly routine that gave the young children the best hope they could strive for, given their lot in life. This struck a personal chord. John's mother was a gentleman's daughter with no close relations, and his father a gentleman. His late father had not been wealthy, however, and his death had left his mother destitute. In fact, if his mother had not remarried Maxwell Aubin, John's own fate might not have been any better than these boys'. The asylum's structure and routine more closely resembled a boarding school in its focus on order and training, though he was unsure if they were taught any skills other than what they were apprenticing for. Reading, writing, and sums, for instance—would anyone teach them those?

He went back to his desk and resumed his seat in front of the most recent ledger, attempting to focus on the numbers and connect them to the expenses, but there was nothing immediately evident to indicate foul play. What madness had he taken on? Did he expect to find something on the first day and be able to resign his position? John tightened his lips, irritated at himself. Yes, that was precisely what he had hoped for. When would he stop being so rash?

As long as he was here, though, he might as well do some good. Perhaps there were areas of the asylum that required better management than what it had thus far received. The walls might be brightened with a coat of paint as a start. He would do his best while he was here. After all, he had not been entirely fabricating his claim about serving as steward to a gentleman's estate. Murray had certainly trained him thoroughly enough in the two years he had worked on his brother's estate. That decision had been satisfactory to everyone concerned, especially once his elder brother made the decision to give Westerly to John. He would need to know how to run it.

John left the orphanage at the close of the day. It was an odd feeling to hold a position as though he were an ordinary citizen and not a gentleman. He had enough to live on with the four thousand pounds he had won from Jack Barnsby—another act that his conscience did not quite sit comfortably with, since he had ruined the man. It had gone far beyond a friendly game of cards between gentlemen, and he should never have let it go so far. He had been egged on by friends, and drunk on spirits and his winning streak. But all that was in the past. What could he do about the matter now?

Besides his own fortune, it would not be long before he was in possession of the income from Gregory's estate. His elder brother was in the process of legally turning over Westerly to John in order to live a quiet life in West Riding with his wife, and act as rector of the local parish. They had been unable to have children and had no need of an inheritance, and his brother Greg had decided *he* would make a better landed gentleman. Whether this were true, John was not sure, but as he soon would be one, it was only natural that he should feel the constraints of his current position as steward.

At last he was able to flag down a hackney cab, and he gave him his direction in Chelsea before climbing into it. The interior was shabby and smelled of laborers, reminding him of how far he had fallen. The days of freedom and seeking his own pleasure were gone. He couldn't live by his whim—heading to Tatts if he wanted to look over the horses there, whether or not he had any intention of buying one. There was no wandering into one of the clubs to see what sorts of games the gentlemen had going on there. And there was no point in going to the opera at night, for it would only involve facing all of society and watching them turn away, one by one. For heaven's sake, none of the society matrons of note would extend him an invitation to their gatherings, even when they were desperate for single gentlemen with good prospects. He knew this without having applied to them.

Chelsea was a fashionable area for the younger set and for nobles wishing to play at the artistic lifestyle. Few knew him there, for he lived on the fringes and avoided places where the more fashionable might frequent. John stepped down in front of his rented lodging and paid the driver his fare, then climbed the steps just as a strange man was stepping out of the front door. There were only two other rented rooms, but John knew who lived in them, and he did not recognize him as one of the lodgers.

The man stopped short and touched his cap. "Do I have the pleasure of addressing Mr. John Aubin?"

"You do," John said, cautiously. He was reluctant to use his last name, now that he had given a different one to the orphanage. And although he would, of course, proudly admit to the Aubin name, he was not lately in the habit of this being well received.

"I've just left a card with your servant but now appear to be in luck since you've come yourself. Name's Ronald Sacks, and I work for Lord Blackstone. I was wondering if I might have a word?"

John climbed two steps until he faced him, all the while cogitating on what he should do. His late interactions with society were prone to bad news, so why should this be different? Although, he supposed, if the man wished to harm him, he was more likely to have waited for him at night and pulled him into an alley.

"May I ask what this is about?"

"Nothing of an unpleasant nature." The man waited patiently, and John threw caution to the wind.

"Very well. Follow me." John stepped past him, opened the

door, and began to climb the stairs to his living quarters. The rooms were cleaned and chimneys swept by a maid, and hot meals were offered for the price of seventeen shillings a week. For the rest, he had a servant who performed the basic services of valet and footman combined.

He opened the door, and Owen hurried forward to take his hat and cane. His valet raised his eyes as the visitor stepped in behind John.

"I was to give you his card, sir, but I see that he has returned."

"Indeed. We will sit in the parlor." His rooms took up the entire floor and consisted of two bedrooms, a small sitting room, a more formal parlor for guests, and a servants' quarters where Owen could heat water and prepare the most basic refreshments, such as coffee and tea.

John divested himself of his cloak and gestured for the man to precede him into the parlor. He did not have the look of a gentleman, but Sacks was representing a peer. And until he knew what the man wanted, he would not offer refreshments—especially when he looked more like he would appreciate a glass of ale at the local pub over a fine glass of claret.

When they were both seated, John lifted both hands in a gesture to invite him to begin.

Sacks shifted more comfortably in his seat, not looking particularly ill at ease in addressing a gentleman. "Lord Blackstone understands that you have been blackballed from White's and Boodle's, and he wishes to offer you a proposition." It was a blunt way to come to the point.

"Is that so?" John hardly knew what to think. The last thing he might expect was for someone to seek him out *because* he had been blackballed. It could not be for any good purpose. "I do not know Lord Blackstone."

"Few do," Sacks replied, with what seemed almost a cheerful air. "He is a viscount. Has an estate in Norwich, but he was blackballed from three clubs years ago. A bit eccentric, he is—it did not worry him a bit, and my lord befriends those who had been blackballed or barred from entering other clubs." He paused before adding, "Provided the reason was not too shocking, mind you."

"And he deems my reason for being blackballed not too shocking?" John asked, in spite of himself. He had a strange urge to laugh.

"I assume so. He generally has a keen eye for those he chooses to reach out to, but you'll have to ask him that for yourself. His lordship does not confide in me."

John felt a rush of some emotion that was too complex to identify, but it seemed to spell out hope that he might have a friend in this world. He would still need to be cautious, for he did not know who Lord Blackstone was. But it had been months since anyone had treated him with a degree of openness and decency.

"You may tell Lord Blackstone that I would be glad to meet him."

Sacks pulled out a card from the pocket of his simple brown waistcoat. "I left my card with your servant, but I was instructed to give you Lord Blackstone's if you agreed to it. Here is the direction to where he stays. Just hand the footman there your card and you will be admitted. Say—any afternoon next week?"

John stood. "I have started a new project but I believe I can come on Friday afternoon, once I've had some time to grow comfortable in my work."

Sacks stood as well and put his hat on his head. "Then I will tell his lordship to expect you on Friday."

Chapter Three

The idea to use some donated cloth to create curtains for the orphanage classrooms had seized Geny the night before as she was falling asleep. It would keep out the drafts while giving the drab rooms a more cheerful aspect. She was plying her needle to this end the next morning when her father entered the drawing room.

"Good morning, Eugenia." He scarcely gave her time to respond before he said, "I came to inform you that I will be leaving for Windsor today. I will be gone for two weeks."

"Will you?" Her disappointment at having to bear an empty house again was tempered by the knowledge that his estate was not far from Eton. Perhaps she might go with him. "Do you plan to visit Matthew then? May I accompany you? I won't be a bother." She hated how desperate she sounded, but the idea of being able to see Matthew was too tempting not to make the push.

"No, it is impossible. We must not allow your brother to interrupt his studies, and he will not thank you for coddling him in front of his classmates."

"No, of course not," she replied, cast down by the immediate rejection. Her father was likely right, even though Matthew had not managed to convince her that he was happy at school the last time he came home for break. And, she supposed, it would be best if she did not interrupt her lessons at the orphanage.

"Besides," her father added, "I have much business to attend to. It will inconvenience me to have you at the estate."

Geny flushed. "I see." She should have been used to his careless barbs by now, but somehow they still stung.

Her father recommended she visit the Elgin Marbles, newly showing at the British Museum, so she could follow the latest topic of conversation in society. He then informed her that the Duke of Rigsby's son would be coming to London, and that he expected them to meet. She must not delay in settling down before she got too old to be desirable, and the marquess was a worthy prospect. With these injunctions, he took leave of her.

She sat lost in thought, the blue hessian curtains on her lap and her industrious spirit temporarily spent. His recommendation to visit the Elgin Marbles had been benign; she never worried beforehand about what she would speak about in society. It was the knowledge that she would eventually have to endure a meeting with His Grace's son. *Lord Amherst, I think it is.* All she remembered about him was that he had small eyes and fleshy jowls, and that his conversation revolved around hunting and eating. She picked up her needle again and tried to put aside the mood of despondency that had come over her.

Later that afternoon, Geny was at home and in sore need of divertissement when Margery Buxton came to visit. Margery often came on Tuesday afternoons, as her socially active mother considered the weekends to start on Wednesday evenings, and Margery required Mondays to recover from them. She wasn't in the least bit feeble but cheerfully labeled herself a most indolent creature. Despite her declaration, Geny could rely upon Margery's help in whatever sewing or knitting project she had decided upon for the orphans.

"I have had tea prepared," Geny said, looking up at her friend with a smile. "And you are perfectly on time, for it is hot and brewed and ready to be poured."

"I have exceptional timing when it comes to tea." Margery removed her cloak and handed that to the servant, then sat on the sofa across from Geny as she removed her bonnet. The tip of her nose was still red from the cold, and her cheeks bloomed with health. Although Margery lived on the fringe of society—brought only into that august sphere by her wealth—she was universally declared a beauty, with hair so blonde it was almost white and a curvaceous figure more suited to the fashions of the last century than the clinging Grecian gowns society women wore now. Even her brown eyes were called luminous and said to be an advantage.

Geny set her sewing on her lap and reached for the teapot. Placing her fingers on the lid, she poured hot tea into a cup for Margery and one for herself. As Margery spooned two generous helpings of sugar into her tea, Geny observed her friend, a smile playing on her mouth. She had just remembered their last conversation.

"What is it?" Margery demanded once she was aware of being observed. Her voice trembled with laughter, as though she already knew what Geny was thinking.

Geny shook her head, still smiling. "I am thinking of poor Mr. Bunting, who must be nursing his broken heart." At Margery's indignant look, she rushed on. "I know, I know. He was not the husband for you, so I do not tease. But I have been wondering how long you will keep at arm's length those who are smitten by you before one of them pushes through your defenses."

"There is truly not a one who interests me," Margery declared, stirring her tea and setting down her spoon with a flourish. "I do not wish to lose my independence. Nor do I want to marry a man who is in pursuit of another possession."

Geny's smile faded as quickly as it had come. In many ways, she agreed. They hadn't spoken about marriage since the season began—only about undesirable suitors. Though she harbored similar fears to Margery, she had the desire to find a worthy husband with whom she would be comfortable and perhaps even find love. Anything must be better than the unbearable loneliness of life in her father's house.

"You are just as aware of the risks of a poor match as I am," Margery said, reading her mind. She reached out for her tea and this time took a sip. "I wish the world was at our feet."

"Isn't it?" Geny asked, thinking of the orphans who would likely prefer a life of drinking tea and doing needlework than worrying about what situation they would gain and how they would be treated there.

Margery shook her head decisively. "It is not. We are pretty birds held captive, and the dealer haggles our price. We will be sold to the highest bidder."

"You are a poet," Geny said. "Why accept the invitations if you feel that way?"

Margery gave her a speaking look. "My mother would do me bodily harm if I thwarted her weekly charade of doting mother and obedient daughter. She already thinks I am sabotaging my chances for a match because I am becoming known as *difficult*." The expression she gave was so full of that dry humor Geny saw plenty of and her suitors little. If they had, they might think twice about referring to her as empty-headed besides a cruel breaker of hearts.

"You have only turned down five offers," Geny said, reverting to her light tone. "That is not so bad. It is not as though you have universally sworn off marriage."

"Eight," Margery admitted. "But Mama only knows of the five that include Mr. Bunting. If only they had not been so *eligible*. She does not like to concede defeat. My mother would attempt to play matchmaker for you if she did not consider such a thing to be grossly encroaching."

Geny smiled. "Your mother is kind. She need not worry, however," she added with a sigh. "My father does a fine job of it on his own."

Margery reached into her basket and pulled out an infant's gown she was hemming. "I have refrained from asking yet this season, for women should have other things to speak of than matrimony. But do you truly have no one who could persuade you from a life of spinsterhood?"

Geny glanced up from her sewing. "I do not fear spinsterhood, not as some do. I don't desire it either. I want to live in a house where people talk to each other and eat meals together." She sent Margery a wry smile. "However, not just anyone will do, and I have not yet met a man who might tempt me into matrimony."

A sudden image of Mr. Rowles assailed her, although why she should think of him at this precise moment defied logic. He was a handsome man, but besides having no claims to the gentry, he was too enigmatic to be someone good. Good men did not hide behind facades.

"What are you thinking of?" Margery demanded. Geny's frowning brow had betrayed her. Her friend knew her all too well.

"It is only that someone new has come to take over Mr. Biggs's position at the orphanage. You remember that Mr. Biggs served as steward since the asylum first opened?" When Margery nodded, she continued. "It is the oddest thing. This man has all the appearance of a gentleman, although he has only worked as a steward for one. I cannot for the life of me understand why he has chosen to work at the asylum. His name is Mr. Rowles. I don't suppose you would have heard of him?"

Margery came from trade, but as her parents had accumulated vast wealth, she was occasionally invited to certain society events. Very often she knew others who lived on the fringes of society, as Mr. Rowles likely did.

Margery thought for a moment. "I do not recognize the name."

"He said he left the gentleman's estate solvent, so it is not that he is running from failure. It is a step down for him to leave that position and accept one in an orphanage. It is unusual." She shook her head. "I do not like it when I cannot understand someone's motives."

"And yet you thought of him when I asked about your matrimonial interests," Margery observed, a smile hovering on her lips.

"Purely a coincidence," Geny said repressively, then laughed. "Although he is handsome, I confess. I will have to see how he does in his position."

"*Mmm.* Handsome." Margery spoke volumes with an arch of her brow. "And…is Mr. Dowling still showing signs of interest?" This came in a light, teasing tone, for she knew her friend's feelings toward the headmaster.

Margery worked slowly, for she stopped to drink her tea while it was still hot and to sample the cakes. Geny was too restless and generally preferred to keep her hands busy, for it brought her relief from an overly active mind.

"I would not say that it is interest, per se." Geny thought about it for a moment. "I do not believe he would attempt to rise above his station." She wished she didn't have such a poor view of him and worried she was being unfair.

Her stomach grumbled audibly, and she laughed as Margery glanced at her from under her eyelashes.

"Very well, I will stop." She knotted the thread and set the curtains down, finally sipping her tea which had cooled. On the plate was an assortment of almond and lemon biscuits, and she selected one of each. "I suppose Mr. Dowling is a considerate man, and I hope he will find an esteemed woman for his wife one day." *Just not me.*

The conversation turned to Margery's younger brothers and sisters, of whom she had five, although the girls were too young to be out. They then discussed the latest gown that Mary Bingly had worn, who always seemed to create trends rather than follow them. On this particular creation, the waistline sat lower than was precisely fashionable, and her ruched sleeves provided the only ornamentation on the entire outfit. They both agreed she had looked very well and that they would likely begin to see more lowered waistlines.

"I wonder where she has her gowns made," Margery mused.

"We should find out. I will send Grace to work there," Geny said, before finishing her cake.

ON WEDNESDAY'S VISIT TO THE ASYLUM, GENY SAW NO ONE other than the orphans she usually taught. She had resisted the urge to stop by Mr. Rowles's office to see how he got on. The day after that, she decided to return to the asylum, though it was not her usual day to do so. She attempted to convince herself that it was not because she was eager to meet Mr. Rowles again. That would be an embarrassing admission to make, and so she simply decided she was not. However, she told Charity that she would wear her white linen gown rather than her serviceable brown one. Other than an eyebrow lifted in surprise, Charity obeyed, and perhaps proving herself a servant able to read her mistress's mind, dressed Geny's hair with more care than a usual daytime outing to the asylum merited.

When they reached the orphanage, Geny alighted from the carriage, leaving Charity to go straight to the kitchen. She was mindful as she walked over the cobblestones. However, the snow was thawing and leaving puddles of mud in its wake. No matter how carefully she picked her way across them to the main entrance, she knew she was muddying her skirt in the process. Before stepping through the wood and glass door, Geny looked down to assess the damage. Her skirt had splatters of mud, and the hem had accumulated smears of it. Charity would not complain at having to clean it, but Geny was impatient with herself for having been so foolish as to wear white.

Sometimes I wear fine gowns to the orphanage, she reflected, trying to persuade herself that it was not because Mr. Rowles was attractive that she had done so today. Usually those times were when the weather was beautiful—and dry.

Her footsteps echoed in the empty corridor, and she heard a mistress correcting one of her protégées on the type of seam to be used on finely woven linen. Geny climbed the stairs, the satin lining of her cloak sounding as it brushed against her gown. As her heart rate picked up, she gave up lying to herself. She *was* interested in meeting Mr. Rowles again. But then, such interest was perfectly natural, was it not? She wanted to learn how he was fitting in, and what his plans were for the latest donation they had received from Mr. and Mrs. Butteridge. Would he view the needs the same way she did?

Mrs. Hastings exited the office and glanced at Geny with an air of surprise. "You have come again today?"

"Yes. I wished to see how little Ben is faring with his cold."

"He appears to be improving," Mrs. Hastings said. "Nurse Ramsey is confident he will fully recover."

"Wonderful. I will see for myself." Geny smiled at her and moved into the office to set her basket on the desk, which she always carried to the orphanage in place of a reticule. She removed her cloak and hung it on the hook beside the door.

From there, she walked through the parlor that connected to the other set of offices and was halfway across the room when she stopped short. *What am I doing? I can't visit a man's office for no reason other than to bid him good day! He will think I am pursuing him. I have gone mad.*

Her odd behavior troubled her, and she turned to go back to her desk. She would merely stop by the nursery to see little Ben as she had planned and then go home. She was nearly at the door leading to her own office when she heard someone addressing her.

"Lady Eugenia."

She turned back to see Mr. Rowles standing on the opposite end of the parlor. His coat had clearly been made by one of the best tailors in London, and it once again sent her thoughts into confusion. *Surely he is a gentleman of substance?* His pantaloons were spotless, as were his Hessians, making her even more conscious of her dirty gown. He bowed.

"Good morning, Mr. Rowles." She remained frozen, half turned and unsure of herself, and this frustrated her, too, for such awkwardness was unlike her. "How have you found your first days at the asylum?"

"Interesting," he said. "However, I have not had a chance to see much of it."

"Did Mr. Dowling not bring you to visit the rooms then?" she asked, surprised. It seemed like something he ought to have done as the first order of business.

"No. In fact, other than Mrs. Hastings inviting me to partake of a midday meal with the rest of the workers, I have not yet seen much of anything." He shrugged and gave a smile. "It is of no account, since I spent much time going through the ledgers. However, I must gain a better grasp of how the asylum is run and visit the rooms without too long of a delay."

"Perhaps I might show you the rooms," she suggested. "That is, if you are not too busy?"

He revealed his surprise with a brief lift of his brows, but what seemed to be his naturally good breeding removed its trace almost before she noticed. "I would be delighted." His tone contained nothing more than professional interest, and if she had any lingering doubts about mixed intentions, his next words were clear. "If I am to see how best to use the donations we receive, it is important that I learn every corner of the asylum."

"Very well." Geny was nervous and feared it obvious. She did not seem to know what to do with her hands. "I am ready if you are."

"Perfectly," he answered and walked to her side.

"Let us visit this floor first. It is where all of the bedrooms are, and some of the classrooms." She led the way into the corridor, trying to discover why she was so nervous around Mr. Rowles, and at the same time trying not to think of him at all. "We will begin by visiting the boys' dormitory."

The asylum formed a full square on the first floor, although the ground floor was interrupted by the gated entrance. In the middle of the square were the courtyard and gardens. The stable and carriage house took up part of the ground floor as well, although these extended some into the courtyard. She led Mr. Rowles into the first room from the corridor, which stretched the length of the building from the offices behind them to the street at the far end. There were beds on both sides of the wall, neatly made although the blankets were thin and some had holes. Blankets were valuable and donations of them rare; the money coming in was not enough to purchase new.

"This is it. And I am reminded that I will need rods to be installed in the windows of the classroom downstairs, as I am making curtains similar to the ones here."

"Certainly. I will see that it is done." Mr. Rowles looked at the beds, sending his gaze to the far end of the room where the curtains had been pulled back. "It is a healthy environment for them," he observed. "Where do they put their effects?"

"They are each given their own box. You can see them under each bed, placed next to the wall."

He nodded in silence, and she took note of his interest in how the orphans were treated. It touched her. As she observed him, she could not help but appreciate his even features. It was not like her to have such a *coup de foudre* for someone. In fact, she had never experienced any of this breathless awareness with another gentleman before.

"How young are they when they arrive?" he asked, bringing his eyes to her.

His gaze scorched, although he would not have meant for it to, and she immediately looked away. It was terrible. She felt like a schoolgirl. Her tongue darted to her lips in her attempt to moisten them.

Act rationally, she scolded herself.

"We find them at all ages. We are not well-known to the poor, and we must keep it that way if we are to limit the number of orphans we can take in and train. We cannot manage babies being deposited on our doorstep, although that does sometimes happen." She paused and when he didn't comment, added, "We depend upon the local parish. Saint Michael's Church receives orphans who are brought to them. The curate there brings the foundlings to us if we have room to take them in."

She led him across the room as there was another door on the far side. He kept pace with her, the sound of their boots echoing with each step.

"The age of the oldest orphans we take in is thirteen. Older than that, we assume they will be able to find some form of work to support themselves. And our youngest are babies. In general, Mr. Vittaly brings them to us, but in February we did have an infant dropped off in front of the gate. It was a fearful time. None of us knew if he would survive because it was so cold."

She stopped, feeling her throat close as she remembered the sorrow and anger when she had found out about it. She could not say who she was angry at, for she understood a desperate mother, likely one step from starvation herself. But to leave a baby—even well-bundled—alone and in the snow seemed unconscionable. Her lips tightened, then she glanced at him quickly before looking away, aware of his silence. "I have been rambling on. I beg your pardon."

"I imagine it must have been difficult to witness such a thing." His voice was low, and she dared another look. He seemed to be genuinely affected by the story. This did nothing to assuage the odd attraction she seemed to have created for him out of thin air.

"It was. In fact, I had been planning to visit Ben before I offered to give you a tour, so you will meet him as well. We must take these stairs to reach the girls' ward, for it is not accessible from here. That, or retrace our steps to the office, but I believe this will be faster. And then we will visit the nursery, if you are amenable to the idea."

"Yes. I wish to see everything, if you please." Mr. Rowles followed her to the stairwell.

She set her hand on the railing but then turned back. She had been flustered. "Oh, I almost forgot. This room behind us is used to train orphans for the services that a footman or valet might perform." She opened the door for him to see for himself the various instruments of the trade that included shoe-shine equipment, silver polish, and sewing kits. Even if there were chips in the plaster on the walls, the equipment itself was in good shape.

"They will arrive fully trained at their position," he said quietly as he cast his gaze to all the corners of the small room. "This is remarkable."

"I think so, too." She smiled, closed the door behind them, and turned toward the staircase.

Chapter Four

John trailed behind Lady Eugenia as they descended the wooden stairs flanked by an iron railing, his thoughts darting from one thing to another. There was much to consider. He had the distinct impression that Lady Eugenia was interested in him as a woman was in a man. There was something in the way her eyes flew from his rather than hold his gaze. And the way she held herself very still when in his presence, as though she feared to make a false step—although, to be fair, he had not spent enough time in her presence to judge her usual comportment.

It would not be the first time he found himself the object of female admiration. He had always had a knack for winning the regard of women from all classes. He prided himself on never taking his flirtations so far as to raise false hopes in the breasts of innocent maidens. If they insisted on hoping anyway, why, there was nothing he could do about that. And for the less innocent maidens, he treated them with a respect that most gentlemen did not. It hardly even mattered that Lady Eugenia was the daughter of a peer. He had had plenty of those fall at his feet, too, when he had been a *ton* favorite.

Well, *ton favorite* was perhaps an exaggeration, since he had always preferred the gentlemen's clubs to the balls, soirées, and dinner engagements. As for Almack's, he had not set foot in the establishment above two times and had not considered himself enriched by either experience. This did not change the fact that he was put out when he stopped receiving vouchers.

Suffice it to say that the fact that Lady Eugenia would seem nervous around him was not an astonishing thing in itself. What was astonishing was that she did not base it on the usual things most women did, for in his present situation, he had no social standing. He was at a foundling asylum in the guise of a paid employee who had no claims to the gentry, which was as far from her station as one could be. He was most decidedly not attempting to charm her. And he had been solemn in all of his interactions with her—his usual mien since he had fallen from favor. And yet, he could only describe her behavior around him as nervous. He was a handsome man; he could not deny it. But he had nothing to offer her in a worldly sense, so the notion that she might find him a subject of interest puzzled him.

Neither of them spoke as she led him through the massive dining hall with pine tables and chairs. This latter element struck him and caused him to remember something else he found curious.

"The asylum has proper beds," he observed, "and chairs rather than benches."

"Yes," she said, pushing in one chair that sat askew as she walked by it. "Since we are training the children to work as servants, some of the more adept will serve as footmen, and they need to practice serving around people who are seated for dinner. And some will become maids who will have to make proper beds. It is better they develop this skill from the outset."

She turned her face to him as she led him from the dining room. "It is also more decent."

The walls in the entrance were painted white, and this public area was the only space where everything looked well-tended. The floors were made of polished wood. The hall was bare of ornamentation, except for a large painting of the earl and what was presumably his late wife. Lady Eugenia bore an astonishing resemblance to her mother, though he refrained from saying as much. She gestured to the set of stairs on the opposite side and at a diagonal to the dining room.

"The girls' dormitory is at the top of this set of stairs. I am afraid you will not find it much different than the boys', but we can still visit."

"It will be good to see where it is situated."

So far, he could make his way around nearly one half of the asylum. He had yet to see the classrooms located underneath the boys' dormitory, but he had glimpsed the meeting hall and chapel underneath his office when he had taken the wrong set of stairs.

As they climbed to the first floor, his mind went to the second thing that had struck him. Lady Eugenia truly cared about the orphans. That fact had been evident when he saw tears sparkling on her lashes as she spoke of the baby who had been dumped at the gate of the asylum. He had never given a thought to the welfare of orphans in London or anywhere else. They were just living the life Fate had doled out to them, and what could he do about that? *He* was not the decider of people's fates. At first meeting, Lady Eugenia had appeared cool and aloof, traits accentuated by her naturally upturned nose and straight hair pulled back in an uncompromising style. Why, she did not even bother to soften it next to her face. He wondered what she looked like when she went to balls, although that was not something he would likely ever see. For her to care so much about children beneath her notice was perplexing in the extreme. But he had to admit that it touched him.

"And here is the girls' dormitory. I warned you that you would not find it much different from the boys'."

He cast his gaze down the length of the dormitory with beds on each side, all of them neatly made. The blankets seemed in slightly better condition than in the boys' room, but they were still thin. And just as in the boys' dormitory, there were boxes underneath each bed. A blue ribbon caught the corner of his eye, dangling from a box underneath the second bed.

He gestured to it. "Not quite. I don't think you would find that in the boys' dormitory."

She directed her eyes where he had indicated and smiled. "It must be Grace's. I think that's her bed. She is a pretty little thing but not the neatest of girls. Fortunately, she has a knack for needlework, so we need not despair of sending her out to be hired as a maid, only to have her sacked." She went over and tucked the ribbon back into the box.

"They have some possessions, then." He would not think that orphans owned anything but the most functional items, even ones who lived in an asylum.

"Only what we give them," she said. And then as though the thought had just occurred to her, she added, "But you need not worry about that for your accounting purposes. I usually manage to find clothing from among members of society; either what they give away or make. Even if they have no time to sew, they are usually happy to donate what their maids do not want, and we can then transform those items into clothing."

He puzzled this over, then glanced at her curiously. "A maid would not want a blue ribbon?" He had seen that one. It had hardly looked used. This was not an article that had been passed from one person to another until it was in shreds.

A flush of pink stained her cheeks. "Well, if it is a small thing, I might use some of my pocket money. I think everyone deserves to own something that has never belonged to anyone else. Something special and just your own. Do you not agree?"

She looked at him with such earnestness, he found himself breaking their gaze first, now uncomfortable. She could not have been doing it on purpose, but it was as if Lady Eugenia was attempting to reveal his own selfish nature by situating it next to what he was coming to see was her pure one.

"I had never thought of it, but I suppose you are right."

"Yes, well." She seemed momentarily at a loss for words. The sound of a baby crying at the far end of the floor caused her to look in that direction. "If that is Benjamin, I shall be very pleased. It means he is doing much better to be exercising his lungs in such a way. Shall we continue?"

He nodded and followed her to the next room, which held chairs where girls of various ages plied their needles. A maid or a teacher of sorts was looking at the work of the youngest and pointing to where the cloth had been knotted. She looked up when they entered.

"Lady Geny," a child cried out.

"It is Lady Eugenia," the worker corrected gently. She was coarse in appearance but spoke graciously, as though she had taken on the gentle bearing of the earl's daughter. Either that or her natural gentleness was at complete odds with her looks.

"It is all right," Lady Eugenia said. "Good morning, Grace."

She went over to speak to the girl of the blue ribbon, who was currently wearing a black band like the other girls. John could only assume they'd all been given a colored one for special events.

Grace had called the earl's daughter "Lady Geny," which suited her. It was somehow more approachable. *Geny*. He thought about what it would be like to be on such intimate terms as to use her Christian name—a nickname, at that. The only thing intimidating about her was her title and, at first glance, an unapproachable air. He was coming to suspect that this was the furthest from the truth. He had never met anyone like her.

Lady Eugenia praised Grace for her work and stopped to examine each one of the girls' stitches. The oldest was pulling a piece of blue thread through a delicate piece of muslin, and Lady Eugenia went over to suggest she not pull the thread so tightly, before setting her hand briefly on the girl's shoulder with a small word of praise. Then she turned to him.

"Shall we visit the nursery?"

John nodded and followed her back into the corridor, eyeing her slim set of shoulders and regal neck. His urge to inquire about her nickname was too strong to resist, and he decided to throw his reserve aside.

"Lady Geny?" he asked, smiling at her.

She turned a startled gaze to him, then blinked before an answering smile reached her lips. "Some of the younger ones have difficulty saying my name, so I told them they could call me Lady Geny."

"Do others call you that?" The words were out before he realized that he was being too familiar. "I beg your pardon. That was impertinent of me. It is none of my concern."

There was a slight pause before she answered in a soft voice. "My mother called me Geny. She was the only one, except for my brother and closest friend."

Not your father? he thought. But now he had a better guard on his tongue and did not speak the words. "Geny is a very pretty name. As is Eugenia," he said, then hastened to add a belated, "my lady."

Good heavens. It was unlike him to be so uncouth. In fact, it had never happened in front of a lady before. Women never overset him. It was not that she did, particularly. True, she was a well-looking woman, and titled, too. But those things had never brought any change over him. If he had been prone to losing his head over status and a pretty face, he would have been married long ago.

Lady Eugenia was too polite to comment on his lapse in urbanity. "Here is the nursery."

The room had once been painted yellow and was much

smaller than the dormitories, having only six cots in it. Three of the bassinets held an infant, and two babies sat on the floor, one of them waving something in his hand. It looked like a wooden ring. There was an older orphan sitting between them, apparently training to care for babies.

"There is Benjamin," Lady Eugenia announced, going over to one of the nurses who held a baby on her lap. "May I?"

The nurse handed him over. "He is faring better than he was yesterday."

John stepped closer to look over Lady Eugenia's shoulder at the baby, taking care not to stand too near and give her more reason to think him overly familiar. It was just close enough to see the baby's face.

Little Benjamin was an unfortunate-looking fellow and had, what seemed to be, a natural scowl on his face. The dark line that made up his hairline was close enough to his eyebrows to make it appear as though he had no forehead. His eyes were mere slits, while his nose and lips looked swollen. Although John had little experience with babies, this one had to be the poorest specimen of one he had ever seen.

Lady Eugenia tucked the blanket under Benjamin's chin, rocking him slightly in her arms.

"Aren't you a handsome fellow?" she asked him, stroking him on the cheek until he lifted a somber gaze to hers. "Yes, you are. But do you see what a fighter you are as well? You ought to be proud of yourself because you have resisted a very chilly night wrapped in nothing more than blankets, and now you have fought off a wicked cold."

She smiled at the baby, and John—who had come around her and now stood facing her—felt like he had been struck a blow in his chest. He could barely breathe, and there was a buzzing in his ears. What had come over him? He stood, frozen, watching her rock the baby back and forth, when suddenly Benjamin began to dribble a startling quantity of milk all over his chin and her gown.

"Oh dear," she said, laughing, as one of the servants hurried to bring her a cloth. The nurse took the baby from Lady Eugenia, and she began to wipe the milk that stained the bosom of her dress. John dragged his eyes away.

She brought a clean blanket over and tucked it around Benjamin. "You feel much better now, don't you?"

The baby's expression appeared to change as he stared at her. He was still somber, but he looked as though he would smile at her. As if the foundling were not sure whether he could, but thought he might just take the chance. John could relate to the feeling. His heart was still hammering in his chest from the disturbing shift that had just occurred.

She glanced at John, her smile slowly fading until only a twinkle in her eyes remained. She looked down and pressed her lips together at the darkened stain on her bosom. He suspected she would appreciate going to cover the stain, and it was this that prompted him to cut their tour short, much as he was reluctant to end their time together.

"I beg you will excuse me, Lady Eugenia. Might we continue our tour at another time? I have forgotten that I have an urgent correspondence I must have sent out."

"Of course," she hastened to assure him, although a crease appeared in her brow.

He bowed. "I am most obliged for the generous gift of your time. I am coming to appreciate the asylum in a way I had not before." He smiled at her, swallowing to cover the unsteadiness that went with it, a sensation he was desperate to hide. "I bid you good day." She returned the farewell, her good humor still apparent. He could almost be jealous of Benjamin for having coaxed such a smile from her. But perhaps he could inspire her to keep it.

She dipped her head in a gesture of grace. "Good day then, Mr. Rowles."

He left her, and as he walked down the stairs to reenter the other wing of the asylum, he allowed his smile to truly break free. He would enjoy coming to know Lady Eugenia. It was an excellent thing she came nearly every day.

On Friday, John headed in the direction of Mayfair with Lord Blackstone's card in his pocket. His prevailing emotion was curiosity. That Lord Blackstone would seek an audience with him was nothing short of extraordinary. In most polite circles, you had to prove yourself and run after other, more distinguished members. No one ever came to you with offers of friendship. He would suspect the invitation was shady beyond anything were it not for the fact that it came from a peer.

As he rounded the corner to St. James's Street, he glanced down its length, uncomfortably aware that he was now in his old haunt. Hopefully, no one would spot him here, for he was not in the mood to be snubbed. The massive house came into view, and he studied its stone facade which stretched five windows across. The entrance was just four steps above ground level, tucked underneath a portico. There were two floors above the ground floor and another shorter floor on top for the servants' quarters. Although the curtains were open, the interior was not easily visible from the street, except for the faint outline of a large bowl of flowers sitting on a table in front of the window.

He walked up the steps and rapped the door knocker, which was in the shape of a crow's head with its metal beak performing the knocking sound. The door cracked open, and a servant peered out at John.

"Yes, sir?"

"I have an appointment to see Lord Blackstone. My name is John Aubin." When the servant made no move to open the door wider, an event he found strange since he had been invited, John reached into the coat of his pocket. "Here is my card."

The servant took it and opened the door wider, peering at a small black book he held in his hand and comparing it to the name on the card.

"Ah, yes. You may wait here. I will bring this to milord."

John obeyed, and as the servant stepped to the side to permit him entrance, he was given a full glimpse of the dimly lit hall. All of the wall hangings and rugs were a deep burgundy red. On the right side of the corridor was a set of stairs leading up to another sober-hued hallway. But it was the left wall, where exotic game of all types were mounted like trophies that transfixed his gaze. The only natural light came from the windows above the door behind him, and the rest was from candles placed in sconces on both sides of the corridor and the chandeliers above him. The heavy colors and multitude of glassy eyeballs staring at him stole his breath.

It did not take long before the servant returned. "Lord Blackstone will see you. Right this way, sir."

John followed the servant through the passage that led to another corridor. The door at the end of it contained Lord Blackstone's study, and he entered on the heels of the servant as Lord Blackstone stood from behind his desk. John had not expected such a courtesy, both because of his recent loss of status and also because he was meeting a peer.

His good manners fled in the face of such odd trappings in the viscount's study, and he only remembered to bow as an afterthought. Above Lord Blackstone's head was a large painting of a beaver donning a morning coat. On his left side a single candle flickered on a table whose legs appeared to be those of a flamingo.

Is this man obsessed with death? John thought. And then—*What does that mean for me?*

"Well met, Mr. Aubin. Please have a seat." Lord Blackstone led him to another part of the office where two leather chairs were placed in front of the fireplace.

John found this corner more settling, away from the staring eyes of the animal trophies. He turned his face to the right and drew back suddenly, for in close proximity were the jaws of a snarling tiger.

Lord Blackstone watched his reaction calmly, not seeming to find any morbid satisfaction in frightening his guests.

"He has just arrived last week. My contacts bring predeceased animals to the taxidermist. Their demise was not done at my hand or theirs."

"Is that so?" John did not feel himself equipped to say more than that.

"I feel it gives them a new life, wouldn't you say?" Lord Blackstone offered a friendly smile. He looked nothing like a peer. At least not one who wished to boast of his status. Whiskers grew on either side of his cheeks, extending a hairline which fell in soft waves. His eyes looked youthful and his smile was cheery, as though he had never known hardship. There was no doubt he was an eccentric.

"I suppose it does," John conceded, realizing that he had better start returning answers if he was not to appear rude. He had not yet uttered a single intelligent word.

"Bring us some brandy," Lord Blackstone ordered the servant. "Or perhaps you would rather have tea? I believe you have been abstaining as of late."

"You seem to know quite a few things," John replied cautiously.

"I know everything." Lord Blackstone threw up his hands, along with the corner of his lips. "I suppose you wonder why I have called you here, other than what Sacks has already told you."

"It does seem a strange thing that you would wish to seek an acquaintance with me; however, I am honored by your notice." There. Nothing could be lacking in his address now.

"Well, you were not an easy man to find, which is why I turned the job over to Sacks. I was intrigued after learning that you found out Lord Goodwin's attempt to ditch his shares in the steam-powered looms after having convinced his peers to invest. It was noble of you to seek out Lord Perkins and try to call Goodwin out on such base behavior."

"Acting nobly—if that was what it was—has certainly not done me any favors," John admitted.

"Nobility is never wasted," Lord Blackstone said.

That sentiment sat for a moment before another thought occurred to John. "How do you know of the venture? And why is it that you believe me?"

"I have contacts who keep me up to date on political maneuverings. It didn't take much to guess that the threat of a steam-duty tax would be enough to frighten Lord Goodwin off of the investment. Now, of course, with the tax law voted out and the boom in trade, he is considered a genius. He's calling for more investors to build a mill and housing for workers up north, and many are joining the deal." Lord Blackstone smiled benevolently at him. "But of course, his success does not invalidate your good actions."

"Well, I appreciate your notice and your validation, but I am afraid it will not do me any good now. I am seeking to recover my reputation after it was unfairly destroyed."

"I know this, Mr. Aubin. If you have taken a position at the foundling asylum, I assume it is to look into the early rumors of mismanagement and see if you can connect them to Lord Goodwin."

John pulled back in surprise. It had not occurred to him

that anyone would figure out what he was doing there. "You seem to be well versed in many things," he managed at last, shaken.

"Only those matters that interest me." Lord Blackstone looked up as the servant brought in a decanter of brandy and two glasses, along with a teapot and two cups. "But perhaps you wish for brandy after all."

John thought about the excessive brandy he had consumed the night before his ill-fated encounter with Lord Goodwin that had led to a series of foolish decisions and opted for tea.

When the servant left, Lord Blackstone turned to John. "I have two propositions for you. The first is that I am inviting you to join my club."

John looked at him, perplexed. The viscount had a knack for catching him off his guard. "Which club? Where is it located?"

Lord Blackstone lifted his hands and looked around. "You are in it."

John didn't remember seeing anybody else when he came in. It certainly didn't resemble any club he knew. He struggled to keep up with Lord Blackstone's strange proposition. "How many members are there?"

"Only two dozen," Lord Blackstone said. "It is small yet. If you wish to join it, you will be made a member straightaway, then I can show you to the rooms where the others congregate. It is composed entirely of gentlemen who have been blackballed by other clubs," he added proudly.

That didn't seem to be a positive attribute. "I should like to meet them first before I decide," John hedged. He had no idea what kind of club he would be getting himself into and wasn't sure he liked the idea.

"That is all very natural. I will introduce you to them shortly. But this brings me to my second point, and that is how to achieve your goal. I would like to help you."

"Why?" The one word seemed to encompass his overall

bafflement since he had stepped through Lord Blackstone's doors.

"Because I don't like bullies," Lord Blackstone declared, and then without giving him a chance to respond, went on. "Therefore, if you are willing, I will secure you an invitation to Mrs. Sookholme's ball tomorrow night. The guests will be far enough from society that you needn't fear crossing paths with people you once knew." It was as though he had read John's mind. "Some of them have invested in the foundling asylum in the past, and you might find your conversation with some of them enlightening. There will be more merchants than gentry in attendance, but I should hardly think that will bother you."

Lord Blackstone waited until John shook his head, still bewildered, before continuing. "It will be an easy thing to begin discussions about the asylum, especially when you mention that you are working as steward there."

This seemed like a hopeful beginning, especially since he hadn't made much progress with the accounting books. The idea of the ball excited him more than the club did. "I would be very glad to attend. However, I must warn you that I am going by the name of Rowles."

"I am aware of it, and I will see that the invitation is sent using the correct name. Shall I show you the other rooms here?"

John sent a surreptitious glance at the untouched tea which would have been welcome since he had not taken any at the asylum. "Yes, that would be nice."

Their visit bore no fruit, however. When they went into the adjoining room, it was empty aside from a large stuffed bear presiding over the space from a corner chair. His noticeable scent made John deduce him to be a new addition. He sent his gaze around the room to the other stuffed creatures before spotting the large bowl of flowers by the window that was visible from the outside. An armadillo shell. Of course.

"Ah, well." Lord Blackstone's voice echoed in the empty

room. "I am afraid there is no one here to meet you just now, and I should not like to bring you into the private rooms until you are sure you wish to join the club. Let us hope we will have more luck later. I will have the invitation sent to your address for Saturday's ball."

"I appreciate your efforts on my behalf," John said.

It seemed as though the interview was at an end, and the servant came in as though he read Lord Blackstone's mind. John was shown to the door, and he left the premises thoroughly at a loss. The place did not seem like much of a club. Besides, what an odd premise for it. Whoever would wish to join it? Could Lord Blackstone be all right in his head? John wasn't sure. But he wouldn't turn down the invitation for the Sookholme ball.

Chapter Five

It was Friday, and Geny resisted the urge to go to the orphanage, although not without a struggle. There was no rational explanation for what had come over her that she should have such an overwhelming desire to see Mr. Rowles—one that was almost impossible to master. But it would behoove her to gain a better grip on her flights of romantic fancy. Nothing was more absurd than the notion that she should show interest in him. After all, he might look the gentleman, but his status was questionable. Besides, was she then to throw herself at his feet? Surely, she was the only one who experienced such forceful—and inexplicable—emotions when they were together. He likely felt nothing, which was even more embarrassing.

She was working on another set of curtains when the sounds of a visitor reached her in the drawing room. The butler came in to announce Miss Buxton, and Geny looked up with a smile. "What an unexpected pleasure. You are usually too tired from the prior night's party to come and visit me."

"Oh, I am tired." Margery plopped herself on the sofa in an unladylike manner, which she only allowed herself to do in front of Geny. Never in public, of course, and never in front of her mother.

"However, I have come to bring you an invitation to a ball that we are to attend tomorrow night. I thought you would like to come because some of those who donate to the orphanage will be there. You will be able to thank them in person." Her demure smile almost hid her look of mischief. "And encourage them to give more. It is at seven o'clock."

Geny sent her friend an appreciative look. "You know me well. That is precisely what I would like to do. However, my father would not approve unless I am to be escorted."

"I have already spoken to my mother on the subject, and she will be happy to have our carriage come and pick you up. Will you indeed come then?"

"You may count on it." The event would be just the thing to take her mind off the asylum's new steward. "Can you stay for a while? I will call for tea."

Margery shook her head. "I am tempted, especially with your cook's delicacies, but I dare not. Besides, I have already eaten more than is good for me today."

Geny chuckled at this. Her friend loved to eat, but any resulting plumpness only seemed to serve to her advantage for it went where it was supposed to. "Well then, I will expect you at seven o'clock tomorrow night. Where is it?"

"You remember Mrs. Sookholme, do you not? She was an early donor with her husband, and when we approached her to ask if she would extend you an invitation, she almost stumbled over herself in her pleasure to do so. I daresay you've never been to her house as it's in Southwark, but she has a very nice residence and a large ballroom."

Margery stopped and puckered her lips. "It is a shame that the *ton* is so particular. There are many who would appreciate such a fine ballroom, and she lays out superior refreshments."

"Well, I am not particular," Geny said. "And I shall look forward to it."

THE NEXT EVENING, GENY HAD HER HAIR STYLED WITH A SOFTER, curled chignon in the back and little curled tendrils near her face. She knew it became her more than her usual severe style, but she found the latter more practical; most days she was not out to impress anyone. She wore her gown of blue silk threaded with gold but left off overt signs of wealth, despite the fact that tonight's guests would likely comprise an affluent set. Instead, she settled for a simple strand of pearls. *I will adorn myself with benevolence and warmth instead.*

On the hour, the Buxtons' carriage pulled up to the front door, and their footman stepped down to open it and help Geny in.

Mrs. Buxton acknowledged her with a bow of her head from where she sat. "Why, you look very fine, my lady."

Margery's mother insisted on formality, although she had known Geny since she was young. She never tried to overstep her bounds, which was likely why Lord Goodwin put up with her, despite the fact that they hailed from the merchant class. Geny's mother, however, had respected Mrs. Buxton, and that would have been enough for Geny even without having Margery for a best friend.

In a sudden jerk, the horses started forward at a trot, and Margery and her mother began to discuss the guests they were likely to see at the party.

"You will pay special attention to Mr. Thompson, now that he has returned from Wales," Mrs. Buxton said. "He is a kind gentleman and well set up in the world besides carrying on the same trade as your father. Honestly, it is not as though I push you toward men who are sixty, or who have strange peccadilloes. I only present you to ones whom I know will take care of you and whom you could love."

"You are very good, Mama. I shall do my best to be interested."

Geny stifled a smile at Margery's outward meekness. The Buxtons' dynamic had not changed since she had known them. Although they pretended to be opposite on many matters, there was no shortage of affection. It cheered her to see their mother-daughter relationship thriving, although she no longer had one of her own.

They arrived at Mrs. Sookholme's house, and Geny lifted her eyes to take in the magnificent residence with candles blazing in all of the windows.

"It is lovely." Geny smiled at Margery and sent an expressive glance toward the ballroom which was visible from the street through the windows, adding in a whisper, "*Much* nicer than Almack's."

Margery grinned at her. She had voiced more than once that she was glad she was not required to attend Almack's above all the other parties her mother dragged her to. They would never be given vouchers for it.

"Here we are, my lady." Mrs. Buxton gestured to the people filing into the house, leaning in to whisper, "I am fairly confident that the guests here will not embarrass you in any way or offend you with their vulgarity."

"I believe I may trust that," Geny replied with a straight face, although she wished to laugh again, conscious of a giddy sensation she did not usually have. Where this came from, she did not know. Besides, anyone who volunteered in an orphanage was not particularly concerned with escaping all that was considered vulgar.

They followed the others inside, where she was introduced to the hostess. "Thank you for your invitation, Mrs. Sookholme, especially one so kindly extended at the last minute."

"We are honored that you've graced us with your presence," Mrs. Sookholme replied with an unaffected smile. She then turned to Mrs. Buxton. "I must remain in place to greet our guests for some time. I hope I may count upon you to see that Lady Eugenia is comfortable?"

"Of course, you may." Mrs. Buxton smiled and led Margery and Geny into the throng.

Mrs. Buxton was a well-liked woman and was soon drawn into conversation, so it was left to Margery to point out the guests she assumed Geny would most like to meet. Mr. and Mrs. Butteridge were expected to come, but she did not see them yet. There was Mr. Harris who had made a significant donation to the orphanage this past year, although Mr. Biggs had explained that the asylum was expensive to run and it was difficult to see the fruit of it. His wife had also donated clothes. When Margery asked if she would like to meet them, she nodded.

"Mrs. Harris?" Margery curtsied when the woman turned to her. "May I present to you Lady Eugenia Stanich? She is daughter to the Earl of Goodwin and takes a keen interest in the orphans' welfare. She wished to make your acquaintance."

"I am honored by your notice," Mrs. Harris said with a curtsy, appearing surprised at the introduction.

"I wished to thank you in person for everything you've done for the orphans, Mrs. Harris. I am aware of your husband's donation, and I received the basket of clothing and other items you had sent for the orphans through Mrs. Buxton." Geny paused for breath and finished by saying, "I must express how thankful I am to meet like-minded people in society who care about those who have so little."

Mrs. Harris smiled warmly at her. "I am not sure everyone would agree with your saying I am a *part* of society, but it is true that I cannot help but think that nothing prevents any one of us from finding ourselves in an unfortunate situation except chance. If I can alleviate their suffering…if I can bring them just a little peace and comfort, then I am quite content."

"I am of the same mind," Geny said, her heart thrumming to hear her own thoughts spoken aloud and to know she was not alone. "As was my mother."

"Will you tell me what sorts of material things are missing?" Mrs. Harris continued. "I know others who are willing to volunteer items, even if their husbands are not yet persuaded to give financially. It is not the case for everyone, of course. Some husbands are as wonderful as mine."

She glanced over at a tall, stocky man who appeared to be engaged in passionate discussion with another gentleman that bordered on a friendly argument, then brought her gaze back to Geny.

"There are some women whose hearts are large but who have little means to give because they must abide by their husbands' wishes. They would be pleased to know that other donations are welcomed."

"There are many things we would find useful," Geny replied and proceeded to list some of the items that were most needed. They spoke for a few moments longer, with Margery waiting patiently at her side, until Geny noticed that Mr. Harris had finished his conversation and appeared to be looking for his wife. She took leave of Mrs. Harris, adding, "I hope you will extend my gratitude to Mr. Harris also."

She and Margery walked to the edge of the ballroom. There was a row of private alcoves all along the peristyle, each containing a couple of chairs, that reminded Geny of a honeycomb. Margery slipped her arm through hers.

"With such a warm heart as you have, you should not be surprised at finding that there are others like you. Although I do think you are the best of them all."

Geny laughed with the words, "you are biased," on her lips, but they died unspoken on her tongue. There, in front of her, stood Mr. Rowles. He wasn't speaking with anyone in particular, and indeed was looking a little out of place as he searched the crowd. Because she saw him first, she was able to witness his reaction when he discovered her presence.

He started in surprise as soon as he caught sight of her, then turned more fully to face her. She could not tell if he was happy to see her or not and feared it made no difference to him. Then he smiled, and it sent the giddy feelings soaring that she had been keeping at bay. Although she returned his smile, she was distressed to have had the reaction of a schoolgirl—and here she was, a young woman of twenty-three. With that smile of his, she could only assume that, gentleman or not, Mr. Rowles was *very* successful with women. The thought made her pinch her lips and rein in her outward display of enthusiasm.

He came before her and bowed. "Lady Eugenia, what a surprise to see you here. Truly, I did not expect it."

"Nor I you, Mr. Rowles." She noticed his glance at her side and remembered Margery's presence. "Please allow me to present you to Miss Buxton. She is a friend of mine."

"A pleasure, Miss Buxton." Mr. Rowles bowed, then turned back to Geny as though she had absorbed his entire interest. The small gesture reassured her because she knew that Margery was very comely. He could have been forgiven for staring.

Margery returned the greeting, then touched Geny's arm. "Would you excuse me for a moment? I can see my mother sending me looks from here, which means she wishes to speak to me."

"Of course," Geny said, and Mr. Rowles bowed again as Margery left.

"How do you know Mrs. Sookholme?" Geny asked before an awkward silence could come between them. She feared it—and feared he would find her uninteresting.

"I was only just introduced to her. A friend had me invited to the party since I am...new to this area. I do not have many acquaintances here."

The fact that he stumbled on his words made her think that he was about to say something else, but she put it out of her mind. She nodded and smiled inanely, a slight panic rising within as her own conversational arts seemed to have fled. Then Mr. Rowles caught her gaze and held it, which steadied her.

"And how do you know our hostess?" he asked. "Have you come with your...family?"

Once again, he hesitated in his speech, and she wondered whether he could be equally as nervous around her. His regard that evening seemed more purposeful than when they had first met. It was as if their brief time together visiting the orphanage had given them cause to become friends. She hoped she was not imagining it.

"I have only just met Mrs. Sookholme. And I came with Miss Buxton, to whom I've just introduced you. She spoke to me of the ball yesterday and secured an invitation for me. There are many people here who have in the past contributed to the finances of the asylum, and some are supporting it still. She thought I might like to meet them and thank them in person."

He studied her, and once she stopped talking, she felt the weight of his regard even more. It made it difficult to breathe or know where to look.

"You are an extraordinary woman, my lady. You truly seem to care for the asylum as though it were the central-most part of your life. Do you not attend parties for pleasure?" He left unspoken what she could only assume. Did she mingle with people of her status?

"I attend Almack's almost every week because my father wishes me to." She stopped suddenly, wondering if he knew what that was. "It is a place where people gather on Wednesday evenings to dine and dance."

Laughter sprang to his eyes, and she did not know the cause

for it but suspected she had committed a social solecism. It should have made her feel more unsure of herself as though he were laughing at her, yet it did not seem as though he were. It also made his expression more approachable.

"And do you attend the opera and other parties?" he asked, making no further reference to Almack's.

"Oh, yes, of course. I frequently attend the opera and am often invited to the musicals held by certain members of society, along with the balls, the routs, the card games. All the usual things." She was rambling.

The laughter faded from his eyes, but his smile was warm. "It is even more impressive, then, that you are so devoted to the orphans. I could not help but notice that it is not a simple duty to you, as though you are doing a good work. I have the distinct impression that nothing could keep you from giving your time there. I do not know many such people."

She turned to him. "Are you not? I would think that the simpler people are, the more they would be concerned with benevolence." She frowned as soon as she spoke the words, realizing too late that she had insulted him by declaring the people he frequented were simpler.

"What I think is that there are good and benevolent people in all spheres of society, whether simple or elevated. And there are, unfortunately for us all, dastardly people in those spheres as well. Those who behave in an ignoble fashion and who set out to deceive others can be found in the Upper Ten Thousand as easily as they can in the merchant class or a village of tenant farmers."

She raised her brows. "You sound as though you are speaking out of experience."

The dark look that had come over him disappeared, and his smile returned. He shook his head. "Forgive me, my lady. I *was* speaking out of experience. But let us set our minds on the people who are good. Like you."

She laughed that he would think it. "Good enough, I suppose. I do not think about goodness or trying to achieve such an impossible standard. It is much better to focus on attempting to love."

Strains of music sounded from the far corner of the ballroom where a small orchestra was seated on a raised dais, and she turned toward it, then cast her eyes to the people setting up for a quadrille in the center of the floor. She hoped he would ask her to dance, and this caused her to return her regard to him where she caught his expression. There was an intensity there, and she wondered at it until the echo of her words rang in her mind.

...attempting to love. Good heavens! She had been talking about the orphans. Not romantic love. But had he assumed she was speaking of that? Or making allusions to himself? Suddenly she was flustered and could feel a deep, burning heat rise up in her cheeks. It was both merciless and flattering, then, that he held her gaze until she blinked and looked away.

"I fear this is presumptuous of me, given the difference in our status," Mr. Rowles said, "but would you do me the honor of dancing with me, my lady?"

Geny held on to every bit of her rigorous upbringing to keep her feelings from springing out in all directions and returned a careful, gracious curtsy. "I would be delighted to dance with you, Mr. Rowles."

He held out his arm, and she slipped her hand around it. As they walked to the floor, she smelled his scent that was like wood smoke, and citrus, and...and grass. *Was that it?* Did he use a soap like that, or was that just his natural scent? She felt the firm muscles of his arm, so unlike other suitors who offered to escort her—or when Mr. Dowling offered his slender arm. Mr. Rowles was likely a man accustomed to hard labor, she reminded herself, attempting to use this as an excuse to forget about any possible future with him. This endeavor was singularly unsuccessful, for she could only think about how much she would like to be wrapped in those strong, protective arms.

She had heard the expression, *love at first sight*, but the words had been foreign. Now, it felt like she had been given the key to the language. She only hoped the surge of accompanying feeling would not steal her speech.

Unaware of the direction of her thoughts, for which she was fervently grateful, Mr. Rowles led her to an open place on the floor and turned to face her.

"I must tell you that meeting you here is likely to prove the happiest moment of the evening."

This caused her smile to bloom. She could feel it, could feel her lips stretching and her eyes glowing. She had not thought herself so easy to read, but she must be if he could speak such familiar words to her. And she could only be grateful that he thought their meeting happy, for it matched her own sentiment.

He led her in the first steps of the dance, and the routine of them brought her back down from the cloud she had been floating on. She knew practically nothing about him.

"You dance very well, Mr. Rowles. Where did you learn the steps?"

"Even the most uncivilized of men can be taught, I suppose," he said smoothly, coming to turn around her. "It was through a dancing master, of course."

The dance gave them little time to continue the conversation, and they did not attempt it. After some time, they found themselves on the side waiting for their turn.

"Did you have a dancing master, then?" she asked. This surprised her. She did not know much of the lives of tradesmen and those of his ilk, but she supposed if they had the money and wished to mingle in society, they would have to hire all sorts of tutors and masters and people proficient in the arts and studies.

"Yes, when I was young," he replied, then laughed. "These were my least favorite hours spent, I confess. My brother felt the same, although such instruction was necessary for a young man's education, of course."

"Where does your brother live?" She wanted to know everything about him and hoped he would not be put off by her questions.

It was their turn to rejoin the dance, and the steps separated them again before he could answer. It was not until they were reunited that he said, "Gregory lives in West Riding. He is married and serves as rector there."

"That is not an easy position to obtain without connections," she observed, thinking that his brother was lucky to have been granted the living. It made her wonder again about Mr. Rowles's status. Perhaps he was a gentleman—son of a doctor or clergyman. "I am sure he must be valuable to his parish."

There was a strange twist to Mr. Rowles's features that was gone in an instant, and she wondered if he and his brother did not get along. Or perhaps he had been offended by her bringing up his lack of connections. She would need to be more careful with her speech, for she truly did not wish to alienate a man she liked so well.

"He is very valuable, indeed. Even his wife serves the poor and organizes relief baskets. She pays the services of the midwife for those who cannot do so. She is…much like yourself." The dance brought them apart, and when they were rejoined, he hastened to add, "As much as a woman who is beneath you in station can be like you."

She settled for a smile until the steps gave her the chance to respond. "You, yourself, said there are good and bad people to be found in both simple and elevated spheres. If she is good, then I am honored by the comparison."

"She has certainly made my brother happy." The first dance of the set had ended without them having rejoined it, and he led her to the edge of the dance floor. "Have you no siblings? No, I believe you once mentioned you have a brother."

"Yes. Matthew. We are as close as he will allow me to be. But I confess that he goes off to Eton quite happily without sparing a thought for his poor elder sister who misses him terribly."

"He is fortunate to have you and will realize it when he is just a little older," Mr. Rowles assured her, his lips turned upwards in a way that chased away her breath. "May I procure something for you to drink?"

Geny looked toward the double doors where servants entered bearing trays with glasses upon them. "Yes, if you please. I am thirsty."

She watched him walk away to retrieve them, as her heart continued to beat a strange rhythm and the candlelight created a warm halo around him.

I understand what it means now to fall suddenly in love. This thought was quickly followed by a second. *And yet Father will never approve. Oh, heavens. What am I about?*

Chapter Six

John had not quite recovered from his initial surprise at seeing Lady Eugenia at a ball in Southwark—not entirely. As much as his visit with Lord Blackstone had occupied his attention in the hours that followed it, his thoughts had never been far from the sight of her holding Benjamin. Here was a poor orphan, with nothing redeeming or attractive about him, and she should have wanted nothing to do with him, but her actions had shown that her interest was genuine. His vast experience with the female population had taught him that such a woman simply did not exist, his brother's wife excepted. And yet, Lady Eugenia had looked upon the foundling with an affection bordering on love. She had not even grown disgusted when the baby had soiled her gown.

In that moment, something had shifted inside of him, like a novel view through a prism. It was as though ordinary objects were painted in vibrant hues and sunlight—colored with beauty. It had been some years since he had had any contact with these finer emotions, and they remained strong even when he was away from her.

"Are you tired?" he asked as he handed her a glass of cold

ratafia. He stood at a respectful distance, although he wished to put his arm around her and shield her from the crowds that seemed to edge too close. "We can sit this next dance out if you'd like."

She sipped before answering. "I am tired, although I should be too young to admit to such a thing." She smiled up at him, and although he could not put his arm around her, he could offer it to her.

"Then let us sit," he said. "If you are active in both society events at night and in your care for the orphans in the mornings, it is only natural you should be fatigued."

The ballroom was agreeably situated with plenty of room for both dancing and conversation; it was a simple thing to lead her over to the chairs in one of the alcoves. The space was almost a small room in and of itself, except for the fact that the open front made it easily visible from the floor. Surprisingly, there was no one else occupying the other chairs in their alcove, so they would be able to speak with a degree of intimacy. Other members of the *ton* would consider the ball too far beneath them. And yet, it was proving to be the nicest ball he had attended in his life as a gentleman, a fact more likely to do with Lady Eugenia.

John turned in his chair so he might have a better view of her, aware of his fortune to be given such perfect liberty to approach her. To converse with one of Lady Eugenia's status. It was as though he had never fallen out of favor at all. This would change in the blink of an eye if ever she were to learn who he was. He was suddenly determined that she would *not* learn it, for he liked her far too well to see a change in her opinion of him.

"Does your father approve of your attending parties like this?" he asked, the unwelcome reminder intruding on his thoughts.

She gave the tiniest lift of a shoulder. "He is not in London. I hardly think he would be pleased with my decision, but he does seem to trust Mrs. Buxton, so I have allowed that to assuage my conscience."

John had a view of Mrs. Buxton on his left. At least, he assumed it was her because Miss Buxton was standing at her side looking slightly bored, and she shared similar features with the older woman.

"Why does he?" He caught himself. "I mean to say, it is none of my affair, of course, but the Buxtons do not seem to be the sort of family an earl would allow his daughter to associate with."

"They are not, I suppose. But my mother liked Mrs. Buxton, and my father respected my mother. The friendship between the women of the two families had been long established by the time my mother died. I suppose my father did not want to take anyone else away from me, so he allowed it to continue."

"That was considerate of him," John replied in a carefully neutral voice. He would have to take care not to reveal any of his true thoughts concerning the earl.

"My father is a considerate man."

Two matrons passed by where they were sitting and stopped to greet another small group, closing off the Buxtons from his sight. As they congregated in front of him, with the heaviest matron standing in the center, the group effectively cut off their view of not only the dancing, but nearly all of the room. John thought about Lady Eugenia's words concerning her father. Did he truly show consideration to his own flesh and blood—or was she dissembling?

The women continued to gossip in front of them, facing the ballroom, and likely never having noticed they were there. He swiveled in his chair to face Lady Eugenia, wondering if she had noticed that they had been granted a momentary private haven.

Despite her perfect posture, she appeared relaxed. Their conversation was of such an easy nature he suspected she was as comfortable with him as he was with her, despite the attraction that seemed to buzz between them. He had long been in the habit of keeping company with ladies of quality, but he had never met one so elevated and natural all at once. She flashed him a smile then, one that went right through him and unraveled his train of thought.

"I do not know what I would do without Margery's friendship." When he looked confused, she leaned in to explain, "By Margery, I mean Miss Buxton."

John froze at her proximity, noticing the perfection of her pale skin, her pert upturned nose, and lips that begged to be kissed. He could scarcely keep track of the conversation, so he uttered a mundane reply, forcing his eyes away.

"She seems like a pleasant companion."

Against his will, his mind went back to his rakish ways when he thought nothing of stealing a kiss from any set of desirable lips that was near enough to make such a thing possible. He glanced at her again, but this time with the stark reminder that she was a gently bred lady, besides being daughter to a peer. It was easy to forget the fact when she was so approachable, and even friendly.

"Yes. She makes me laugh, and I don't always have much of that." Lady Eugenia had not moved from him, and it occurred to him that perhaps she longed for the closeness as much as he did. This time the temptation proved great, and he allowed his eyes to rest on her face.

"Do you like to laugh, then?" His lips quirked upward as soon as he asked it. There was much he wished to know about her, but suddenly this was the thing he wanted to know the most.

"I love it," she said, smiling, and suddenly he saw it. He saw the warmth and humor bubbling up like a spring out of the earth. She was not a cold person. Certainly, her posture was stiff, and her beauty of the glacial kind. When she was unsure or when meeting someone new, as in their first encounter, she appeared to be distant. But now he noticed that her smile caused her eyes to sparkle. He could not stop staring into those eyes now.

"If I were in your life, I would attempt to induce such smiles all the time," he said. "They are very pretty."

Her blush deepened. The sounds in the room became indistinguishable, and the candlelit atmosphere impossibly romantic. Never had he been so powerless, so prey to the influence of a temptation that he was ready to surrender to it as though his own will was as weak as straw. He could not help himself as he leaned in, almost closing the distance between them so that his lips were a hand's breadth from hers. Her eyes widened, and her mouth formed a perfect "O."

Two of the women in front of them broke away, and with the influx of sudden light, the room came back into focus. Along with that was the sight of the people who might have witnessed their indiscretion had his intention to kiss her not been interrupted. He had been hopelessly lost to their surroundings, and the fact disconcerted him. When had that ever happened to him before? Such a thing could not be permitted now, not when he had much to lose.

He dared to glance at her, and her eyes were trained straight ahead. The pink tinge had not left her cheeks, yet he could not guess at her thoughts.

"Why are you working at an asylum?" she asked without looking at him. At first, he was too flustered to understand her question, but when its meaning reached him, he grew wary. He had forgotten himself and let down his reserve.

She dropped her gaze to her lap before looking ahead at some distant point. "I know you said you have your personal reasons, and I do not wish to pry. It is only…"

When she did not go on, he could not help but to prompt her. "It is only?"

She turned her eyes to him then, answering softly, "It is only that you seem so very much a gentleman."

The words pierced him with guilt and confusion and brought him fully back to his real situation. It was not a good beginning, not if he wished to redeem his reputation. And he *had* to redeem his standing in society. It was all he had.

He hesitated—wrestling within himself—before turning back to her. "I assure you, I am no gentleman. I am sorry if that is unpleasant news to you."

She sighed softly, placing her hands between her knees, rocking them back and forth in a way that seemed out of place for a ball, and for an earl's daughter. It seemed like something a young girl might do, and it only endeared her more to him.

"It is not unpleasant, no. I do not care so much, as long as you faithfully manage the orphanage and find a way to use the donations to help more children."

He had the overwhelming urge to ask her if she found it unpleasant on a personal level because she could not entertain any thoughts of courtship if he were no gentleman. She could not—could she? Surely he would never have a chance with her as plain Mr. Rowles, working as steward at the asylum?

He could not ask her that, though. His misfortune had changed him. Perhaps the man he once was would have done so, for he had always liked nothing more than attempting the outrageous. Besides that, he liked and respected Lady Eugenia too much to engage in anything like idle flirtation. If only he could know something of what she was thinking.

"Do you find it unpleasant that you must keep company with a man of my caliber?" he asked, instead.

She glanced at him, a crease between her brows. "No. That means nothing to me. A person is defined by their character, not by the title or situation they were born into."

"And do you find my character...acceptable?" He smiled, but

it was only the barest tug at his lips. It was a nervous smile as he waited, breathless, for the answer.

This was a dangerous conversation, for it danced into the space of intimacy which was something he could not, at present, afford. Despite knowing this, he could not stop. Somehow, the dawning possibility of friendship, forbidden though it was, made him want to hope. She would not have given anything of herself if she didn't like him, at least a little. He had gathered that right from their first meeting.

She turned in his direction and met his look with a perceptive one of her own. "You know very well I find your character acceptable—what I know of it at any rate. I would not be sitting here talking to you if I did not, for there are many other people I had hoped to talk to tonight."

Her admission sobered him, even as it made his heart race with the implication. He could no longer stay silent.

"I should not say this, for it is most ridiculous coming from one who is beneath your notice, but..." He covered the tips of her fingers with his, and she looked up in surprise. "I find your character beautiful—and without equal."

Lady Eugenia was fair and nothing could keep her blush from burning bright when something incited it. He found even that touching, and beautiful. He had never come close to experiencing anything like what he felt for this woman in so short a time. And he was not without experience in consorting with the fairer sex.

"That is a very kind thing to say."

The music ended, and John had no choice but to help her to her feet. They stood unmoving for a moment before he came to his senses. "May I bring you to Miss Buxton?"

She nodded.

He was reluctant for their moment to end, but he had no choice in the matter. Even if he had still been society's darling, he would have to limit his dances to two. However, instead of attending her in her drawing room the next day—something he had never felt compelled to do when he lived as a gentleman, although he had accompanied friends who did—he would meet her at the asylum.

They reached the Buxtons, who both broke off from their conversation to smile at him and Lady Eugenia. He bowed a greeting to them, and then turned and bowed to her.

"Good evening, my lady."

She nodded in reply, her smile warm and speaking, as though their relationship had grown in her eyes the same way it had in his. He turned and let out a silent exhale. He was in danger of losing his head over this woman, and he could not have settled on a more complicated choice if he tried.

The next morning, John was disappointed when Lady Eugenia did not come but thought that perhaps the fatigue of the night before had kept her home. When she still did not come in the afternoon, he began to doubt what he had been coming to view as the beginning of a mutual attachment. Such a connection was hopeless, of course. She was his social superior, and he was posing as a common man, not even a gentleman. Not only that—unbeknownst to her, he was trying to expose her father. Those facts alone should have doused any ardor or hopes he had in her direction, but they hadn't. It was the first time he actually liked a woman enough to pursue her. Everything in him dictated that he put on blinders and not consider what complications the future might hold.

There was another cause for dissatisfaction. At the dinner party the night before, the hostess had introduced him to two men who had donated to the orphanage in its early days and had not done so since. He had been given a chance to ask them in quite a natural way whether they had enjoyed seeing the fruits of their investment. Both had seemed content with the way their donations had been handled and were proud to have contributed to the future of such a fine institution. Meanwhile, after a week of looking through old ledgers, he was getting nowhere with his attempt to expose fraud.

If there was any desire to give up, it was thwarted by the knowledge that this was his only chance to regain his standing in the *ton*. That, and the fact that if he left now, he was not going to see Lady Eugenia again, for he would never cross her path at any society event. He would not be invited to the places she went to, and she was unlikely to attend a ball such as the one they had met at last night.

Lord Blackstone had given him an open invitation to return to the club if and when he wished to meet its members. He was just curious enough to see what sorts of members there were, and besides, he might be given a chance to dig a little more into Lord Blackstone's identity. The viscount was eccentric, but he seemed to be extraordinarily well connected. Perhaps he would assist John in other ways than by simply procuring for him an invitation to a ball. Perhaps Blackstone would give him concrete information about Lord Goodwin. At the very least, he could see if such an opportunity arose.

This was how he found himself in front of the club at the close of day, when the lights were already lit inside. The bowl in the window had been replaced by a statue, which resembled an elk's antlers. He looked at the other window, but this one had been curtained and there was no view inside. Grasping the crow's head, he rapped at the door.

This time it was Sacks who answered the door, and he stared a minute before recognition dawned. Then, he smiled broadly. "Come in, Mr. Aubin. Come in. I am watching the door while Plockton is away. Lord Blackstone will be glad to see that you have returned."

John handed Sacks his hat and coat with an irrational

misgiving that the man was going to place it on the boar's head mounted on the wall to his left. He did not. He opened a door that appeared to have a rack for such things, then led the way to Lord Blackstone's office. When John did not follow him, he turned back.

"Are you coming? Did you want to see Lord Blackstone?"

"Yes," John said, faltering. "I assumed you wanted to inform him of my visit first."

"No need for that. He is in the drawing room with the other gentlemen. When he's there, no need to announce you. You may go straight in."

"I see."

John trailed behind the servant, on edge to learn who the members of the club were. Sacks opened the door to the drawing room, and the men immediately in view stopped their conversation briefly to look at John. Then they turned back without a word. He should have felt uncomfortable, but it was rather nice not to be given particular notice, especially when this had not been positive in recent months.

"Mr. John Aubin," Sacks announced to the room at large before retiring. There were a few murmured replies of welcome.

Armchairs and sofas were set out in various places throughout the room with small tables at each side for those who wished to read alone or sit together and talk. Lord Blackstone was in one of those chairs, deep in conversation.

John looked around but did not recognize any of the other gentlemen. He chose a seat that was near enough to two of them that he could be included in their conversation if they invited him, but not so close as to be intrusive. One was a young man who had only one leg—the other was a nicely carved wooden stump. A pair of crutches sat at his side. The other was an older, distinguished gentleman who seemed to be someone John might have met at White's.

"Afternoon, Aubin," the younger one said. "My name is Harold Smart. I should probably commiserate if you are in this club, except that we have too glorious a time to regret having joined it."

"Aye, that's the truth," the older gentleman said in the nearby chair. "I am Sir Humphrey Baskerton. I'm one of the original members from when Blackstone first had the idea to start the club."

He followed John's gaze to the wall where a thick python was nailed to it, a brass candleholder perched in its mouth. "Ah, you'll get used to it. It's Blackstone's doing. He has a penchant for not letting any deceased being wither away into nothingness. He's a natural-born collector—even of misfits." Sir Humphrey laughed, and Mr. Smart joined him.

"Most of us know of each other's reasons for being blackballed, although there are some who will not tell. Me, for instance, I was accused and cleared of mutiny, but society did not appreciate the lingering stain." Mr. Smart smiled at John in such a natural way, it set him at his ease. "Feel free to unburden yourself if you wish. And call me Harry—everyone does."

John hesitated. He did wish to unburden himself. He had not even done so with his brother—not fully—although he would have to do that at some point. He just didn't want Gregory to talk him out of his plans for revenge. As a result, he had no one he could talk to about his expulsion from society. At least the men here would be able to relate to him. In that moment he decided.

"I overheard Lord Goodwin attempting to rid himself of some worthless shares in a private equity deal after he had learned of inside information. It would not have concerned me were it not for the fact that he had been encouraging other members of the *ton* to invest, and he had no intention of making them aware of their upcoming loss."

"Goodwin." Sir Humphrey gave a sound of derision between a bark and a huff. "That doesn't surprise me."

"Does it not?" John asked. "Everyone else thinks him the portrait of benevolence."

"Is that what happened?" Harry asked. "You made his perfidy public and it did not go well?"

"Exactly so," John replied, his tone dry. "I only spoke to Lord Perkins, who I knew was one of the investors. But he did not believe me."

"And let everyone else know you were the voice of doubt impugning the character of a peer," Harry surmised. "Except Goodwin did not call you out because he is known to be a poor shot."

"Was that the reason?" John asked. "I was told it was because he would not meet someone whose character as a gentleman was in doubt." Remembering those words still stung.

"The steam duty tax was not levied by Parliament, and open trading has brought more orders in, making the venture lucrative. Therefore, Goodwin's reputation is still pristine," Sir Humphrey announced.

John turned to stare at him. "You seem to know quite a bit about the situation."

"I keep my eye on Goodwin's comings and goings and report them to Blackstone. I have my own reason for doing so. He and I do not have an amicable past." He met John's gaze. "No, he was not the one who had me blackballed, but he would surely have found a reason to do so if someone else had not done it first. We are not friends."

"What happened between you and Goodwin?" John asked. Perhaps in Sir Humphrey he might have an ally.

Sir Humphrey's expression grew dark. "He ruined a young woman on my estate and left her to fend for herself."

John paused in surprise. He found that Lord Goodwin could indeed sink lower in his esteem.

"I see. And so you confronted him on the matter."

"I made him aware of my discontent, yes. And he did not appreciate having his sins exposed."

"So what got you blackballed then, Sir Humphrey?" Harry asked him. "You're such a fixture here, I've never thought to ask."

Sir Humphrey shrugged. "Oh, that was years before. I challenged Lord Aberdeen to a duel because he attempted to elope with my betrothed, who was the daughter of a duke. Word got out, and *I* was accused of dragging the lady's name through the mud. Needless to say, we never married, she and I."

John stared at him, waiting for more. "And Lord Aberdeen for convincing a duke's daughter to elope? Was he blackballed, too?"

"Why, no." Sir Humphrey sent him a droll look. "Society liked him better than they did me, and society is a fickle beast."

"Too bad Blackstone can't stuff it and mount it on the wall," Harry said with a snort.

Chapter Seven

When Geny returned to Margery's side, she fully expected to be pressed with questions she would have trouble answering. And although her friend raised her eyebrows with a speaking look and left her mother to step over to her, Geny thought she detected something else in her gaze that she could not fully discern—a warning. Had Margery been watching them?

Perhaps Geny had only imagined that Mr. Rowles had been about to kiss her. His face was close to hers, and there was a focus in his gaze, enough that her breath left her chest. But the idea was pure folly on her part, for surely he would not do such a thing. How could he when they had no understanding and were in such a public place? At least, she did not think he would do it. If only it did not trouble her how much she had secretly hoped he would. That longing would be for her to privately mull over while she lay her head on her pillow that night.

Alas, there had been no time for private confidences because Mrs. Buxton was fully engaged in performing the duties of watchful mama, while remembering to introduce Geny to the people she thought she would most like to meet. Since Margery was unable to pepper her with the questions she clearly wished to, it was unsurprising to hear the sounds of her arrival the next day.

"Mother was gracious enough to spare me for the afternoon so I might come and visit." Margery removed her bonnet and cloak and handed those to the footman, then faced Geny with laughter in her eyes. "Although I suppose I did not give her much choice in the matter."

Geny turned to the footman, who hovered by the door waiting for instructions. "Adam, have some tea brought for us. That is all we will need."

Margery sat across from her and waited until the door closed behind them before piercing Geny with an intent look. There was still a hint of a smile on her face, and her eyes sparkled with interest. "Now who is he?"

Geny did not pretend ignorance. "*He* is the new steward," adding the emphasis although she was sure her friend would remember.

"From the asylum. I was sure I had remembered the name!" Margery exclaimed.

"Exactly. I was astonished to find him at Mrs. Sookholme's. He said that a friend had secured an invitation for him to attend. What did you think of him?"

Margery sat back and cast her eyes up, as though attempting to conjure up his image. Geny did not need any such assistance to call his face to mind. Throughout the evening, she had glanced in his direction more than once, as he stood in conversation with two of the gentlemen she recognized as having donated to the asylum. Thankfully, he was facing away and did not see her pointed interest. She hoped no one else did. Then, at the end of the night, he caught her regard before leaving and dipped his head in a bow. The small gesture of recognition had sent a surge of delight through her.

"He is a handsome man, I will give you that." Margery

brought her attention back to Geny. "Truly, I have never known anyone to catch your eye before, and that is what intrigues me the most. Unless, of course, you are hiding a score of suitors at the various balls I am not invited to."

Geny laughed. "No, you know of every one of my suitors—of which there are precisely none."

"There have not always been none," Margery reminded her. "There was Mr. Saxton—"

"Who said he found orphans to be nasty little creatures," Geny finished for her.

"And then there was Mr. Davidson, who has fifteen thousand a year—"

"Who spit at me when he talked," Geny said, pulling her mouth down in distaste. "So you see why I have not been interested in any of the ones my father has put before my notice."

"I do. There is only one thing that worries me," Margery said.

Her friend hesitated, her face more serious than Geny was accustomed to. She did not like where this was going—did not like the idea that Margery would find fault with Mr. Rowles and thought she knew where the hesitation might be coming from.

"It is only because he is not a gentleman that you seek to put me on my guard. But you are being more prejudiced than I," Geny protested. "If anyone should find fault with the disparity of our station, it should be me or no one."

Margery shook her head. "No, it is not that. I only wish for a husband who is worthy of you and who loves you, nothing more. As much as I am in doubt of finding such happiness for myself, I feel certain you will find your perfect match. It is only...do you remember the gentleman my mother was speaking to last night when you came up to us?"

"She spoke to a great number of gentlemen—unless it was the one she was urging you in the carriage to favor with your attention?"

"The very one. Mr. Thompson. She has hopes in his direction, which of course must be dashed."

Margery paused and swiveled to look as Adam entered the room, carrying the tea platter, a maid trailing behind him. Together, they set out the tea and cakes before withdrawing, allowing Margery to continue. "Mr. Thompson said that at first glance he mistook your Mr. Rowles for another gentleman by the name of Mr. John Aubin."

Geny waited for more, and when nothing was forthcoming, replied, "It is natural to mistake a person for someone else."

"That is true, which is why I do not hold much stock in what he says." Margery dropped her gaze to her hands in a rare sign of reticence. "However, he did say that Mr. Aubin was chased out of town. In essence, he was shunned by society and blackballed by the clubs he was a member of. Mr. Thompson doesn't know him personally, for he does not mingle in those circles. But his friend pointed him out at a boxing match amidst the spectators in January." She smoothed the gloves she held on her lap, then raised her eyes to Geny's. "Mr. Rowles bore a decided air to the gentleman he had seen there. He admitted that it was at night, and he had only a brief glance, which allows that he might have been mistaken."

"Well, there you have it." Geny shrugged. "It is no more than a rumor or a mistake."

"Yes." Margery dragged out the word, then drew in a quick breath. "I am sure it is that. I would not worry about it were it not that this Mr. Aubin is reputed to be a terrible man. A hardened gamester who cleaned out another gentleman in one night by cheating, thereby ruining him. A frequenter of the less reputable establishments. A penchant for strong drink."

It was strange that Margery would so insist on a chance remark. Besides, Geny could not picture any similarities between Mr. Rowles and such a man. He was nothing like that Mr. Aubin. She sensed his kindness and his stability and trusted it to be genuine. She crinkled her brows. "Even so, you said that Mr. Thompson admitted he was probably mistaken."

"'Tis true. My concern comes only from a sense of protectiveness for you, but if you think the suggestion preposterous then I believe you." Margery studied her expression until a smile appeared. "It appears you have already given your heart to Mr. Rowles, haven't you?"

For the sake of something to do—something to manage the feelings that were too new and raw—Geny leaned down and stirred tea leaves into the pot, then sat back. She was nervous. Excited. It was hard to contain such emotions, and she could not for the life of her hide them from her best friend.

"I don't know what it is, for I hardly know the man, but each time I am in his presence, I cannot help but like him more. Yes, he is a handsome man, but it is beyond that. There is a quality to him impossible to explain. I can't help but be drawn to him. And I *do* like him." She briefly covered her face with her hands to hide the laughter that escaped her lips, then sat back upright, as though her governess might still be watching and ready to scold. "He said that he found my character beautiful and without equal. I have not stopped thinking about that."

"Did he?" Margery's widened eyes showed just what she thought of the compliment. "I must like the man too, then, for he clearly has good taste. Another reason to ignore Mr. Thompson. He is no judge of character."

Geny laughed. "Do not be so hard on Mr. Thompson. It was an innocent mistake." A comfortable silence fell between them and Geny poured tea for them both.

"Well, then," Margery said, accepting her cup. "I hope I shall have a chance to know Mr. Rowles better, for if you like him, then so must I. At least the fact that he is not a gentleman ensures he is not likely to snub me."

"He would not dare," Geny said, narrowing her eyes with mock fierceness.

On Monday, Geny went to the orphanage as usual, and although she had Charity style her hair into a softer arrangement, she wore a more sensible gown in the color of rifle green. Once again, the simple act of climbing the stairs to reach the office she shared with the head matron left her breathless in her anticipation of seeing Mr. Rowles. Mrs. Hastings was at the point of leaving the office, and she stepped back to allow Geny to enter.

"The foundling baby appears to be completely on the mend, I thought you might wish to know. He even smiled at Nurse today." Mrs. Hastings was rather severe overall, but Geny knew she had a soft spot for babies.

She hung her coat on the hook and turned to face the head matron. "That is wonderful news. I had planned to visit him this morning."

Geny only taught the five children reading and writing once a week, which gave her the freedom to attend to other matters in the asylum. She had insisted upon teaching one class, however, for although she did not have the time to devote many hours, it was her favorite time of the week. She also planned to visit Gabriel and see how he was coming along with his training. He was a good-natured twelve-year old boy who had a bright future ahead of him.

Mrs. Hastings left for her errand, and Geny went over to her desk. There was nothing precisely she had to do, which left her with time to spare. She sat, prey to her state of indecision—prisoner to her desire to see him while wrestling with her good sense. It was impossible to go directly into Mr. Rowles's office. She had no reason to do so and therefore must look ridiculous should she attempt it. However, nothing that she had planned to do at the asylum today seemed as important as this. She could not imagine leaving without at least exchanging a few words with him.

She sat for a while, knotting her fingers, the only sounds in the orphanage muffled and coming from far away. Then, an idea sprang to her mind that was so clever it caused her to inhale sharply. She would go to Mr. Dowling's office first, for she did have a reason to speak to him. He had recently placed Betsy as a kitchen maid in Mrs. Strathmore's household. The asylum had the practice of checking in two weeks after a placement to make sure the situation was working well, and she could ask him about it. From there, it would only be natural to step into Mr. Rowles's office to wish him a good day.

She wondered if he would be glad to see her and was already smiling in anticipation. He had said her character was beautiful, and that was quite the loveliest thing anyone had ever said to her.

Having decided upon a course of action, Geny stood and went to carry out her mission. She went through the parlor and was almost at the doorway of the meeting room when Mr. Dowling appeared through it, causing a near run-in. They both drew back in surprise.

"I thought I heard your voice, my lady." He bowed and smiled at her. She did not know why his presence always made her want to flee. "How do you do?"

Her initial disappointment was overpowering, for now she had no reason to visit Mr. Rowles's office. She might be forced to leave the orphanage without having spoken to him, and she would not be given a clue if he felt anything like she did. Was it only she who thought about him constantly? Did he return her regard? All of these thoughts and sensations flew through her mind in the space it took for her to return a polite smile and civil nod.

"I am very well. I was wishing to speak with you—"

He did not let her finish before saying with an arch smile, "I do not know what I could have done to have merited any space in your ladyship's thoughts."

Geny paused in exasperation. She was accustomed to such fulsome behavior from him, although her wintry reaction to it would have signaled to a more intelligent man that it was not welcome. "I was wondering if you have been to the Strathmore residence to see how Betsy is getting on?"

He looked momentarily nonplussed at her question, as though he did not even remember who Betsy was. Then a look of comprehension dawned on his face, and he rallied. "I have not yet done so, but I had plans to do that this week."

This caused her irritation to rise. Mr. Dowling paid attention where it was not welcome and lost it where it was most needed. She put on a cultivated look of surprise that she hoped would depress his pretension.

"But it has been a month since Betsy was placed, Mr. Dowling. Usually this step is something that must be accomplished after two weeks."

Her displeasure was evident should he choose to note it. She could not be certain he would, since he seemed to have a particularly thick skin.

An oily smile returned to his face. "I have been busy arranging other interviews for the orphans who will soon complete their training. But I have not forgotten about Betsy, you may be assured of it, my lady."

Geny was certain he had but merely responded with, "Very well."

There had scarcely been time for a natural pause in the conversation when she had a sudden urge to leave—to walk around the asylum and see that all was in order, as much to get away from Mr. Dowling as to expend her nervous energy. A bold notion of how she might shake off Mr. Dowling struck her, and she seized it before thinking overmuch.

"If you will excuse me, I must meet with Mr. Rowles. A part

of the stable wall is beginning to crumble opposite the chapel. I must bring it to his attention so he might have it repaired."

"Allow me to perform the service for you, my lady," he quickly replied.

This taxed her ingenuity for only the space it took her to remember that she was an earl's daughter and needn't ignore her own wishes out of a self-inflicted obligation to be polite.

"I thank you for your offer, but I will do it."

Mr. Dowling stepped back as though he would give way and act like a sensible man. At the last minute, he held up his two hands in a cautionary gesture, thereby blocking her exit.

"If you will allow me to give you a word of warning, my lady. I am not sure how befitting it is for you to visit the stable in Mr. Rowles's presence." He glanced down the corridor, judging whether he might be overheard, before turning back to her and continuing in a lowered voice. "He is not a gentleman by birth, you see. And therefore, I think you ought to be cautious with him. Who knows what his code of conduct may be? One cannot predict the behavior of a man who is nothing but a commoner."

Geny pressed her lips together and took a moment to control her annoyance. Mr. Dowling was a gentleman in name. He was the fifth son of an impoverished gentleman, and she privately thought that he had taken this position because no other was open to him. It certainly could not be out of interest in the cause that he did so, for he could scarcely perform his duties with less enthusiasm. She did not think his words deserved a reply, and so she waited.

"Besides," he continued in a low pitch, "all I ever see him do is to look into the old account books. He hasn't placed any orders or begun any new repairs. Where is the money Mr. Peyton is handing over to him? Not only does Mr. Rowles lack a gentlemanly status, he does not even behave like a steward. Perhaps we should approach Mr. Peyton with our concerns, for I have doubts that he is performing his role adequately."

Her irritation rose to a pitch, concealed under an impassive face. That Mr. Dowling thought himself properly positioned to give her a warning bothered her more than anything. She hoped he would never lump her into his use of "we" again. It took everything in her to hide her disdain.

"I thank you for your observation regarding Mr. Rowles. I will bring the notion up with my father," Geny said.

In truth, the earl never cared about issues that involved the people working in the orphanage. She had tried in the past to draw his interest there, and it had always been without result. However, she could speak directly to her father's man of business herself if needed. Mr. Peyton oversaw the orphanage, after all. And she was sure that Mr. Dowling's words were spoken more from jealousy than anything else.

"As you wish, my lady." He seemed disappointed.

"As for your warning, you need not concern yourself with my affairs. Mr. Rowles and I will visit the stable in the groom's presence. Besides, I am able to care for myself." It required considerable effort, but she smiled at Mr. Dowling and moved to step past him. "Now, if you will excuse me..."

She let the rest dangle and left him to go to Mr. Rowles's office, her relief palpable as soon as she had escaped, although she felt Mr. Dowling's eyes on her back.

She walked in quiet steps down the corridor, stopping in front of the doorway of Mr. Rowles office and looked in. He sat at his desk in his shirtsleeves, poring over the account books, just as Mr. Dowling had said. To her untrained eye, these books did not look new, so there might have been something in the accusation. But Mr. Rowles was likely trying to make sure everything had been noted correctly.

He looked up and smiled broadly when he saw her, which made her forget any doubt the headmaster had tried to instill in her. Mr. Rowles stood and bowed before glancing down at his appearance. His smile fled, replaced by a panicked expression.

"Forgive me," he said, reaching for his coat in a hasty gesture. "I should not have removed my coat in such an improper manner. But I was growing too warm."

"I do not mind it," she said, hiding her smile. *On the contrary. It only shows you to advantage.*

She stepped back into the corridor to give him privacy and allow him to finish dressing, thinking what an intimate thing it was to be standing in the same room with a gentleman as he buttoned his coat. When he cleared his throat, she stepped back into the office. For the first time, Mr. Rowles appeared to be flustered and did not meet her gaze. It was nice to see him uncertain for once, which was how she felt each time she was in his presence. It caused her heart to flutter, and she bit her cheeks to keep from smiling.

"How may I assist you, my lady?" he asked, his smile sheepish but with a warm light in his eyes.

"You may accompany me to the stable," she said. "That is, if you can spare the time. There is a matter there requiring your attention. Part of the wall is about to crumble and needs to be repaired."

Mr. Rowles gestured forward. "I am perfectly ready to accompany you. Let us attend to it now."

"It should not take long."

They walked in silence past Mr. Dowling's office, where he sat at his desk, only glancing up briefly as they went by. They continued into the corridor and down the stairs leading to the courtyard. When they stepped out on the cobblestones, he held out his arm.

"Please allow me to escort you. The ground is uneven here, and I would not like for you to turn your ankle."

"You are very kind." Her stomach gave a little dip as she slipped her arm into his. Yes, it was just as firm and solid as she had remembered it.

An unwelcome thought accosted her as she wondered for

the first time what her father would think of Mr. Rowles and whether he would countenance the match. She was certain he would not and did not dare to imagine what it would be like to go against her father's will.

"So, I am no gentleman and therefore cannot possess a basic code of conduct that would safeguard you against unwanted advances," he said, pulling her thoughts from the unpleasant direction in which they had gone. For a moment she was confused, unable to make sense of his words, until she realized that he had overheard Mr. Dowling from his office. His gaze was trained ahead, and when she glanced at him, saw a brief quirk of his lips that let her know he was amused more than anything.

"You heard that, did you?" She gave a quiet laugh. "But you will have noticed that I did not take the warning seriously."

"Did you not?" he asked. "I will have to take your word for it. Only Mr. Dowling's words reached me. I heard none of yours."

The smile still sounded in his voice, and she replied tartly, "I am here with you, am I not?"

"You are." He gave an ever so slight pull toward him so that she felt the warmth of him through her pelisse. "And I thank you for the trust you have placed in my common decency."

She glanced at him again and, although he still wore a teasing look, she was fairly certain there was some sincerity in his words.

Chapter Eight

"Careful, my lady." John steered Lady Eugenia away from a puddle in her path, reminding himself to pay more attention and not lead her straight into one. There was something about her that made him forget everything else.

Ever since the Sookholme ball, he had been unable to pull his thoughts away from Lady Geny—for that was what he had begun to call her in his mind. She was a beauty, that much was clear. But she had also been surprisingly easy to talk to when they were at the ball together. He had never before enjoyed such a simple, natural exchange with a woman. Usually, women were for charming, and he knew the easy victory of winning them over simply for the sake of being able to do it. Lady Geny, however, was no easy victory; he could not view her in that light.

True, he had sensed, and had been nearly certain of, her interest in him from the beginning. The open way she had spoken with him that night confirmed it, as did the way she froze when he had nearly lost his mind and kissed her in public. She had been as affected by the mood as he was. The fact that she had disregarded Mr. Dowling's words of caution only reinforced which way her heart lay.

But this could bring John no satisfaction, for she was far above his touch. It was not that she was a daughter to a peer—he had never cared for such a thing. It was the way she loved the foundling infant and all the orphans. The way she had seemed to accept him from the beginning without having proof of his status. On the contrary—she believed him to be nothing more than a common man with no ties to the gentry. And yet, she treated him with a manner that was beyond cordiality. She showed warmth and interest. He did not deserve a woman like that, not with his less-than-pristine past.

"Mr. Dowling does not appear to like you," she said as they neared the stable.

"I believe we view each other with an equal degree of prejudice," he replied, careful not to say that he had taken an instant dislike to Mr. Dowling. It had been immediately clear the man was bent on winning Lady Geny's regard, though he would never succeed. John did not like to boast about himself, but he knew enough about women to know that she would never respond to Dowling's flattery.

They stepped into the cool, dim interior of the stable, and she held on to his arm for seconds more before dropping it and pointing eastward.

"It is there. The stable hand informed Mr. Biggs of it in his last week as steward. I believe he did not have the mind for repairs that he would not be around to finish."

They walked in the direction she indicated, the straw and distinct smell of horses teasing John's nostrils. They passed one of the stalls where a roan horse bobbed his head up and down at Geny, and she reached into the pocket of her cloak, pulled out a bit of apple, and fed it to him.

"Yours?" he asked, smiling at her. She and the horse had such an instinctive way between them that he was certain she must know it.

"My father's. And here is the other half of the pair. Hero." She reached up and gave the second gelding a bit of apple as well.

"You are well prepared," he observed.

"Always." She flashed him a smile, showing two deep dimples on either side. How could he ever have found her cold?

He had frequently bought and sold horses when he was living as a gentleman—when he was surviving on gambling wins, the small inheritance from his mother, and the expectations from his brother's estate. Now, he kept only one pair for driving and a stallion for riding. The stallion he had left at his brother's estate.

That reminded John of the letter from his brother he had tucked into the pocket of his cloak, which he had not yet read. His fondness for Greg had been submerged by feelings of guilt at how low he had been brought in life. He was unworthy of the gift of the Westerly estate. Since he had fallen out of society, he had become significantly more restrained in his spending. But that didn't atone for the way he had been living for the years before it, when he had plowed through his small fortune with wild living. His brother did not know even half of his exploits and was as yet unaware of his expulsion from society. The thought of telling him sent his mood plummeting.

"This is it," Lady Geny said, pointing to a portion of the wall, and he followed her gaze up.

The ceilings were as high in the stable as they were on the ground floor of the asylum. The weak portion of the wall was visible above his head, and on the other side of the wall was the chapel. It did indeed need to be dealt with as soon as possible, for if the stones fell, it could injure both horses and people. When he had sought the position of steward, his mind had been bent only on revenge; the idea had not occurred to him that he would be required to oversee such projects. That had been naïve.

"I do not have the contacts at my disposal to begin the repairs immediately," he said, before he had thought the better of it. He may as well admit he had no experience as a steward.

"Yes, I imagine they would be different in London than where you were before. Where did you say you were from again?"

"Surrey," he answered, prey to a mix of feelings. He was grateful that she had seen the best in him and assumed that his lack of knowledge came from his not hailing from London. There was also the fear that the more information he gave her about his life, the more likely it would lead her back to finding out who he truly was. He wished he could have known her before his fall and pursue her through traditional means.

But then, her father would not have allowed it—not even then.

"We will have to anchor it with a pattress plate and connect it to the opposite end of the stable with a tie rod." He knew that from experience on his stepfather's estate, for it had been done on the wall around the dower house.

"Then we must tighten the bolt until the wall straightens." He shot her a glance, smiling wryly. "But of course you do not care how it is to be repaired. You simply wish to see it done."

"I cannot argue with you, Mr. Rowles." There was humor in her eyes when she looked at him. "And yet, you described it so knowledgeably, I am ready to express my admiration."

He chuckled. "Good. Now, I have seen it, and you may leave it in my hands." He turned toward her, unwilling to leave the quiet haven of the stable. It was cold and damp—dark even—and yet he was happy to be in her presence.

With reluctance, he turned toward the entrance and indicated with his head. "Shall we?"

She took a deep breath and pivoted as well. Was he mistaken, or was she as reluctant to leave as he was?

"Did your mother come to the asylum as often as you do?" he asked, wishing to know more about her. He could hardly imagine that any of her goodness came from her father. Lady Goodwin must have been a paragon.

"Yes." She smiled in reminiscence. "She did not permit me to accompany her each time, but I enjoyed our visits when she did. She once told me she was unfashionably interested in the foundling asylum and the fate of the orphans. However, she was too high in society for anyone to cut her for it."

"Your mother sounds like a remarkable woman. You must miss her."

John thought about his own mother, remembering the shock he had experienced at the age of seven when the attending physician announced he would never see her again. She had only been married to John's stepfather for five years, and John had been two when they tied the knot. Gregory had experienced both the loss of his own mother, though scarcely old enough to remember it, and then his stepmother who had been kind to them both. John and Gregory's bond might have been merely that of stepbrothers, but they mourned John's mother together with equal sincerity.

"I do miss her." Lady Geny sighed as they approached the light streaming into the stable from the opening. "There was a time I thought I would not survive her loss. My father is not an affectionate man, you see." She stopped short, and her face took on a guilty expression. "I should not have confessed that to you."

She did not say, *because we are not on intimate enough terms to do so*, and somehow he did not think she thought it either. This comforted him.

He wished to say something that would lift her spirits. "You must take after your mother, then. For I do not think I've met a woman with more affection."

He turned and looked into her eyes, knowing he was acting recklessly. He came dangerously close to flirting, although he meant every word. "I do not mean to be familiar. It is only that I have seen the way you are with the orphans, and it is clear you possess a warm and sympathetic heart."

A stable hand chose that minute to enter the stable leading a horse, and she returned only a quick smile before stepping to the side. "Thank you."

When the stable hand passed by, John held out his arm to lead her back to the orphanage, where they would each have to return to their own affairs. He wished he had a reason to spend more time in her company. It was becoming the most challenging aspect of his current situation. He knew how to pursue a lady in society. One needed only to take her riding in the park —or visit her drawing room.

He quashed a bitter laugh before it erupted as he imagined what it would look like to show up in Lady Eugenia's drawing room. How Lord Goodwin would turn apoplectic to see him there. He did not know if the earl would simply have him thrown out, or if he would attempt violence on his person for the audacity. Then again, did not the member at Blackstone's inform him that the earl was too cowardly for such a thing?

It left John discouraged because there was no way he would be able to attempt an honest pursuit of Lady Geny. How could he? Even if she were able to make her own decisions, her father would have good reason to turn her against him, for his own presence here was a lie. Once she found out, she would cut all ties.

He glanced at her, aware that he had said nothing as they crossed the courtyard. He would not be able to persuade her to do anything at this rate. "Have you been to check on the baby—on Benjamin?"

"Mrs. Hasting said he is doing very well. I have promised to visit him and will do so afterwards." She sent him a glance. "It is only that I wished to speak to you first about the wall, which I considered to be an urgent matter."

Was that true? Or had she done so to spend time with him? "I am glad you did. I will see if I can have someone come and look at the wall within a week."

They had reached the entrance, and a line of boys filed past them. Lady Geny gave them an encouraging nod then turned back to him. "Those are the boys training up for the indoor positions, such as footman."

"Do they have anyone teaching them arithmetic?" he asked.

She thought for a moment. "To own the truth, there has been no talk of it yet. Perhaps because we've had no one offer to teach them. Mr. Biggs was a very kind man, but he was not skilled with children."

"I would be happy to train ones that show promise, if you think it would serve." His offer had come out quickly before he had thought it through. He could only credit it to his desire to please her.

She turned to him, a gleam in her eyes. "Would you indeed? The more possibilities we have for their placement, the more likely we are to see them well situated. We can ask Mr. Dowling to provide a room for you to teach them in, similar to the training room for the footmen."

"That would be excellent," he replied, thinking that her look of gratitude had made his offer worthwhile.

At the same time, he hoped he hadn't indulged in folly to have promised to teach orphans. What did he know about such a thing? And yet, it was not only Lady Geny that had prompted the offer; he knew it would please his brother that he should try. The idea brought him a sense of satisfaction he had not felt in a while.

"I may not need a room, though. I believe I might take two of them in my office, for it is large enough. Perhaps we will start with just the mornings? I can teach them some basic sums, and then we can go over the account books together so they learn how it is used."

She clasped her hands. "Mr. Rowles, that would be wonderful."

Her look of pleasure warmed him, but as soon as he had spoken of balancing the accounts, it occurred to him that he might have overcommitted himself. How was he going to look for discrepancies in the account books if he had a pair of orphan boys watching his every move?

He managed a smile and bowed, his hands clasped behind his back. "I wish you a very good day, Lady Eugenia."

"And I you." She dipped her head and paused ever so slightly before turning away in the direction of the nursery.

John's thoughts were full as he climbed the steps to his office. With all his heart, he wanted to pursue her. He was sure of it, but didn't see how he was to accomplish such a thing. He entered his office, went over to where his cloak hung and pulled the letter from Gregory out of its pocket, then walked over to the window to read it.

John,

I had to learn from Murray that you spent nearly three months at the estate and have only just left it to return to London. May I draw the conclusion from this unprecedented event that you are eager to settle into your new role as landowner and have been making adjustments to that end? Well, I have good news for you. Mr. Wyndham has written to tell me that the papers are finalized and that Westerly estate is officially yours. He will, of course, reach out to you directly with the documents, but he felt it only proper to relay the news to me first.

I do not desire a reply with your thanks, heartfelt or perfunctory, as I've oft told you. Anne and I will have no children of our own, and there is no point in having the estate go to you or your son after I have departed this earth—not when I have no desire to care for it while I am still here. It is better all around this way, and I believe even Father would have agreed. That said, although I do not desire a letter with your thanks, I do desire a letter. You are, after all, the only family left to me, and it matters not that there are no blood ties. Anne sends her love, as do I.

Yours—

Gregory

John stood staring through the window, his thoughts dull rather than overjoyed by the news. He would need to write to his brother—yes. But he would also need to come clean about his former manner of living. To begin such a letter seemed insurmountable.

He resumed his seat where the account books from the foundling asylum's commencement lay open. He used the first portion of each day to see what he could find in the old books, then spent the second half in what was more honorably part of the position he had taken on. Unlike what he had overheard Mr. Dowling accuse him of, he did spend time each day drafting letters to Mr. Peyton who handled the finances for the asylum, placing orders, and carefully recording where the money was being sent.

From looking over the account books, he gathered that Mr. Biggs had been honest in his work. His accounts were meticulous and most added up. But some of the donations the asylum had claimed to have brought in were not showing as having been disbursed. And there were other expenses in recent months that were listed as redirection for mill works, which were likely related to the mill Sir Humphrey had spoken about. But any investment that went into that project should have been kept completely apart. These were currently his only leads into mismanagement. It would be good if he could speak to Mr. Biggs. Perhaps he might find out more.

As much as he disliked having any conversation with Mr. Dowling, he would rather ask him how to find the old steward than visit Mr. Peyton, who might wonder at his curiosity. It would also be faster. John stood and went to the headmaster's office, where he was sitting at his desk, indulging in a cup of tea.

"Mr. Rowles," he said, with a nod of his head.

He did not get to his feet, which was meant as a snub. John did not care overmuch, but it lowered Mr. Dowling in his esteem. Not that his impression was all that favorable before.

"Mr. Dowling," he replied, equally civil and with no more warmth. "I was wondering if you could tell me why Mr. Biggs left his position and where he is now."

Mr. Dowling left him standing while he continued to sip his tea. "Why, I do not know that it is any of your business."

John had expected such a reply, although he had optimistically thought it might be delivered with more respect. "I wish to ask him about a donation that was brought in. The pledge listed five hundred pounds, which is a great amount. However, I have not seen the equal sum in the accounting books. Perhaps the money had been used for repairs without being recorded in the ledgers. That is why I wished to see him."

"Who was the donation from?" Mr. Dowling asked.

John schooled his face, although his irritation rose. He decided he would not bring up the entries that talked about redirecting funds for a mill and instead answered Dowling's question. "Sir Edward Burbank."

"I see."

Mr. Dowling gave the appearance of one who seemed to consider it, but John suspected he had no idea of the financial aspect of things. It would not make sense that he did. If only John knew his own place better, he would have been bolder in responding to such impertinence.

"This is why I wished to have Mr. Biggs's direction. Did he leave London, or can he still be found in the area?" John stood his ground, waiting for Dowling to respond.

Dowling sniffed and glanced up, rubbing the side of his nose. "I am sorry to say, I do not have that information."

John nodded and turned to leave. There was no sense in continuing the conversation or even taking a more civil leave. He would have to seek out Mr. Peyton. The only inconvenience was that he didn't have time to visit the agent until the following week, so it would have to wait. This was not the sort of thing to handle by correspondence.

Chapter Nine

Geny wondered if Mr. Rowles had been able to find a mason to repair the wall in the time since their conversation the week before. He had seemed disconcerted by the fact that he did not know anyone local, so when her father's man of business called, only to find the earl away from home, she took the opportunity to ask him if he knew of laborers who might perform the task. He sent a message the next day with the names of two masons who were located a short drive from the orphanage.

Repairs should not have been her concern, but with the house so quiet, she did not have anything to occupy her mind apart from the asylum. That, and, well—Mr. Rowles. When they visited the stable together, he had been all that was proper, but his praise still echoed in a heart that received so little of it. And she could not forget that moment at the Sookholme ball, still wondering if he had indeed wished to kiss her. Her initial disbelief had begun to give way, and it began to seem possible that he had. After all, he had said he found her character beautiful and had followed this gem of delight with even warmer praise.

Although she was not the best judge of these things, she was nearly certain he had not been flirting when he'd told her she possessed a sympathetic heart. In fact, he had appeared quite sincere. From an impartial view, Mr. Rowles had taken many more liberties than Mr. Dowling had, but they never felt like liberties because she welcomed his notice.

Mr. Dowling never spoke to her in anything approaching intimacy but would allow his regard to linger on hers, even when she gave him no encouragement. He knew he was beneath her notice and therefore did not attempt an overt courtship, but rather hinted at his interest with insinuations. Such behavior made her squirm.

The comportment of Mr. Rowles, who in technical terms was even further beneath her notice, only left her with a desire to spend more time with him. She decided she would seek him out at the orphanage the next day and see if she could assist him in his quest to find someone to do the work. It seemed unlikely that he had a carriage, but she could offer the use of hers. Her father could not object to the excursion, since it was for the good of the asylum.

In the meantime, she and Margery had planned a trip to the Pantheon Bazaar to purchase more textiles that the children could use to practice sewing.

Mrs. Buxton played guardian for such visits, and this was another reason Geny suspected her father allowed her to spend so much time with Margery. He was not inclined to such a role himself, and it was not practical to include the spinster cousin whom he supported financially for these smaller errands. Miss Edwards did not live at the house—the earl did not like her well enough for that—and was only called upon to accompany Geny to the evening society events that would admit her. For the day visits, however, she had Margery.

At precisely two o'clock, the Buxtons' carriage pulled up in front of Geny's house, and she tied on her bonnet as she descended the steps, then went over to where the footman stood holding the door to the carriage.

"Good afternoon, my lady," Mrs. Buxton said, as the footman helped Geny inside to claim her seat next to Margery. Mrs. Buxton always insisted on taking the rear-facing seat so the young ladies might sit side by side. Margery smiled at Geny and grasped her hand in an affectionate clasp.

"Good afternoon," she replied and then turned to Margery as the carriage moved forward. "My father has encouraged me to visit the Elgin Marbles exhibit. Would you care to go with me on Thursday?"

"If it is all right with Mother, I will," she replied with an inquiring glance at Mrs. Buxton, who said she would permit it.

Geny wondered if Mrs. Buxton regretted her daughter having a friend whom she felt obliged to escort everywhere. Despite the fact that Margery's mother was determined to see her daughter successfully settled, she had never encouraged the friendship in order to elevate her daughter's status. Geny suspected it was more in memory of her mother, the late countess, that she did so. Whatever the reason, she had been unfailingly kind in all the years Geny had known her.

When they arrived at the Bazaar, Mrs. Buxton gave instructions to the groom for when to come for them before trailing behind Geny and Margery. By now, Geny knew where the best cloth was to be found, and they wasted no time in going to that corner of the market. Mrs. Buxton knew it, too, and followed at her own pace, sometimes stopping at other tables that caught her interest.

"Miss Buxton!" a gentleman called out from behind them and was heard over the din. Geny felt Margery freeze at her side, and she glanced at her curiously before they both turned.

"How do you do, Mr. Thompson?" Margery offered the gentleman a tight smile as she curtsied. "I believe you must remember Lady Eugenia Stanich from Mrs. Sookholme's ball?"

"Of course. How do you do, my lady?" Mr. Thompson bowed.

He was a well-looking man. Nothing like Mr. Rowles, of course. He was not as robust or as tall. His smile was not as warm, nor his eyes the kind you could lose yourself in. For all that, Mr. Thompson was a confident man who seemed capable of appreciating her friend without fawning over her. He also did not seem to be the type of man who would easily be put off by Margery's show of disinterest, and she would need someone like that. Geny could like him for that reason. He turned back to Margery.

"What a pleasant surprise to see you here, Miss Buxton. Perhaps I might escort you both to wherever you are going?" He followed Margery's searching glance behind him and perceived Mrs. Buxton, who had just arrived. He bowed. "Mrs. Buxton, how do you do?"

She returned his greeting and answered the question he had asked Margery. "You may escort my daughter and Lady Eugenia if you would be so obliged. I had hoped to visit a stand on the opposite end of the bazaar that sells soaps."

Margery brought an enigmatic gaze to her mother that held a degree of irritation to those who knew her. This caused Geny to turn away to hide a smile. She could read her friend very well and, despite the challenging look, she quite suspected that Margery was not as opposed to Mr. Thompson's suit as she let on. Geny had never seen her friend show anything but indifference to suitors in all the years they had known each other, but Mr. Thompson seemed to unsettle her.

"I am happy to oblige," he replied, smiling at Mrs. Buxton. He turned a teasing gaze back to Margery, as though he knew she was disgruntled about this turn of events, and gestured forward with a smile. "We will not be successful in walking three abreast. I will follow both of you."

"You are most obliging," Margery replied in a dry voice, and

Geny turned away to swallow the laughter that rose up. When she looked back, Margery sent a look warning her not to tease. It would be difficult to restrain.

Under other circumstances, Geny would be the first at the table heaped with cloth to sift through it. She was in search of both rags for samplers on which younger orphans might practice their stitches, and the finer cloth that could be used to sew clothing and other articles. The younger orphans practiced sewing pinafores and serviceable skirts that could be worn, and the older ones made more complex garments that would train them for working with a modiste if they became skilled enough.

There was only enough space in the crowd that had gathered for one of them to squeeze in and sort through the cloth, and Margery turned to her.

"My lady, you will be pushed and shoved. I know precisely what you are looking for; I beg you will allow me to find it."

Margery did not give her a chance to protest, and Geny submitted to it, once again concealing her amusement. Her friend was quite determined to avoid Mr. Thompson. As for Geny, she was not likely to receive a better chance to learn why this was and was determined to seize it.

"Mr. Thompson, how are you acquainted with the Buxtons?" she asked. People streamed past them, but Mr. Thompson held his ground and somehow shielded her from the unceasing flow of humanity.

"My father was friends with Mr. Buxton before my father's death. They were rival merchants in ceramics but could never be bothered to dislike each other."

He grinned, and Geny returned it. Oh, she would most definitely tease Margery. What was there not to like in this man?

"So you have known Miss Buxton since...?" She allowed the question to dangle.

"I suppose our whole lives. But I have been away for many years—much of the period of time that she would remember me. I was learning the trade from my mother's brother in Wales."

"Oh." Geny could not hide the surprise in her voice. "So your mother is Welsh."

He shook his head. "No, but my uncle moved to Nantgarw and started a factory there. Although my father's talent lies in earthenware, it was my mother who brought the knowledge of finer ceramics into the marriage. She wished me to learn porcelain painting from my uncle, so I might improve on the designs she was already helping my father with."

"That is most interesting," Geny said. She glanced at Margery, pressed on both sides but undaunted in her search. "Have you found topics of interest with Miss Buxton, then? Considering that both of your families are in the same trade."

"I am well aware of how close you and Miss Buxton are, Lady Eugenia. Without wishing in any way to be impertinent, I believe you must already know the answer to that. Miss Buxton *never* speaks of trade if she can help it."

Geny laughed. "It is much too fatiguing, I am sure she tells you."

"Indeed." He, in turn, glanced at Margery, who kept her back to them as though the cloth selection interested her very much. The general buzz from the crowd gave their conversation a degree of privacy.

"She speaks of all the balls she attends, assuring me that dancing is the only thing that interests her. Dancing, new gowns, and jewels."

"It sounds very much like her, but I wonder if you are aware that it is not truly who she is."

Mr. Thompson looked intrigued. "To own the truth, Miss Buxton puzzles me exceedingly. She informs me in so many words that she is uninteresting and shallow. And yet anyone who can say such a thing could not be uninteresting and shallow, could they? For someone who is both of those things would not know it."

"Miss Buxton attends balls to oblige her mother. She enjoys sitting quietly with me and talking, and she enjoys making clothing or stockings for the orphans." She smiled at him. "So you see? Not quite the frivolous nature she would have you believe."

"Why do you suppose she does it, then?" he asked—humbly, Geny thought. "As much as she pushes me away, I do not have the feeling her heart is engaged elsewhere, or that she is truly bothered by my presence. If I thought she were, I would cease to pursue her so openly."

"Ah, Mr. Thompson. As much as I *could* answer your question, I do not think I shall." Geny tucked her hands behind her back, a smile hovering on her lips.

"The solidarity of two females, I suppose," he replied, looking resigned.

She nodded. There was a comfortable pause in their conversation, and as much as the bazaar was active around them, Geny was protected from it by Mr. Thompson's presence. No space in front of the table had opened up, and she could see that Margery was haggling with the vendor over a pile of cloth she had chosen. Geny turned back to look at Mr. Thompson, suddenly growing nervous. She wished to bring up what he had said about Mr. Rowles and felt that fate had given her a chance to do it now.

"Margery told me that you believe to have recognized Mr. Rowles, the man who works as steward in the foundling asylum—only that you believed him to have been a Mr. Aubin at first?"

"That is so." He furrowed his brows. "If Miss Buxton had not insisted that his name was Mr. Rowles, I would have been certain it was he. However, I cannot credit my memory—especially under such unfavorable circumstances—enough to discredit a lady's word. It is only that they share a great likeness."

"And this Mr. Aubin, who is he?" Geny asked. Margery had mentioned a few things, but she wished to hear it directly from Mr. Thompson. It was not that it made any difference, but she could not help her curiosity over anything that related to Mr. Rowles.

"I know very little," Mr. Thompson admitted. "I have a friend who runs in society some, and he was in a club with the man. The fellow was barred from the club for unsavory behavior. I believe he ruined a gentleman through fraudulent means and spread lies about another."

"He sounds horrid," Geny admitted.

This relieved her mind. There could be no confusing such a person with Mr. Rowles. There might be a bit of natural reticence to him, but he was not so base as to seek a man's ruin, and he would certainly not be the type to spread false witness.

"In a way it relieves my mind, though. Mr. Rowles shares no characteristics with such a man, and I am glad. I should not like for the asylum to be in such unscrupulous hands."

"Then I am relieved for your sake," Mr. Thompson said, looking up as Margery turned toward them. A smile lit his face, but it was lost on Margery who would not look in his direction.

"I have triumphed," she said, holding the pile of fabric up for Geny. Then, as though remembering the figure she had adopted before Mr. Thompson, added, "There is nothing I like more than shopping, even if it is not for my own purposes."

"I can see that," he said gravely, but there was a twinkle in his eye as he looked at her. He took the pile of textiles from her hands and tucked them under his arm.

"You have made quick work of it," Geny said.

"Of course," Margery replied with a tilt to her chin.

Geny shook her head fondly, full of good humor. It had been a satisfactory day. For one thing, she had been able to tell Mr.

Thompson more about who Margery truly was and didn't feel the slightest bit of guilt over betraying her friend in such a way. If he wished to pursue her, he would do so—and perhaps with less discouragement than he might otherwise have felt, now that he knew she was merely difficult to win over and not truly superficial. If he was the man for her, he would push through and win her. And if Margery chose to ignore his advances, then that was her own choice. But Geny did not think she would hold out for long.

Another element contributed to Geny's good humor. She was now confident the man Mr. Thompson had thought Mr. Rowles to be—Mr. Aubin—was most assuredly not him. The two men could not be more different. A man like Mr. Aubin would never add to his own workload by offering to teach orphans. Why, he would not be working as a steward in the first place, for Mr. Aubin was apparently a gentleman. It just went to show one that gentlemanly behavior was not limited to those who possessed the title of it.

GENY HAD ALWAYS LOVED HER TIME AT THE ASYLUM, BUT SHE HAD never set off for her visits with such eagerness until Mr. Rowles had taken on the position. She stepped out of the carriage and tilted her face to the sky. The spring sunlight had begun to grow warm, and tulips blossomed all along the plot of land that the gardeners were working. They grew vegetables, of course, but from the beginning, the countess had suggested they grow flowers as well. There was enough earth for it, she had said, declaring that everyone needed a bit of beauty in their lives.

Charity went on her way to the kitchen, where she would help out until it was time to teach the duties of a lady's maid to the three orphans in training. Geny went straight to the classroom where her small students awaited her. She and her maid had been stuck behind a cart carrying root vegetables that had turned over, and it delayed their arrival. She had had no time to go upstairs and remove her cloak and bonnet. Never mind. It would be her reward to see Mr. Rowles when she was finished.

I wonder what his first name is.

Jack, the one orphan boy in her class, was waiting for her by the door, and when he saw she carried no basket, he looked disappointed. She pretended not to notice. It was better that they not grow accustomed to thinking there would be a treat at every class. They should learn that it was enough simply to live safely with their share of food, care, and instruction. One could not eat sweetmeats every day of the week, after all.

"Good morning, children," she said and assembled them into the half-circle to begin reciting from their readers. Today she would be teaching them to write three-letter words on the blackboard for the first time and knew they would be astonished to discover they could write something that someone else could read. It thrilled her to think of their futures, of what they might become. She hoped they would be cheerful and industrious, thankful for their chance in life.

The forty-five minutes usually passed quickly, but today Geny constantly had to force her mind back to her students. She wondered if Mr. Rowles knew that she was here, and if he was as eager to see her as she was to see him. At last, her class ended, and she sent the children off to eat the midday meal the orphanage provided them while she stayed behind to tidy up the books.

Alone, Geny looked around the small room, folding her arms around her waist, as she thought about how best to approach Mr. Rowles with her idea. Her plan was to ask him if he wished to accompany her on an errand to seek out the two masons the steward had recommended, and see if either could be found. It embarrassed her to be so forward as to propose it, but she decided to do it anyway. On the days she did not see him, she *missed* him.

Geny went over to the blackboard and picked up the rag beside it. The only tricky part was how to accomplish this without Mr. Dowling catching wind of the errand—him or anyone else in the asylum who was likely to talk. If she went to his office, Mr. Dowling would overhear and likely summon the audacity to question her on what she was doing.

A knock on the door interrupted her meditation, and she turned from where she had been wiping the blackboard to see Mr. Rowles. In her surprise, she knocked over the tray of chalk that was next to the board.

"Allow me," he said, darting over to help her pick up the chalk, now broken.

She bent down at the same time, flustered to have him in the room with her, despite it being the very thing she wished for. Her hands trembled, and he gently took the tray from her. She straightened, and without forethought, touched her fingers to her cheeks to try to cool them as Mr. Rowles collected the last bits and stood upright.

"How do you do, my lady? Forgive me, for I fear I startled you." Mr. Rowles smiled, then he stilled as his gaze rested on her face. He pulled a handkerchief out of his waistcoat pocket, handing it to her.

"You have…you have chalk on your face, I believe."

"Oh." Geny could feel the heat in her cheeks and was glad for the distraction. She took the handkerchief and began to wipe at her cheek.

"It is not there. It is…" He pointed to the other side.

She wiped her other cheek and glanced at him in inquiry. He nodded and she handed back his handkerchief, their bare hands brushing as she passed it to him. It sent her heart rate pummeling her chest.

"I was walking by the classroom when I saw you here," he

explained. He looked as self-conscious as she felt, and she guessed that he had not spoken the entire truth. She did not think it was by accident that he had come to the classroom at this hour when he would know where she was.

The knowledge that he wished to see her caused her heart to soar. They were surely engaging in some sort of quiet courtship, were they not? It was not the loud Hyde Park romance that was followed by a trail of buzzing gossip. It was the courtship of two souls who had the same values and cared about the same things, never mind that their situations in life were different. She began to hope that he found her as admirable and attractive as she found him.

"I am glad you stopped to greet me," she said, absently tidying the pile of books on the desk. "I was wondering if you have had any luck in finding masons to repair the wall in the stable?" She held her breath, hoping the answer was no.

"I am sorry to say I did not have the time to search." His look was one of pure chagrin as though he disappointed her by not being in advance on his duty. How little he knew! It was precisely what she had hoped to hear.

"I inquired because I took the liberty of asking my father's steward if he knew of any masons in London, and he gave me two names. I was wondering…" Her voice trembled, causing her to pause, suddenly aware of how forward she was acting and doubting whether it was indeed wise.

"What is it, my lady?" His eyes were intent upon hers. She had never been so drawn into the depth of a stare before, but his held kindness and warmth. There was also a familiarity that should not have been there with so little time to be acquainted, and yet it was. This was what gave her the courage to continue.

"I thought perhaps I might accompany you to visit them. Or at least we can try to see if we can find one at home. I can instruct my groom to take us there now if you wish."

He set the chalk tray on the desk, which he had still been

holding, his grin suddenly boyish. "That would be excellent. I am ready to set out whenever you are. I am much obliged to you for inquiring on my behalf."

She returned the smile, adding shyly, "It is only that you do not know London well, and I wished to help you."

A shadow flashed over his face that she couldn't read, creating an odd, uncomfortable moment. She did not know why it would be. Perhaps he felt embarrassed by how little cosmopolitan he was. She would reassure him that such a thing mattered little if only she knew how. It was a brief pause, however, before he turned and gestured toward the door.

"Shall we go?"

She nodded.

Chapter Ten

They went to the stable together, Mr. Rowles claiming he wished to see the wall for himself once more so he could accurately describe it to the mason. Geny had considered asking Charity to accompany her for propriety's sake, but after wrestling with what the correct course of action should be, she decided against it. Charity would be teaching the duties of a lady's maid to a small group of orphans, and Geny feared to make a bigger deal of the outing than it truly was. She was merely performing a service for the asylum alongside one of the workers. It was like going somewhere with a footman, she reasoned, and then tried not to think about how little she viewed him in the guise of a footman or any other worker. She also refused to admit how much she was looking forward to their conversation during the short outing.

Geny went to the carriage house where she found her groom and gave him orders to have the horses put to again. Mr. Rowles then excused himself to see the wall before retrieving his hat and cloak, and she found herself pacing nervously inside the stable as she waited for him, unable to stay still. Her unruly emotions were somewhat akin to a runaway carriage; she had no control over them and no idea where they were headed.

He returned just as the groom had readied everything. When a stable hand stepped forward to assist her, Mr. Rowles put up his hand, indicating that he would do it. He held her hand in a firm grip, allowing her to climb in, and she was suddenly seized by some nonsensical notion of the princes and princesses she'd read about as a girl. She slid over on the seat, and he took the place across from her, then closed the door. With an inquiring look, he raised his hand to tap the ceiling, and she nodded. The carriage started forward.

Her goal had been to assist Mr. Rowles in finding a mason, with the added benefit of spending more time with him. But now that they sat across from each other, all she could focus on was how nervous she was. This did not extend to mistrust; although she did not know what they would discuss, she knew she could trust being alone with him in the carriage.

"So this Adam Cook is located in Clerkenwell?" Mr. Rowles asked. He had overheard her giving instructions to the groom.

"Yes. And John Smith lives only a few streets away if Mason Cook cannot do the job. This was one reason Mr. Laurier recommended them both, besides their skill. The odds are greater that at least one of them will be free to take on our project without traveling the whole of London."

He nodded and brought his gaze to hers, a smile lurking in his eyes. "I am happy to have your company, although I fear I am abusing your goodness."

"You are not. I do precisely what I wish to, and I wanted to come." It was forward of her to admit to it, but she could not lie. Never had she behaved thus in the presence of a man—with so little filter for saying exactly what she thought.

A silence settled between them until his lips turned upwards. "You look very fetching today, Lady Eugenia. I should not say it, but I keep thinking it."

Geny ducked her head to hide the smile that sprang instantly to her lips. "You have a sweet tongue."

He chuckled softly. "I do, perhaps. But in this instance, I am only stating the absolute truth."

"*Hmm.*" She pinched her lips together and attempted to plug the joy that bubbled over.

Mr. Rowles took a deep breath. "Have you given any thought yet to which orphans will train under my supervision?"

"As a matter of fact, I did wish to speak to you on the matter, because I have two boys in mind. I suppose I should consult Mr. Dowling first since it is his domain." She let out a sigh. "I confess that I have not been eager for that conversation."

A dry laugh escaped him. "I think I can imagine why. Although, I would rather hear it from you than assume I know its cause."

"Mr. Dowling is a strange mix of familiarity and fawning, and I find it uncomfortable. On one hand, he will easily approach me on any matter he deems must interest me and will stand closer than I would like him to. And in the same instant, he will speak of the social distance that separates us as though he is not worthy of breathing the same air. It shows how little he knows me, for social disparity is not something that offends me. Being overly familiar, on the other hand, does."

"He does not look upon me with any fondness," Mr. Rowles admitted. "But the feeling is mutual. I suppose I should be the one to ask him about the orphans to train. After all, we do work together."

"Perhaps. If he gives you a difficult time, please let me know."

Geny fiddled with her gloves and glanced at him under her lashes. When he caught her regard, he smiled wordlessly. His smiles were open, but she wished he were not so mysterious about the details of his life. The only thing she knew about him was that he was from Surrey and that he had a brother.

"Were you close to your parents?"

"I was too young to remember my birth father. My mother remarried when I was only two years old. I remember loving her very much, and she died when I was seven."

"Oh." Her heart sank at the thought of him losing his mother at such a young age. "You poor thing. It was hard enough for me to lose my mother, and I was already sixteen."

"It was dreadfully hard. I suppose what brought me comfort was that my stepfather and stepbrother had a true fondness for me, as though we were related by blood. My stepfather never remarried after her death. I think having two wives predecease him was enough for him. He died four years ago."

"I am sorry to hear that. And your brother?" she prompted him. "You mentioned he is living in the north with his wife. He cares for a parish there, I believe. Do you visit him?"

"Not as often as I should." He sighed. "I have been thinking that I should have gone to see him before I took on this position. It will not be so easy to get leave to do so now."

"It is not too late. Fortunately, the asylum is not a workhouse, either for the children or its stewards." She smiled at him. "Perhaps you might go this summer?"

"Perhaps," he said as the carriage slowed and came to a halt. It was probably just as well their conversation was interrupted, for although he had answered her questions, he did not seem eager to offer more than he had to. She did not want to offend him by continuing to pry.

The groom opened the door. "This is the address, my lady."

"Thank you."

She waited until Mr. Rowles stepped down and lifted his hand up to take hers. The strength of his grip sent a tingle through her. He held her hand for just a second longer as though to make sure she was firmly set on the ground before he released it.

Geny looked around them. In the distance, she could see some tenement housing, but here the road had more space, and there were houses along it that seemed to belong to people who earned a correct living. A small forge sat by the side of the humble house in front of them, and a man plunged the glowing iron into a stone basin of water, causing it to sizzle loudly. He set it down and, wiping his hands, came over to see them.

"Mason Cook?" she asked.

"Ay. 'Tis me."

She glanced at Mr. Rowles, who stepped forward.

"I am the steward for the foundling asylum in Bloomsbury, and a part of the stone wall in the stable needs to be repaired urgently. Do you have the time and competence for such work?"

Mason Cook was a wiry gentleman with grizzled hair and a deeply lined face, and he seemed to reflect for a moment before answering. He turned when a younger man stepped out of the house.

"Carl, we have some Quality here needing a repair on a stone wall. Can you do it?" The man nodded, and Mason Cook turned back to Mr. Rowles. "'Tis my son. He'll be a better man for your job, though he can't come until Monday next week."

"Excellent." Mr. Rowles glanced at the younger man. "Have you something with which to write? I will give you the direction to the asylum."

Carl tapped his head with a meaty finger. "I'll remember it."

Mr. Rowles accepted this without question and gave him the directions, adding, "I will see you Monday next."

"I DID NOT EXPECT TO MEET WITH SUCH IMMEDIATE SUCCESS," HE said when they had resumed their places inside the carriage again.

"Nor I. I suppose we will not need to visit the other mason." Geny was conscious of a vague sense of disappointment, for it meant they would not have an excuse to spend more time together.

"No, I do not think that is necessary." He smiled at her. "Thank you for your assistance, my lady."

She smiled back. "Of course."

As the horses moved forward, Geny reached into the reticule that lay on the seat at her side. "Even if this is Mr. Dowling's domain, I did wish to show you the list of boys I thought might suit for training in arithmetic—although I think only the first two are truly suitable. I've listed their ages and talents."

He took the paper from her and unfolded it, then squinted as he tried to read her writing.

"I have difficulty reading this with the light coming in from the west end." He glanced up at her. "Thank you. I will look it over as soon as we reach the orphanage.

Without forethought, Geny slid over on her seat and patted the place next to her. "The light is better on this side. If you were able to read it now, I can answer any questions you might have."

She had not intended to invite more intimacy with Mr. Rowles. It was just that she was a practical woman and was in the habit of using each opportunity that was given. Besides, she felt instinctively safe with him. But she did suffer a moment's embarrassment as soon as she realized what he might presume of her suggestion.

Fortunately, he did not hesitate and moved to sit beside her in the most natural way. That gesture alone caused her heart to start beating pitifully. Although she had had no designs when she suggested he sit by her, now that they were side by side, she could feel the warmth of his arm next to hers. It was a comforting, inviting sensation, and she understood why such proximity was generally avoided between unmarried ladies and gentlemen. She also suffered a pang of conscience that she had *not* insisted that Charity accompany her.

Mr. Rowles skimmed the paper and pointed to the first name. "Gabriel seems to be an interesting choice. If he has such a prodigious memory, he may have a knack for more than just sums. I am less certain of Timothy, but I certainly trust your judgment, for you know them well."

He turned to look at her and froze, as though he had only just been made aware of their closeness. With his gaze intent upon her, she could not answer for the space of a heartbeat. It was as though her breath had been knocked from her lungs.

She licked her lips and that drew his eyes downward, although this, too, had not been her intention. Suddenly, despite the fresh air of springtime pouring into the carriage, their confined space had grown too warm.

"Gabriel was the first person I thought of." It was not without a struggle that she managed to get the words out, and not for the life of her could she pull her eyes from his. After she swallowed over her dry throat, she reached over with her gloved hand and pointed to the second name. His gaze followed reluctantly to where she pointed, and she drew a deep breath, striving for normalcy.

"Timothy is perhaps not as bright as some others, and certainly not as bright as Gabriel. However, he has an understanding of the way things work. He can fix just about anything, and his solutions are innovative. For that reason, I would like to see him have a chance at a position that will put these talents to use."

"I will certainly follow your recommendations on this matter since you know the orphans better than I do."

Mr. Rowles lifted his head and turned back to her, then went still as his regard held her captive. They remained like this for a charged moment, their gazes locked.

"My lady, forgive me for saying this, but I find that you unsettle me." His voice was soft, but every word rang out like a bell and resonated in her heart.

Geny was breathless. "In what way?"

"You are unlike anyone I have ever met." He broke the gaze, then immediately brought it back. "I confess that I am developing feelings for you that are inappropriate, given our difference in station."

"I am not sure… It is perhaps unladylike of me to admit this, but…" Geny stopped, heart pounding, and yet unable to refrain from saying the rest. "I admit to feeling the same way."

Something flashed in his eyes then. "Since that night at the Sookholme ball, I have longed to do this." Mr. Rowles reached over and grazed his fingers along her cheek.

She closed her eyes and leaned into his hand. And as if he needed no more invitation, she flickered her eyes open just in time to see him bend his face downward. He touched his lips to hers, and white flashes like bursts of light came from behind her eyelids. He brought his other hand up and cradled her face as he continued to kiss her.

Geny's heart pattered in her chest like the wings of a sparrow, and she rested one hand on his arm, leaning forward into the kiss. He slipped his other arm around her waist and focused only on kissing her, his fingers caressing the skin on her cheeks and neck. For one heavenly moment, she knew only the tenderness of his kiss. Not how lonely she was, not the difference between their stations. Inhaling deeply, he pulled her closer.

The carriage jerked forward, throwing them nearly onto the seat across from them. Outside, the groom cried out an oath, and the carriage rattled to a sharp halt. Mr. Rowles placed a protective hand on Geny's side as he settled her back into her seat, his worried eyes examining her for injury. The carriage tilted, signaling the groom's descent from the box, and Mr. Rowles leapt to the seat across from her, his chest heaving.

The groom opened the door and peered in with concern. "My lady, are you well? You appear overset. My apologies. A cow-handed gent cut off my path and left me with no choice but to rein in suddenly."

"I am flustered," she said. "But I do not blame you. Pray, do drive on." Before he could close the door, she asked, "How much longer until we reach the asylum, Higgins?"

"In two minutes we'll be there, my lady."

The door shut, and they were once again in the dusky interior of the carriage. Geny folded her hands and attempted to regain her composure, a nearly impossible feat but one that must be done.

"My lady," he began.

She feared what he would say and held up her hand, smiling feebly. "Please do not say anything about…that." She could not bear to hear that he regretted having kissed her. It would spoil everything. "Would you tell me instead? What is your first name?

He looked at her in surprise, and then smiled faintly. "My name is John."

John. Somewhere in her subconscious she recalled that Mr. Aubin's Christian name was John as well. Margery had told her that the night after Mrs. Sookholme's party, and she remembered it because she liked the name. It was a solid, reassuring sort of name. What an odd chance it was. She received his confidence with a smile but did not make free use of it.

Another shout came from outside, but this time it was followed by the sounds of iron gates being unlocked and opened. The carriage rattled over the cobblestones into the interior courtyard and came to a stop.

John and Geny locked eyes for a brief moment. He opened his mouth as if to say something but seemed to decide against it. The groom opened the door a second later, and he climbed out. Then he held out his hand to assist her, so she might alight.

In the full view of everyone, he became formal and bowed

over her hand. "My lady, I wish to thank you for your assistance. I will bid you good day and return to my work."

Geny nodded and mumbled something inarticulate about it having been no trouble. The disappointment of such formality after their closeness threatened to crush her. The fact that he could hardly have behaved in a different manner did not weigh with her, not when it came to her emotions. She wanted to prolong their time together and discuss what had just happened—to see that he had been affected by what they had shared as well. She wanted to know if…if they had a future together after such intimacy.

She turned to watch him walk toward the entrance and suddenly could not leave the asylum quickly enough. She called out to the groom, who had begun to lead the horses to the stable.

"Higgins, there is no need to unhitch the horses. I will stand here with them. Charity should be in the room where the girls are setting stitches. Fetch her for me, if you will."

The groom touched his cap. "Ay, my lady." He went off, and Geny reached up to pat Hero's nose. He eyed her, seeming to sense her distress.

"Yes, you have guessed it," she whispered. "And I do not know what will happen now." The gelding nudged her, and she allowed herself to be consoled by him so she would be ready to face her maid with a degree of calm.

Chapter Eleven

John had taken a hasty leave of Lady Eugenia. Perhaps it had not been well done of him, but he was eager to reach the sanctuary of his office and be alone with his thoughts. That...thing that had just happened in the carriage was nothing short of monumental. As soon as he closed the door and sat behind his desk, he dropped his face into his hands.

What had he been thinking? When had he ever lost his head in such a way? It was unthinkable to kiss a woman of gentle birth that he could not marry, and he had never had even the slightest desire to do so before. It was only that her eyes had been so large and lovely, and he had already fallen for her heart, for it was something to love. It had seemed in that moment that he was incapable of resisting.

He knew it was not simply carnal attraction, which made it all the more dangerous. His feelings for her, although they had developed in a brief period, ran deep. He closed his eyes and relived the feeling of her lips underneath his, his hand around her waist, and the gentle touch of her fingers resting on his arm. He needed only to remember their closeness in that moment, and he thought his heart would pound right out of his chest. How was it that she smelled so fresh? There was nothing sweet and cloying about her. Just a simple citrusy scent that he found irresistible and which made him want to keep kissing her. The altercation with the other carriage had proved to be a fortunate thing, because it had stopped him before he completely lost all reason.

John exhaled and rubbed his eyes. It was as though he had been plunged right back into his days of debauchery, as though he had not learned his lesson. It was inadmissible to have taken such liberties with her, and he was going to have to apologize and hope she accepted it. It did not matter that he was, in truth, a gentleman by birth and in status, because he was pursuing her while attempting to bring her father to his knees. That alone was enough for a gentleman to pull back from pursuing her.

He lifted his head as the full weight of his folly was brought upon him. He did not want to imagine the look of disappointment on her face when she discovered who he was, and he hoped she never would discover it. At the same time, that would mean disappearing from her life without a trace, and this he was increasingly unable to do.

Even so, he would have to break things off with her—whatever *this* was. He had allowed an ease and intimacy to grow between them that simply could not continue. John stood and paced in his small office. It would be one of the hardest things he had ever done. Everything in him wanted to pursue her until he won her. For marriage? *Maybe*, he thought. *Yes—I think so!* But such a thing was impossible, and he had better put it out of his mind.

They did not meet again that day, and John arrived at the orphanage the following day after a sleepless night. Despite his best resolutions, his heart beat faster at the thought of seeing Lady Geny. By way of distracting himself, he decided to begin training the two orphans she had suggested and went to find the headmaster for that purpose. There was no need to lay the additional burden on her of speaking with Mr. Dowling.

The headmaster was just arriving in his office and had removed his hat when John came to stand at the doorway.

"Lady Eugenia has informed me of the various positions the orphans are training for, and I have offered to train two of the more capable boys in learning sums. I wish to start as soon as possible with their morning instruction." John waited patiently as Mr. Dowling appeared to ignore him in the act of putting away his effects. "Lady Eugenia suggested Gabriel and Timothy as the most suitable options."

Mr. Dowling patted the pockets of his waistcoat as though he were in search of something. John suspected he was in search of an excuse to stall for time.

"It would have been better had you come to me directly instead of disturbing Lady Eugenia with these notions. After all, training and placement is my domain."

John studied Mr. Dowling, careful to keep his face free of the dislike he felt toward the man. "The conversation came about naturally. I would not be so impertinent as to approach her with such an idea of my own volition."

"Nevertheless, Lady Eugenia is daughter to an earl and therefore has little to do with you. You had best leave all concerns regarding the asylum for me to address with her."

John leveled a gaze at him. "Do you suggest that if Lady Eugenia speaks to me that I should not answer her? If she makes a suggestion or asks for my opinion, that I should reject her overture?"

"Of course that is not what I mean," Mr. Dowling replied impatiently. "I am only saying that you should not put yourself in her way so that she feels obliged to converse with you."

John directed his gaze to the wall beyond Mr. Dowling. "I shall keep that in mind. And now, do you wish to bring Gabriel and Timothy to me, since Lady Eugenia recommended I begin training them? Or shall I report back to her that you were not in favor of the idea?"

After a tense silence, Mr. Dowling capitulated, most likely realizing Lady Eugenia would not take kindly to such opposition. "I will bring them to you today."

John expected Mr. Dowling to bring the orphans within the hour, but he did not. He had not heard the carriage bringing Lady Geny either and hoped he had not scared her away. Despite knowing they could not build a future together, the idea of her no longer wishing to see him would be a difficult disappointment to overcome.

John looked over some of the early donations one more time. He could not find any more discrepancies in the books and it frustrated him, for if the rumors were there, would there not be some truth to them? Especially now that he now knew something of Lord Goodwin.

If only I could verify that these were all the donors from the asylum's beginning and could be sure of the exact amounts donated. All he had to go on were the names listed in the ledger and the fact that the orphanage remained in a humbler state than it ought to be with so many wealthy people pouring donations into it.

While he sat contemplating how else he might come by incriminating evidence—and wondering if there might be a member of Blackstone's who would have this knowledge—Dowling walked in, trailed by boys.

"This is Gabriel." Mr. Dowling indicated one well-favored boy and then gestured to the other, who had the look of an urchin who would survive on the streets if he needed to. "And this is Timothy. I have informed them that they will train under you each morning."

"Excellent." John pulled out his pocket watch and glanced at it. "We have only an hour or so before you will have your soup. Let us see what you can do with some basic sums."

"Yes, sir," Gabriel answered, a gleam in his eye. Timothy looked wary and returned no answer.

Completely ignoring Dowling, John pulled a small table away from the closet and put it closer to the window. He then brought the chair up to it before looking back at the headmaster. "I will need another chair."

This seemed to wake Dowling out of his stupor, and he responded with thinly veiled irritation. "You will find one in the meeting room next door." He turned on his heels and left.

Good. John's goal had been to get rid of Dowling, and he had done so. He turned to the bigger of the two boys.

"Timothy, go next door and bring a chair from there." The boy went out in search of one, and John went over to his desk and brought out two blank ledgers and receipts that he had already calculated. He wanted to see how they fared with simple calculations.

When Timothy returned with the chair, he said, "Sit, and we will begin with a basic lesson in accounting."

When they did so, he set the ledgers on the narrow table that had just enough room for them both to write, then paused, thinking he ought to learn more about each of them. He placed his hand on the stack of ledgers.

"Tell me about yourselves. How old are you, when did you arrive at the orphanage, and where were you before?"

Gabriel spoke first, looking up at John with a surprisingly clear-eyed gaze. "I am twelve, and I came to the orphanage six years ago when it was first built. Before that I lived with my mother."

There was something in his look, a slight tremble to his lips that softened John toward him. "I am sorry to hear that you lost your mother." After a slight beat, he turned to Timothy. "And you?"

"I'm thirteen. I came four years ago." Timothy looked belligerent, which John suspected was a front. "They caught me on the streets, even if I was doing fine on my own, and they brought me here."

"Are you glad they did?" John asked, although he wasn't sure if he would be given a truthful answer.

Timothy twisted his lips in a grimace. "I suppose. Even though I'm not like Gabriel here." He jerked a thumb in Gabriel's direction, and John waited for him to expand on it. He didn't.

"How is Gabriel different from you?" John glanced between the two of them, and Timothy was still scowling, while Gabriel tipped his chin up in a manner that seemed oddly genteel for an orphan. He clammed up his lips, and it was Timothy who answered.

"*He* gets his own room. *He* has a sponsor—a gentleman from the looks of it."

"I see," John said slowly.

Lady Geny hadn't mentioned any orphans having their own rooms. He had not visited the third floor and could only assume that the room—or rooms—would be found there. He wondered if other orphans were in such a privileged position. It occurred to him that he hadn't seen any record for sponsored orphans, either, which was peculiar. It would bear some looking into, and he would have to have a better look at the ledger from the year Gabriel arrived.

In the meantime, there were lessons to attend to. He explained how to record the simple receipts he had created for the mock ledger, and how to add them, then allowed the boys to begin their work.

John knocked for the third time on the door of Blackstone's club, determined to make a decision today about whether or not he would become a member. There was no point in continuing to go if he was not going to invest in the society there. The two gentlemen he had spoken with the last time seemed pleasant enough, but it took more than two gentlemen to know if a club was right for a person.

Plockton opened the door and recognized him at a glance, bowing and addressing him by name. John was relieved that he wouldn't have to undergo the little black book scrutiny of the last time, which reminded him all too forcibly of his rejection from the other clubs.

"Come right this way, sir. Lord Blackstone is in his study and asked not to be disturbed. There are plenty of other members present today, and you will find them in the various rooms."

Plockton was in a talkative mood that day, which was another strange distinction of the club. The servants seemed to be on nearly the same level of informality as the members.

He added in a conversational tone, "You can decide if you wish to play billiards or sit at cards—or you might go into the drawing room." Perhaps Plockton thought he was already a member, because these rooms had not been open to him before.

"Be so good as to show me into the billiard room," John said.

He did not know where to find it but thought it might be a good idea to seek out a different room and company than what he had seen the last time. They entered the room, and Harry Smart was mid-game with another gentleman, and he raised his hand in salutation. Three other gentlemen watched the game idly, one leaning against the wall and the others seated.

"Good to see you again, Aubin. I was beginning to fear you would have been turned off by the strange company, both dead and alive, and refuse to come back." Harry grinned and leaned down to take his shot. It proved to be a good one, for he hit both object balls. He gave a crow of victory, then came over and shook John's hand.

"Allow me to introduce you to everyone. That over there is Sebastian Drake; he is new as well. These two are Mark Riordan and Grant Bell. And this"—Harry added, pointing to the older gentleman who was his opponent—"is the Earl of Hollingsworth. Come to think of it, he is just the person for you to meet, because he's had intimate dealings with Goodwin. Or he did have in the past."

John greeted the other gentlemen before turning to bow to the earl. "Lord Hollingsworth, it is an honor to make your acquaintance."

He glanced at the others present, aware of how unusual it was to speak openly of one's affairs in front of strangers, but it was Harry who had brought it up. "If you are so inclined, I would be glad to know what dealings you've had with Lord Goodwin in the past, for the knowledge might help me."

Harry had missed his next shot, and Lord Hollingsworth let his gaze rest on John for a moment before smiling and walking around the table to take his own shot. When he had accomplished this with less success than Harry, he stood.

"I was in love with the Countess Goodwin before she held the title and had hoped to make her my wife. Lord Goodwin stole a march on me, and I was never able to realize my ambition."

John did not know what to make of such openness or its implications. He could understand what it was to be thwarted in love, but was that all there was to create such animosity between them? He searched for something to say. "I have seen a portrait of Lady Goodwin, and she was comely."

Harry joked with the man leaning against the wall, pulling the others into his raillery. None of them appeared to be overly interested in his conversation with the earl. John was glad for it.

Lord Hollingsworth sighed. "She was indeed, but it was her goodness that held my heart captive. I am a rogue, always have been. It was her noble character that tempted me for the first time to bring a lady to the altar. A shame it did not come about, for she might have been the making of me."

Harry walked back to the table and took his shot, contributing nothing to the conversation. Lord Hollingsworth appeared to be able to follow both conversation and game, for he marked a point for Harry.

"What happened to lead her to choose Goodwin, do you suppose?" John inquired. "If it is not too forward of me to ask such a personal question."

"Tell me first what you have against Lord Goodwin, and I will tell you—possibly." The earl turned to Harry. "That was a foul."

"Yes, my lord," Harry said in a mocking tone. "I was about to call it." He did not appear to hold peers or his elders in any particular reverence.

John was in a surreal world where people spoke of their personal affairs in front of others. Well, why not answer? All of society knew of his anyway—or at least, those in the clubs did. He waited until Hollingsworth returned his attention.

"Goodwin had me blackballed from the clubs—ousted from society, in fact—for having exposed his scheme to offload some worthless shares of a private equity deal. The other investors were peers that he had persuaded to join in." John hesitated before adding, "Unfortunately, Lord Perkins did not believe me. Then, later, the shares ended up being lucrative for its investors, so I was made to look ill on all counts."

Lord Hollingsworth examined the tip of his cue. "I wonder if this is damaged, and that is why I am playing so ill."

John recognized stalling when he saw it and waited until the earl saw fit to return to the topic at hand. At last, he did.

"Your misfortune does not surprise me, nor do Lord Goodwin's actions from what I know of him. In my case, Lady Goodwin—Miss Beatrice Watson as she was then—believed in his appearance of goodness, whilst I remained a rogue in her eyes. She was persuaded to throw in her lot with Lord Goodwin. I do not know if she ever saw his true colors before her death, but I suspect she did."

As John had no idea, he could only surmise. "Do you know of any other ill dealings besides the one I learned of?"

"Only rumors." Lord Hollingsworth resumed the game, taking his shot and having more luck this time. Harry nodded and added a point to his score. "Although, I do run once again in the same circles as Lord Goodwin, for I was reinstated in the clubs."

"Were you?" This surprised John, for he would not have expected anyone to remain a member in this eccentric club if he were able to frequent the more standard ones. He hadn't seen him at either White's or Boodle's. Perhaps Hollingsworth was eccentric enough to find more of a home in Blackstone's than White's.

"I scarcely go, however—except to the Cocoa Tree. I like it here," Lord Hollingsworth said, adding inconsequentially, "and I mourned Lady Goodwin's death, even though she never did accept my proposal."

John murmured some appropriate reply, then a dreamy look came over Hollingsworth's face. "However, I have seen the young Lady Eugenia in society, and she resembles her mother. Nearly the same look, the two of them, and I hear she possesses a similar character to her mother. I have been considering trying my luck with her instead. I suspect Goodwin would welcome my offer despite our past history."

The idea was so shocking, so alarming, that John cried out his protest. "But my lord! You are more than twice her age."

A pregnant silence fell as the gentlemen in the room exchanged glances. So they *had* been listening. John felt exposed.

"Felicity in marriage is not always based on similarity of age," Lord Hollingsworth countered, perfectly at ease. "But I am to gather from your objection that you have made Lady

Eugenia's acquaintance and have built some hopes in that direction."

John had walked into a trap of his own making. Now, he attempted to rein in his words.

"I have come to know Lady Eugenia from working at the foundling asylum alongside her. I wish only the best for her." It was an anemic statement considering the strength of what he actually felt for her, but it was all he would say.

Lord Hollingsworth raised an eyebrow. "So you have infiltrated the asylum. Very clever of you."

John had always possessed an easy way in society. It had been a simple matter to make friends even from youth, and he had never stumbled in his words or suffered uncertainty about his actions. But now... Ever since he had fallen out of society, he had not only lost his good standing, it seemed as though he had lost his self-possession—his dash. He was beginning to fear he would never regain his full confidence from before. Since he was finding himself out of his depth, he thought it prudent to end the conversation.

"I believe I have taken enough of your time. I must allow you to resume your game, Lord Hollingsworth. Perhaps I will see what conversation there might be had in the drawing room." He forced himself to speak naturally and not show himself to be in any rush.

Harry called the gentleman leaning against the wall over to the table. "Drake, you may have the next game. I am weary of playing." The newest member wandered over, a look of ready humor on his face, and took the cue from Harry.

John entered the hallway with Harry not far behind him. He slowed to allow for Harry's infirmity, although he was unsure if he wished for the company.

"I encourage you not to be uneasy on Lord Hollingsworth's account." Harry glanced at John adding, "He may be a rogue still and more eccentric than he lets on, but he is known to be a loyal fellow. He will not pursue a courtship if another club member has already made headway in that direction. Hollingsworth is a man of honor."

"I thank you for your disclosure. That does put my mind at ease." John offered him a polite smile.

Ronald Sacks stood at the entrance to the drawing room. His role in the club was not very clear, for he was certainly no gentleman, but he appeared to move freely amongst the guests. It was an eccentric club to belong to, but John had made up his mind to become a member. If for no other reason than to keep Lord Hollingsworth away from Lady Geny, he would join. Harry walked into the drawing room and greeted members there, but John paused at the entrance.

"Sacks, would you be so good as to inform Lord Blackstone that I wish to have a word with him as soon as he is at liberty? I do not plan to leave the club anytime soon, so I am quite at his disposal."

"Will do, Mr. Aubin."

John went to sit down and wait, taking a newspaper with him and calling a servant over to bring him a coffee if it could be had. At least the decision about whether to join Blackstone's had not been a difficult one.

Chapter Twelve

It had taken every bit of Geny's self-mastery to remain at home instead of visiting the asylum the next day. She longed to see Mr. Rowles—John—to see if she had misinterpreted his leave-taking to mean he regretted the kiss they had shared. She could not have thought it possible, for there had been *feeling* in that kiss. But then he had been so formal when he bid her good day. Perhaps he was afraid of being found out, or afraid of her reaction, or...worried that others might have detected the closeness that had grown between them. Oh, if only she could know for sure!

She held fast to her dignity and decided she would not go. Perhaps John had not shown outward signs that he had been changed by the kiss, but she had been. Never in her life had she experienced such a sensation—the intimacy of two lips joining, the sweetness as he held her in his arms and cradled her face as though she were someone to be cherished. It was the first time since her mother died that she had received anything in the way of physical affection. It was certainly the first time she'd ever felt cherished by someone who asked nothing in return. She knew John was a good man. He was not pursuing her for personal gain; she could sense it. And yet, he had made it clear that he not only sought her company, but admired the woman she was.

"Excuse me, my lady." The butler opened the door to the morning room where she was sitting. "Lord Caldwell has just arrived. He has returned from school."

"What—Matthew?" She leapt to her feet and hurried to the door, running out into the hall where her brother stood with a grin. She hugged him, which he submitted to, even returning her embrace for a moment before pulling away.

"I am home. It's a jolly good piece of luck, is it not?"

"Yes, but why are you?" She examined him. "You have grown taller by at least two inches since I last saw you. Does Father know you are here?"

"Yes, for he was the one who sent for me. There was a measles outbreak in the school, and he did not wish for me to catch it." Matthew held out his hat for the butler to take.

"Did he bring you back himself then? Is he here?" She looked behind her brother but saw no one. How wonderful it would be for Father to have surprised her by returning early.

"He could not be spared. He sent Brantley to get me. He's still in Windsor."

"Oh." Geny was conscious of a strong sense of disappointment. She had had the unreasonable hope that they might have a family dinner that evening. Her father had been concerned enough to have her brother brought home when he'd heard of the outbreak. That was good, but she would have been better satisfied had he come home, as well.

"Never mind then. So there was a measles outbreak, you say?" Suddenly the implications of the danger he had just escaped hit her.

"Yes. Five lads caught it, and before I knew it, Brantley appeared at my door. The headmaster must have contacted the families to bring us out of there before it spread."

"I only hope you are not sick," she said, instinctively feeling his forehead, which was cool. He brushed it off, and she looked at him fondly for a moment. "Hungry?"

"Aren't I just? I'm as hungry as a hawk!"

"Come on, then." She led the way to the kitchen. Cook would be happy to dote on Matthew while he sat at the kitchen table as he had when he was still under the care of Nurse.

The day passed quickly as Geny looked over his trunk and pulled out the clothes needing to be repaired or washed. They then spent a very pleasurable evening playing chess and spillikins after dinner. Normally her evenings were so quiet, but she couldn't keep her joy from bubbling over each time she heard him laugh. She had missed Matthew so.

"I am going to the orphanage tomorrow. Do come with me. You have not come for at least a year," she coaxed before they went up to bed.

Matthew yawned and stretched his arms wide. "Perhaps. If I am awake."

"Very well," she said, knowing it did no good to insist.

At least he had not said no outright, which meant there was a chance he would come. He used to love the asylum and had come with her regularly, playing with the orphan children on their short breaks. Besides, she thought it would be good for him not to be idle for the entire time he was at home, and no one could guess how long that might be.

The next day Matthew woke earlier than expected and came willingly enough with her and Charity. He likely sensed his alternative would be boredom.

Geny's thoughts had been given a reprieve from revolving around Mr. Rowles, but once they entered the courtyard, those feelings, accompanied by her fears about seeing him again, rose to the surface. They were difficult to put aside, which was inconvenient because she wished to introduce Matthew to him and hoped she could do so without appearing flustered in any way.

They entered the hall, and it was Mr. Dowling rather than Mr. Rowles who was the first person she met. He crossed the hall to greet her, stopping to bow.

"Good morning, my lady." He turned to Matthew. "How do you do, my lord. Home from school, are you? I hope you were not sent down," he added in a jovial tone.

"No."

Her brother deemed it unnecessary to give a more elaborate response than the one word. With anyone else, Geny would have admonished him to be more civil in his greeting, but she could not blame him, for she knew he had also not warmed to Mr. Dowling.

Matthew turned to her. "I wish to visit the stable and carriage house."

"Very well, you may go. Just stay away from the back wall in the stable, for the stones are coming loose, and I should not like for you to be injured." He gave a nod and sprinted off.

She found herself alone in Mr. Dowling's presence, a situation she was eager to remedy. She offered a polite smile and turned toward the stairwell.

"My lady, if I might breathe a word of warning in your ear."

This unpromising beginning wormed its way under her skin, and she paused with her hand on the guardrail and looked at him, waiting.

"I believe Mr. Rowles deems himself to be nearly on par with you—or at least he does so to the degree that he suffers no qualms about encroaching upon your goodness. He informed me about the request he made to have orphans assist him in his labor." He offered her a patronizing look that was clearly meant to be kind. "I have taken steps to ensure he will no longer do so and have instructed the steward to approach *me* on all matters in the future."

Geny breathed in through her nose. *On the contrary, Mr. Dowling, it is not he who encroaches on my goodness, as you choose to call it.*

The meaning of his words struck next, causing her to furrow her brows. He had claimed that Mr. Rowles wanted orphans to assist him and not that he had offered to train them. She decided not to bring this up and paused only for the brief moment it took for her to decide how she would respond.

"You are very good, Mr. Dowling. Please do not concern yourself with me. I can handle my own affairs, and Mr. Rowles has been nothing but civil. I do not mind being of assistance to him in this small way when it cost me nothing to do so."

As she took a step, she saw out of the corner of her eye that he lifted a hand, and it caused her to tense. But he dropped it, and she was able to leave without being accosted.

She climbed the stairs and, as soon as she had removed her cloak and bonnet, went directly into Mr. Rowles's office. Gabriel and Timothy were already there working on the accounting books Mr. Rowles had provided them. She greeted them, a smile in her eyes as she acknowledged John, who had come to his feet to bow. His Christian name came to mind as soon as she saw him, for how could she think of him formally after what they had shared?

The two orphans stopped their work to look up at her, Gabriel with a solemn gaze and Timothy with a speculative one. She praised them for what they had written, fully aware of John as he stood behind her. She had enough presence of mind to notice his handwriting on the boys' ledgers. He was indeed training them. She shook her head at Mr. Dowling's impudence, then drew a breath, turning just as John moved his gaze from her to the orphans.

He gestured for them to stand. "Boys, you may go outside for fifteen minutes to have some exercise. If anyone says anything to you, you will tell them I've given you permission. Your sums will be waiting for you to return, however."

Geny was secretly thrilled that he had sent the boys away, for it revealed his wish to speak to her, which was precisely what she wanted. She called after the boys.

"My brother, Lord Caldwell, is in the stables if you wish to greet him. You remember Matthew?"

"Yes, my lady," Gabriel answered for them both, and they ran off.

She turned to John, who closed the distance of a few steps between them with a smile that matched hers. "Your brother is here then?"

"Yes—unexpectedly so. There was unfortunately an outbreak of measles at Eton. My father thought it judicious for him to come home immediately rather than risk being contaminated. At least, I hope he will not grow ill."

John's brow creased with concern. "Indeed, I hope he will not…and that you will not."

His gaze lingered on her face and there was warmth in his eyes. She could not help but smile more broadly, although she fought the urge to be so utterly transparent. It was just that she felt so happy in his presence.

Without warning, the light in his eyes faded and his expression grew somber. He lowered his voice. "My lady, I am afraid I took a great liberty the other day, one I—"

She was already shaking her head before he had finished his sentence, and he stopped short when he saw it. She wished to tell him that he had not taken any liberties because she had welcomed his kiss. But how could she say such a thing?

When nothing more was forthcoming, he added, "I beg your forgiveness. It was unwise, and I will ensure that it does not happen again."

Disappointment froze her speech, but she finally managed to nod. "Of course. Of course it will not."

She smiled again, a rigid one that felt every bit as painful as the look on his face. He did not seem to like this any more than she did, so why must he say it was a mistake? She took a deep breath and turned behind her to glance at the doorway, now hearing the sounds of Mr. Dowling in his office. Surely their quiet speech could not have carried?

"I should go and see how my brother is doing." She wanted only to escape, but he stepped to her side, surprising her.

"I should very much like to meet your brother, if that is all right with you."

She lifted wary eyes to his and assessed his expression. This was not a man who looked as though he wished to rid himself of her presence. The thought carried comfort, though it was small.

"I am sure he would be glad to meet you. If you will excuse me for a moment, I must retrieve something in the office."

He murmured his assent, and Geny escaped from his office to collect herself before they walked outdoors together. She had not thought that he would be so eager to dismiss what they had shared. The fact that he had would take some adjusting to. Upon reflection, she was convinced that she was not the only one to have felt something. He must have been pulling back because of the difference in their station. It was noble of him, perhaps, but she did not ask for nobility in this instance. What she wanted was a simple love between two people with similar ideals—a man and a woman who shared the same beliefs about what was important without a concern for where they stood in society. A tear had escaped, and she wiped it hastily as she grabbed her cloak.

Whirling around, she came face-to-face with Mr. Dowling.

"My lady, are you well? You seem overwrought."

Was she to have no peace? Geny could not answer right away. He had infringed on her private moment, even before she could wipe away signs of her distress. It took every ounce of her good breeding to respond civilly.

"I am fine, I assure you." She buttoned her cloak back in place. "I am to show my brother the changes we have made since he was last here."

An eager light came into Mr. Dowling's eye. "I shall gladly accompany you, then. After all, if I may speak immodestly for a moment, I have been at the root of many of these changes. Why *is* Lord Caldwell home from school?"

Now, it required more than civility; it needed all of Geny's ingenuity to politely decline Mr. Dowling's offer.

"There has been a measles outbreak in his school, and my father thought it better to bring him home rather than allow him to suffer the risk of becoming contaminated."

"I should say so." A look of alarm had come over his features. "And if he should already be contaminated? Why, my lady, you might be at risk. And those of us who work at the asylum might be at risk."

"And the orphans too," she added pointedly. She knew he did not value the lives of the orphans as much as he did of those more happily circumstanced. "However, I do not believe there is any danger of that. He had already been quarantined in school, and we think enough days have passed that he would have manifested symptoms."

Mr. Dowling had inched back. It was hardly enough for her to notice, but she had. He cleared his throat. "I have forgotten that I have an urgent correspondence I must attend to—"

"Lady Eugenia, if you are quite ready, then so am I," John's voice came from the doorway. When Mr. Dowling turned, John bowed politely—in appearance every inch the gentleman. Mr. Dowling did not return it and only frowned.

"I am. Shall we?" Geny walked past Mr. Dowling toward the stairs with John trailing behind her.

They exited into the courtyard, which was empty, and walked toward the stable. Geny's mood had sobered further. This was different from the last time they had walked these steps, for that stroll had held promise. This time, he had nipped in the bud any possibilities for a courtship before it could bloom. There was something so depressing about that finality—and something so frustrating because she could do nothing to convince him otherwise. She dared not attempt it and so lose all dignity.

"I fear I upset you earlier." John's voice carried quietly to her ears.

She stopped in the middle of the courtyard, knowing that this was not a conversation for anyone else's ears, nor would she like for their exchange to be noticed by others. But she had to respond.

"I am upset, but it is not at the liberties you claim to have taken. It is rather at having learned that you regret it."

He looked stunned at her admission "I...I do not regret it—at least I cannot say I do. I regret only having done such a thing when I cannot see it through."

She looked at him steadily. "Can you not?"

She held her breath, waiting for his answer. She could not lay her heart bare before him any more explicitly than that.

"We are of such different worlds," he began. "Such different stations—"

"And if that does not bother me, why should it bother you?" Geny was dancing dangerously close to proposing to the man herself. She knew it, but she did not want to lose potential happiness based on a misplaced sense of honor.

"It is more complicated than that," he said.

She drew back. These words struck her even more harshly than the ones he had uttered in his office, for his reticence was clear. She had openly given him her heart, and he still did not want her. Blinking, she glanced away, and a movement in the upstairs window caught her eye. Mr. Dowling was watching them from the office she shared with Mrs. Hastings.

It was not for nothing that she had been strictly trained to move in society, for she could hide all vestige of pain at will. She lifted her chin.

"I see."

"Geny," he said softly as she turned away.

She resumed her walk to the stable with measured steps, carrying what shreds of dignity she had left.

Matthew came running out of the stable just as she neared the entrance. "Some stones from the wall have fallen—there is now a hole!"

"I warned you that it was in danger of falling. I hope you did not go back there." Despite seeing that Matthew was unscathed, Geny had a sense of foreboding and hurried into the stable as John reached her side.

"No, not very close. I just wanted to look at it. But when I pointed it out to Gabriel and Timothy, Gabriel took a pole and poked at the loose stones before I could stop him."

Geny drew in a sharp intake of breath and hurried past the stalls of horses toward the orphans. John ran ahead to where Gabriel and Timothy stood looking up and pointing. The long pole was still in Gabriel's hand. Then there was a rumbling sound.

"Gabriel! Tim—!" John's words were cut off by the sound of the entire wall crashing down on top of the boys.

Chapter Thirteen

John ran through the settling dust and caught a glimpse of both orphans. They appeared to be clear of the pile of debris, but Gabriel was lying on the ground groaning, his arm at a funny angle. Timothy stood by him.

"I'm sorry, but I had to move you," Timothy said, glancing up at John as though for reassurance. It was the first time the orphan had dropped his swagger and appeared afraid.

Though he did not yet fully understand what had happened, he set his hand on the boy's shoulder to reassure him.

"You did very well, Timothy." He got to one knee beside Gabriel. "You are uncomfortable now, but it looks like Timothy here saved your life."

"Thank you," Gabriel said, his eyes closed in pain.

"Never mind that." Timothy bent down and patted Gabriel's other shoulder, causing him to wince.

"Let's leave him be for a moment." John stood and turned to tell Geny to keep her distance, but she was gone. In her place was the boy he presumed to be her brother. "Where has your sister gone? Did she go for help?"

"She went to get Mr. Dowling," the boy replied.

"Very good. Stay back, my lord." He gestured to Timothy. "And you, too. It is unlikely for there to be more danger, but it is better to be safe."

John put his hands on his hips and surveyed the pile of stones, then looked at the remainder of the wall, which now had a large opening in the middle. He surmised that any stones that were likely to fall had already done so. Through the hole, they had full view of the chapel. What appeared to be a heavy wooden sculpture of a saint lay at the top of the stones that had fallen into the stable. The wooden cross was still standing on the table inside the chapel, but the reredos had fallen into the stable and splintered to pieces. A smooth slab of stone was visible, leaning against the base of the table. Figuring there was nothing else he could do, he knelt back down again.

Gabriel's eyes were filled with pain, and John held his uninjured hand, instinctively knowing that physical touch would help the boy to be less afraid. "Lady Eugenia has gone to get help. You need not worry about anything."

John glanced behind him again, and still did not see Mr. Dowling. He had expected for him to have come running. The earl's son had gone back to stand at the stable entrance, and he called out to him, "Do you see them yet?"

"My sister is returning, but Mr. Dowling is not beside her," he called back.

"Go fetch for me one of the saddle blankets," John said, forgetting for the moment that he was addressing a peer of the realm. The boy did so without hesitation and ran over to John carrying one, which John then placed over Gabriel. "It's a bit uncomfortable now, but you will soon be as right as a trivet."

Lady Geny arrived, looking pale. "Gabriel broke his arm?"

"I believe so, but were it not for Timothy, it could have been worse. Where is Mr. Dowling?"

Her face flashed in anger. "Missing. He had said he had an urgent correspondence to write, but he is not at his desk and I could not find him anywhere. I will fetch the surgeon myself. I know where to find him."

John hesitated. He should be the one going on such an errand, but he did not know where the surgeon lived and they needed to move quickly. He turned to her brother.

"My lord, you will accompany your sister." It was not a question and not quite a command, but the boy went with her without comment.

Minutes after Geny had gone, Mr. Dowling finally made his appearance and stopped to stare at the gaping hole in the wall that revealed the humble benches inside the chapel. He stepped up to the blanket covering Gabriel. "I have just heard what happened. Lift the blanket so I might see."

John did as the man asked without comment.

"It looks broken. I will go and fetch the surgeon."

"You are late for that," John said dryly. "Lady Eugenia has already gone with her brother to fetch him."

"Why didn't you stop her?" Mr. Dowling asked, turning on him. "The daughter to an earl should not be traipsing about the streets in search of a doctor."

John raised his eyes to Mr. Dowling. "I believe Lady Eugenia's compassion is too great to allow for any loss of time when it comes to an orphan who is suffering. I did not know where to find the doctor. Had you been on hand, I am certain she would happily have left the errand in your care."

"Are you accusing me of something?" Mr. Dowling asked.

John looked down at Gabriel who was watching the exchange with dull eyes. "Of course not."

For something to do, he laid his hand on the boy's forehead, feeling for a fever, though he did not think one could get a fever from breaking one's arm. The boy did feel hot. Dowling hesitated briefly then left, and John relaxed slightly.

Timothy was kicking at one of the stones, and he came over to them. "Why'd you go and poke at the wall, Gabe?"

John held up a hand. "That is something we will go into later when Gabriel has been taken care of by the doctor."

He sized up the hole. It was now imperative that the wall be fixed as soon as possible, and he hoped that the mason would be up for the challenge. Although it did not appear to be a full load-bearing wall, there was surely structural damage that needed to be remedied if the orphanage was to be safe.

"I was just curious," Gabriel said through gritted teeth. "I saw plaster through the hole and wanted to see if it would hold. 'Twas stupid of me."

"I'll say," Timothy said, and John silenced him with a look.

At last, the surgeon arrived, and Lady Geny's brother stood nearby in rapt curiosity, watching everything he did. John gave up telling them to stay back, for he did not think that any more stones would come loose. The surgeon lost no time in setting the bone, which caused Gabriel to fall into a swoon. John glanced over at Timothy who looked as though he were about to do the same.

"You are relieved of your lessons for the morning, Timothy. You may go and join your friends, and I will see you tomorrow morning."

The orphan was off like a shot, and John turned to Lady Geny's brother. "You seem to have a stomach for this sort of thing. You are not queasy at all."

"Not really," he answered, flashing John a smile. "I found it more interesting than anything else."

The surgeon picked up his tools and stuffed them into his bag. "Shame you are going to become an earl, then. You might have made a fine doctor." This caused the boy to beam from the praise.

Geny had been watching everything, and she stood and gestured to two servants coming from the stable entrance. "He is here. You will need to have him brought to his bed and inform Nurse Ramsey about his situation."

"Yes, my lady," one of them said. This was easily done, especially since Gabriel was still unconscious. John got to his feet, his knees stiff, and the earl's son turned to his sister, his hands on his hips.

"Geny, shall we tour the asylum now? We can begin with the chapel." He jerked a thumb in the direction of the hole in the wall with a broad grin.

Geny met his look with narrowed eyes. "Yes, indeed. But we will go through the door, like civilized people." She turned to John. "Mr. Rowles, you have been set back in your work by this incident. We will not trouble you to escort us."

Her smile was distant, and John understood why. But it didn't make it easier to see the change. He had been trying to protect her from himself, and of course he could not tell her about his true purpose here. He had no choice but to keep his distance. If only she knew how much it cost him.

He bowed. "Very well. But take care, if you will. This hole has weakened the structural integrity of the building on this side. I would avoid the chapel, and the meeting room which is upstairs, until I can have a look at it."

Lady Geny nodded her understanding and put her arm around her brother's shoulders. Together they left the stable. John turned again in the quiet to survey the damage, finally noticing the empty stalls. In the confusion, he had not noticed the flurry of activity as the grooms and stable hands had rushed over to the horses to calm them. They had already led the horses to the far end of the stable, away from the dust and commotion. He was alone on this end.

He walked over to the pile of stones and circled it, examining the statue more closely. It did not appear to be broken. He wondered if this was what had caused the stones to fall—if it had not been properly anchored on the side of the chapel. Otherwise, he found nothing but stones and the broken plaster that had once held it together. There was also the smooth plaster from the inside of the chapel.

He walked around the pile to the other end and found the same thing on the ground, except for the smooth stone that was sitting at eye level on the side of the chapel. He went over to examine it, pulling the loose stones away to have a better look. It appeared to be made of marble—a plaque, it seemed, that had been hidden between the decorative screen and the wall. It sat between the bare stones and mortar on the side of the stable and the smooth plaster on the side of the chapel. He tried to turn it over, but it was too heavy.

"Hey!" He lifted his arm to wave to a stable hand, who came running. "Give me a hand turning this, will you?"

The stable hand attempted to help, but they ended up needing a third person to pull it loose. They turned the plaque to view the opposite side. On it were names, some of which he recognized as being early donors. Next to the names were numbers in pounds, presumably the amounts that had been donated.

"What's this?" He had spoken his thoughts out loud, and an older servant who had wandered over to see what they were about leaned in.

"This used to hang in the chapel, but I ain't seen it in years."

John looked up at him, drawing his own conclusions. "You've been here since the asylum opened?"

"Ay."

John returned his regard to the plaque, thinking it might offer some clues that the ledger books had not provided. Perhaps that was why it had been hidden—although, then why have it made in the first place? He glanced at one of the two stable hands who had assisted him. "Can you get another sturdy fellow and have this brought to my office?"

"Yes, sir," the man said.

Chapter Fourteen

On Thursday, Geny was downstairs waiting for Margery so they might visit the Elgin Marbles. When the knock came on the door, she tied her bonnet under her chin and grabbed a parasol. The weather was fine, and she would not need to bring her cloak. The butler opened the door, and Geny stepped forward to exit but discovered Mr. Thompson rather than Margery standing on her doorstep.

"Oh!"

He lifted his hat and bowed. "Miss Buxton is in the carriage, and I took the liberty of coming to knock on your door. I hope you don't mind my company today, as Mrs. Buxton was otherwise engaged."

Geny had recovered from her surprise and smiled, taking his presence to be a welcome sign. It meant that he was making headway into Margery's heart, whether or not she realized it— or even wanted it.

"On the contrary, I am delighted to have you accompany us," she replied, descending the stairs at his side. "I am sure Mrs.

Buxton is gratified to do something more restful than accompanying two troublesome young ladies around London."

He grinned at that. "I am not certain Mrs. Buxton ever rests. As for two troublesome young ladies, I must dare to contradict you."

He opened the door to the carriage, where Margery waited inside. She shot her a look of resignation, but Geny was not fooled. She knew her friend well by now, she was almost certain Margery returned Mr. Thompson's feelings—or was well on her way to doing so.

As they started toward the British Museum, Geny turned to her. "I must tell you—Matthew is home from Eton. There was an outbreak of measles there."

"Oh dear." Margery's fair brow puckered. "Do you fear he has been exposed to it?"

"I don't believe so. My father sent our footman to bring him home, and he didn't seem to think Matthew was at risk since they began the quarantine early."

"I am glad for you that you have his company then," Margery replied, squeezing Geny's hand.

After a brief silence, Mr. Thompson opened the conversation. "I have longed to see the Marbles ever since I learned that the earl had sold them to the museum. Now I can combine two pleasures in one."

"And what is the other pleasure?" Margery asked, clearly without forethought. He gazed at her with a gleam in his eye, and she caught herself. "Never mind. I do not wish to know."

Geny laughed quietly and looked through the window as they passed the streets of London. Mr. Thompson managed to coax an unwilling conversation out of Margery by allowing her to argue with him. Geny remained quiet, letting them have their pleasure until the carriage deposited them in front of the museum.

"There is a frieze along this wall from the Parthenon,

although I believe it's only a partial." Mr. Thompson led them in the direction of the exhibit. "I hope you will not think me too high-handed in directing the tour, but I did some research in advance and this was the suggested route for best enjoying the Marbles."

"Thank you for arranging a pleasant day for us," Geny replied, catching Margery's eye. "Very considerate of Mr. Thompson, was it not?"

Her friend returned a look that told her to leave off teasing. It was only fair, she supposed, because her heart was not in the right condition to endure any teasing on the subject of Mr. Rowles. She had not yet told Margery about the kiss, and she wasn't entirely sure she would. It felt so private. Then again, if she would have to mourn what could not be, she would need the support of her closest friend.

They followed the stretch of marble frieze along the wall, and Geny leaned in to examine more closely the marble, which was expertly crafted though much of the detail had been eroded from the faces. Beyond the frieze were statues of people and horses in various poses. Many were missing limbs or heads, and one statue of a horse's head had been cut off above the neck. She wondered when they had been destroyed, and whether it had happened in transport or during centuries that had passed.

"Lady Eugenia, what a pleasant surprise."

Geny turned to find that the voice had come from Miss Lucy Purcell. They frequently met at society events, although Geny never encouraged a friendship to grow between them. A nearby gentleman turned back, and upon seeing Geny, acknowledged her with a bow. It appeared Miss Purcell was walking with Lord Amherst, the Duke of Rigsby's son—the one whom her father had encouraged her to spend time with.

"How do you do, my lady," the marquess said with a deep bow. He stood upright, and Geny was able to have a clearer look of him. Her opinion of him did not change since the last time she'd seen him five years ago. If anything, age had not been kind to him.

"It is indeed a pleasant surprise, Miss Purcell," she replied, greeting both with a curtsy. "How do you do, my lord. I believe you have only just returned to England?"

Margery and Mr. Thompson had moved on, likely assuming their presence would not be welcome to Miss Purcell or Lord Amherst. They would be right, but Geny did not care for such pretension. She did not know why she was so different from the rest of her set regarding who was considered proper to know and could only credit it to her mother's influence.

"I see that you have been seized with the notion to visit the Marbles as well," Geny said, determined to be amiable and conversational. Her father might not be able to force her to marry a man of his choosing, but there was no reason to act churlishly toward someone whose company she did not particularly enjoy.

"Indeed, indeed." Lord Amherst continued, "I had hoped to bring you to see them, but I did not receive a response when I left my card at your residence and therefore had no chance to invite you."

An awkward silence fell as even he realized his blunder, and a dull flush spread from his neck up to his cheeks. He had just announced to the woman he was walking with that she was his second choice. Geny would have found it funny had she not felt some pain for Miss Purcell. She might not wish to deepen their friendship, but nor did she wish her ill. She searched for something to say that might bring harmony back to their conversation.

In end, it was Miss Purcell who smoothed over the blunder. "My lady, will you be attending the opera tomorrow night? I have not seen you lately. What have you been keeping yourself occupied with?"

Lucy Purcell was a gentleman's daughter, and although she

had no claims to the peerage except through a distant cousin, she was extremely wealthy and ran in the same circles as Geny. Therefore, she did not suffer the same fear as many young ladies of appearing too familiar. In truth, Geny had not attended society events lately because her father had not been there to force her too.

"I have been busy with the foundling asylum. As you know, it is a project dear to me. However, I will indeed be attending the opera. My father returns tomorrow morning from our estate and has expressed a wish to go."

"I hope you will allow me to come and visit you in your box," Lord Amherst said, dipping his toe back in the conversation.

"Of course you may," she said, perfectly aware that it was precisely what her father wished for, even if it was not what she did. She turned to Miss Purcell, adding, "And I hope you will come too."

There! She had succeeded in showing favor to Miss Purcell and tempering the marquess's thoughts in her direction by making it clear she had no designs to share a private conversation with him. If she could help it, she would not be forced to refuse a proposal she did not encourage or wish for.

"Excellent." Lord Amherst looked around. "But, may I ask, with whom have you come today?"

Geny cast her gaze over the exhibit and found Mr. Thompson and Margery on the far end. She pointed in that direction. "I am with Mr. Thompson and Miss Buxton standing there."

"Thompson? I don't know the name—unless it is the Thompson whose name appears on the underside of my tea set." He chortled at his own joke.

"Precisely the one," Geny said with a broad smile. "Mr. Thompson's family is in ceramics." She challenged him with her gaze, and Lord Amherst's flustered look returned.

"Now, if you both won't mind, I will rejoin my friends and leave you to enjoy the Marbles."

She dipped into a curtsy and walked away, but not before catching some of the murmured words that Miss Purcell let fall on not being too careful about one's company. Geny did not even mind that. If it had not been for her own mother's kindness, she might very well think exactly as Miss Purcell did.

"This is quite the fashionable place," Mr. Thompson mused when she rejoined them.

"It is all the rage. My father said I must go so that I would have a topic of discussion at parties." Geny exchanged a droll look with Margery, and they both smiled. Margery could read exactly what she was thinking.

They continued along the exhibit, and as they went, marveled at the age of the statues and how wonderful it was that they could look upon something that had been created so many centuries prior. When they had seen everything, Geny was satisfied that she would be able to tell her father she had indeed visited the exhibit when he returned. It was an agreeable feeling when her father was pleased with her, and she attempted it as often as she could while remaining true to her convictions.

She turned to Margery. "I had forgotten to tell you. Part of the wall in the stable came down, and it hurt one of the orphans. Do you remember Gabriel, who is now twelve?"

Margery thought for a moment. "Is he not one of the sponsored orphans?"

Geny nodded. "He was standing too near the wall when it fell, although I believe he poked at the hole with a stick, which was not the wisest of him. He is a good boy, and I regret that this should happen to him."

"Is he all right?" Mr. Thompson asked.

His concern caused Geny to send him a grateful look. There were too few gentlemen who were truly concerned with an orphan's welfare. Her mind went back to the way John had sprung into motion when it happened. He rushed over to see that Gabriel was more comfortable and seemed annoyed that he was not able to fetch the surgeon for himself. The memory brought a sensation of longing and chagrin. That she should have such strong feelings for him—and that they should have shared such an intimate embrace without a proposal or any promise—was not only shocking, it was agonizing, for she could do nothing to bring a proposal about.

"He was hurt," she told Mr. Thompson. "He has broken his arm, but the surgeon set it easily and promised he would have full use of it afterwards. So he was very lucky. It could have been much worse if he had been hit on the head, for instance."

"What a relief," Margery exclaimed. "I would not like for anything to happen to him, or any of the orphans."

"Matthew was there," Geny said, remembering it with a shudder. "I warned him not to draw near and thankfully he heeded my advice."

"Will your father be able to repair the wall?" Mr. Thompson asked her. They had begun walking toward the entrance of the museum, and he offered an arm to both women.

"The steward—Mr. Rowles," she added, glancing at him to see if he recognized the name. He nodded as though he did. "He and I had found a mason to repair the wall when it seemed there was only a little work to be done. Now the budget for fixing it will be much greater, for the foundation will have to be strengthened in addition to the repairs. I am concerned that the donations are not enough at present to undertake such a large project."

A look came over Mr. Thompson's face that she would not have caught had she not been looking at him then.

"I hesitate to say this, my lady. Actually, it is not in my nature to…" He looked uncomfortable, and Margery's curiosity must have overcome her, for she pulled him to a stop and peered up into his face. He looked at her, then Geny.

"Last week, I donated five hundred pounds to the orphanage, and I am hoping that this will be enough to cover the project. It should be. There should be no problem with the asylum's finances at the moment."

"You donated to the foundling asylum?" Margery asked, a look of disbelief and admiration in her eyes.

He nodded and lifted his hand to rub the back of his neck, as though he did not like the attention. Geny was very sure he did not, but she would not hold back from expressing her gratitude.

"Please know how very grateful I am that you have done such a thing. We are greatly in your debt."

"Well..." Mr. Thompson seemed unsure of what to say next and cast his gaze around desperately, then his look brightened. "I have just had a splendid idea. Let us go to Gunter's and have some ice, shall we? The day is warm enough for it, wouldn't you say? And I heard there is even pineapple to be had."

Margery and Geny exchanged another glance and both nodded and smiled at him.

"That sounds lovely," Margery said. She was the first to slip her arm back into Mr. Thompson's.

The next day, Geny waited for her father in the sitting room for fear she would miss his arrival, and he would closet himself in his library without seeking them out. Matthew strolled in minutes before their father's voice sounded in the entryway.

"It's Father," he said, starting toward the door.

He was still young enough to expect to be received with paternal affection; she had cause to be more wary. Then again, he was the heir and did receive more consideration than she.

"Well, Son, no signs of illness, I hope," the earl said.

"None, sir." Matthew grinned up at him. "But I will likely need to stay at home for another month or two to be sure."

The earl gave as close to a smile as Geny ever saw. "A month, you say? It sounds more like you are trying to shirk your studies. However, I am not eager to send you back until there is no risk of contagion, so you may rest easy." He looked at Geny. "Eugenia, how have you been? Have you visited the Marbles?"

"I have, Father." She stopped short, neither wishing to say in whose company she went, nor wishing to say who she met while she was there, lest her father remind her of his expectations. He did not need the reminder.

"I have not forgotten that I want to have you spend time with Lord Amherst. We will invite him for dinner. See Cook about preparing a menu. Let's say for next week."

She sighed quietly. He had remembered. Perhaps if she informed her father about his request to visit her at the opera, dinner might be avoided.

"As a matter of fact, Father, I crossed paths with Lord Amherst at the British Museum, and we spoke for a bit there. He said he would come to our box at the opera tonight."

Her father moved toward the drawing room, and they followed. "Very good. You may extend the invitation to him then if you wish."

She did not wish, and an oppressive air seemed to settle in the room. Her father had never been so intent on a match as to force a dinner invitation. He rarely entertained after her mother died, and when he did, it was his own friends that were invited.

"A part of the wall fell down in the asylum," Matthew said, bringing her back to the moment. "It will have to be repaired, as it weakens the structural integrity, the new steward has said."

"I trust him to take care of that. That is precisely what I pay him for." Their father took out a glass and poured some brandy. Their butler had rushed to see that it was ready, knowing the earl's habits well.

"I was there when it fell, Father," Matthew continued. "One of the orphan boys got hurt."

"Did he?" Lord Goodwin took a sip of his brandy, then went over to sit.

"Yes, you remember Gabriel Smith?" Geny said. "He is twelve."

The earl's eyes flicked upward, and she noted a look of surprise in them. It must have been because Gabriel was one of the first orphans to arrive that her father remembered him.

"Was he gravely injured?" her father asked. Although his tone was casual, she thought he seemed intent on the answer.

"He broke his arm, but the surgeon said he will make a full recovery." Matthew took the seat next to the earl, prepared to launch into as much discussion as their father would allow.

Lord Goodwin's features eased, and Geny was touched to find he cared so much about the orphan. However, his patience for children came with limits. He put up with Matthew's conversation for the time it took to finish his brandy and then said that he had work to do in the study. A look of discouragement came over Matthew's face, but he bravely hid it.

That night, Geny waited with her companion for her father to come into the drawing room so they might attend the opera. She had not needed Miss Edwards while her father was away, since she had not gone out for even one evening, apart from the Sookholme ball. Her companion was a timid woman—speaking little and only when the earl was not nearby unless it was to answer a question—and they waited in silence.

Lord Goodwin entered the drawing room and gave Geny an appraising look. "That color suits you." He gave a nod of acknowledgment to her companion.

Geny warmed under the praise. She did look her best tonight in a silk champagne-colored gown simply adorned but of the finest material. Her father did not spare any thought for how she dressed during the day, but he expected her to be well turned out when they were seen together in the evenings. He had already reminded her that she would be meeting the marquess that evening and that she should look her best. She privately thought the effort was wasted on Lord Amherst and wondered what John would think of her appearance. Would he be tempted to kiss her again despite declaring that it had been a mistake? This sent a wave of frustration and longing through her again.

"Did you accomplish everything you wished to at the estate?" she asked, once they were settled in the carriage.

"Yes." He pulled out his timepiece and glanced at it in the dim light, then snapped it shut.

"I am glad." And the conversation died from there.

The opera was thronged with people, because they were to hear Mozart's *Don Giovanni* for the first time. Not even her father had heard when it debuted in London thirty years prior. She followed the earl to their box seat, allowing him to navigate the crowds while Miss Edwards clung to her arm. Geny appreciated the opera more than she did the parties and balls, for she liked music. And she could lose herself in its notes while not being required to converse with anyone. Other than the commonplaces she exchanged with her companion, she was able to do just that until the first intermission brought their first visitor.

"How do you do, my lord?" Lord Amherst bowed, and her father returned the greeting, warm with praise. She did not know why he had settled on this man above all the others. She had not thought her father so exalted as to choose a match for her simply because the man was heir to a dukedom.

Her father had leaned in to speak to Lord Amherst, but she was able to catch his words.

"I shall not bring up investment matters here, but the time to purchase the shares is running out, and you will certainly regret having missed them."

Out of the corner of her eye, she saw the marquess glance her way. "I might be persuaded to do so under certain conditions."

"We have much to discuss then." Her father spoke in a more audible tone. "Well, I shall take advantage of the intermission to drink some champagne while you enjoy time with my daughter. After all, is that not why you are here?" He left the box, just as Miss Purcell was entering it. She curtsied and murmured her excuses, then pulled back to allow him to leave.

Geny resigned herself to a dull intermission, although she was grateful that Miss Purcell would be there to remove some of the tedium and focus from her. She had launched into a story, when Geny glanced down into the pit, allowing her gaze to roam over the crowd. One face was turned upwards, and his eyes seemed to be fixed on her. She held her gaze there until recognition dawned. Mr. Rowles.

She gasped and jumped in her seat.

"What is it, my lady?" Miss Purcell asked as Miss Edwards laid her hand on Geny's arm.

Lord Amherst took a step toward her. "Are you quite all right? I hope no one has had the temerity to stare at you," Lord Amherst said, glancing down into the pit, as though he were ready to challenge the man.

"No, no." Geny could no longer see John in the crowd, but she was sure it had been him. "I merely...thought I saw someone injured in the crush, but it turns out I was mistaken." She turned back to Miss Purcell. "Please, do go on."

Now, her eyes were fixed on Miss Purcell, but her thoughts were fully consumed by Mr. Rowles. He had not only been at the opera, he had been staring at *her*. That meant he could not be as indifferent as he claimed to be.

Chapter Fifteen

The day after the opera, John spent a rare morning at home in his rented lodgings in Chelsea. He had not bothered to attend service since he had been ousted from society, except when he was in Surrey away from prying eyes. So he had nothing to do except think through the events of the night before. He reminded himself that the fact that he was at the opera could hardly unmask him, for he was sitting in the pit where people of his supposed status would be.

He had decided to risk attending the opera because he was a fan of Mozart's work. The temptation to hear an opera that had not graced the English stage for so many years was very great, and he could not resist it. Of course he did not purchase a seat in an area where he might be discovered, even though he still bore the risk that some of his former friends might cut through the pit on their way to visit the opera dancers during the intermissions.

He had suspected that Lady Geny would be at the opera that night, and she was. She sat in the box with her father and an older, nondescript woman whom he guessed to be her companion. As he looked up at the stretch of box seats, he easily found her in the crowd and watched from the shadows as her father left during the intermission. His eyes were drawn to her so magnetically, he found it astonishing that he did not know her when he mingled in society. Surely such a woman would have captured his eye.

A man he did not recognize, but who appeared to be a leader of society, entered the box and settled his attention on Geny. It had not been wise to fix his gaze upon her so steadily, for of course she should catch his eye once she chanced to look down upon the crowd in the pit. It had not been John's intention to be discovered, but he froze in place when recognition dawned on her face. If he was not mistaken, she had jumped in surprise, for she had immediately to answer to the gentleman in her box and —he supposed—explain what had caused the alarm.

John, who had been circumspect in his regard when Lord Goodwin was in place, could not help but keep his eyes on Lady Geny during that conversation although he moved farther from sight. It was jealousy that caused him to do so, which was stupid. He himself had told her that nothing could come of the attachment they had for each other, despite having shared a very memorable kiss. And although he still knew this to be true, it was a quandary he could not see his way out of. She would not refuse him even were he of low status—he knew it with a certainty. But she *would* most certainly refuse him if she knew he had tried to expose her father and was continuing to attempt it. Not only that, but that he was working in the orphanage under false pretenses.

Early in the afternoon, a knock came on the front door, and Owen went to answer it. As soon as John heard the visitor's voice, he remembered that he had requested the solicitor to visit him on a Sunday, despite how irregular the practice was. He had explained that he was not at liberty to meet any other day of the week, which was mostly true. He stood, hoping he looked like a man who had been expecting the visitor he had invited.

"Come in, Mr. Wyndham. I apologize for making you work on a Sunday, and thank you for troubling to come to my lodging."

"Good afternoon, Mr. Aubin. It is of little trouble. My wife is away visiting her sister, so the house is empty."

The solicitor drew out papers from the bag as he spoke. This alerted John to the fact that they would need to sit at the table, for he would have to sign them. It was a shame he had not sought a nicer and more spacious living quarters while he was staying in Chelsea, but he had not expected to spend much time in the place and had certainly not intended to receive anyone. He had preferred to save his money.

"Owen, bring us a bottle of claret, if you will. Please have a seat here, Mr. Wyndham." John indicated the round table and took the seat across from him.

The solicitor sat and pushed the stack of papers toward him. "My visit need not take up much of your time, unless you have questions. Nothing has changed since the last time we spoke about the terms. This is just the formality needed to make it legal."

John nodded and began to read the document. The solicitor leaned over and pointed to two clauses.

"As discussed, this clause states that if for some reason your brother succeeds in having an heir, you will set aside the living attached to Westerly. And if he should have more than one, you will settle three thousand pounds on each of his issue for their own private uses. Should there be any girls, they will each receive a dowry of two thousand pounds. These sums are held in trust."

"Yes, of course. That needs no reflection." He had only accepted the inheritance because Gregory told him they were medically unable to have children. He did not go into the details, and John did not ask, but nothing would stop him from showing every consideration to his niece or nephew should Gregory be so fortunate as to sire children.

He began to review the contract, although he knew the terms almost by heart. They had discussed this idea for two years before seeking to make it official.

"I am glad to hear you say it, Mr. Aubin. If you will permit me to say so, Mr. Gregory Aubin possesses a most generous nature. More often than not, I am called upon to arbitrate for siblings who are fighting over inheritances, even when the matter of who inherits should be a simple one. It destroys the bond between them." Mr. Wyndham looked at him with kindly eyes. "It is refreshing to see brothers acting in so contrary a way, and brothers not even bound by blood."

The praise should have brought him pleasure. Instead, John was seized with guilt over the way he had treated his brother in the past by living a wastrel existence far removed from Greg's moral integrity. He lifted his eyes from the papers in front of him.

"I am well aware of my luck in being able to call Mr. Gregory Aubin my brother. I will do nothing to harm the relationship—with him or any of his children should he be so fortunate."

Mr. Wyndham held up both of his hands, looking slightly alarmed. "I did not mean to imply that you would. Indeed, I did not."

This caused the corner of John's lips to tip upwards. "I did not think you were. It is only that I wished for someone else to bear testimony to my promise, for I intend to keep it."

He read the documents through once more. There was nothing new, and it was left only for him to sign his name, which he did after he asked Owen to bring him the inkwell and pen. Then he proposed they drink a glass of claret together before the solicitor collected his belongings.

"I will leave this copy for you and will send one to your

brother in Mossley. The third I will file. I am sure Mr. Gregory Aubin will be glad to know that this affair has been happily concluded, since this was his wish."

John thanked him, still wrestling with his conscience for having so ill repaid his brother's generosity with foolhardiness and deceit.

"I will send him a letter of my own as well to inform him that everything went forward as planned." They bid farewell, and Owen showed the solicitor out.

John stood in his small sitting room, folded his arms, and looked around, dissatisfied. His life in those years since school had not been much different than that of many gentlemen, but that brought little solace. He had wasted his money on gambling and women and—were it not for his win from Barnsby—spent the entirety of the small inheritance he had received from his mother. He had not gone to visit his stepfather when he had first fallen ill and had only arrived after his death—a fact he could scarcely contemplate without being consumed by self-loathing. He scarcely paid heed to his brother's attempts at closeness, except for fulfilling his promise to learn how to run the estate. But that had been self-serving. And yet, somehow, Greg had not come to detest him. Even his wife seemed to view John with undimmed affection. The remorse that he usually managed to keep at bay now bit at him.

Sobered by these reflections, John thought that there was no better time than the present to write to his brother. It would not be too soon.

Gregory—

I have just signed the legal documents for Westerly, and although any show of gratitude of mine will fall short of what I feel you deserve, I must attempt to express it anyway. I have wished to come and visit you and still hope to do so soon. I am staying in Chelsea at the moment, for I have found myself in a bit of a situation. My direction is in this letter should you wish to write to me here.

Please do not worry about me, and know that for once my troubles are not of my own making — at least it is not a result of my folly. But I prefer to explain it to you in person and promise to come as soon as I am able. In the meanwhile, I am compelled to send you a short letter to let you know that I am well, to thank you, and to send my affection both to you and to my dear sister, Anne.

Yours truly,

—John

The next day, John was in his office, with only Timothy sitting at his desk working on sums. Under John's focused tutelage, he had grown more proficient at them, but he would never be at Gabriel's level. However, John had no doubt that both had a bright future ahead of them and a more promising career than they might otherwise have, had they not landed in the asylum.

He glanced at the marble plaque that he had discovered hidden when the wall came down. It was astonishing that the falling stones had not broken it. He read the engraved names, taking more time to note the amounts associated with each one. It was in going through them methodically that he noticed, for the first time, Lord Hollingsworth's name listed next to the amount of seven hundred fifty pounds.

After Timothy's revelation about Gabriel being sponsored, he had eventually located the ledger from the year Gabriel arrived. Lord Hollingsworth's gift was the exact sum of the anonymous donation that had gone to sponsor the boy. This detail caused him to speculate for the first time that perhaps Lord Hollingsworth knew the former Lady Goodwin more intimately than he had let on.

The more he thought about it, however, the more John had difficulty in crediting the notion. If the late Lady Goodwin was anything like her daughter, her integrity would be too pure to permit such a thing. He wondered if this might be a matter to bring before Lord Hollingsworth to try to get to the bottom of the misappropriation of funds. After all, Lord Hollingsworth's name had not appeared in the early books either.

John looked up when he heard the sounds of footsteps approaching his door. Mr. Dowling appeared with the mason standing behind him.

"Mason Cook is here to repair the wall, although I told him that the damages are more extensive than when you first spoke of them."

John had moved away from the marble plaque as soon as he had been aware of Mr. Dowling's presence. He did not want him to be overly interested in its contents.

"Thank you. Let us go and examine it now." He gestured to the mason, and also to Timothy, to follow him to the stable. As they crossed the courtyard, he elaborated on the damage.

"It is as the headmaster has said. A large part of the wall has crumbled, and this has created a hole between the chapel and the stable. It looks like the foundation will need to be strengthened. Is that something you can do?"

"I will need to see it," the man replied.

John said nothing further until they were standing in front of the hole. The mason went over to pull one of the stones in the pile and finger the plaster that had attached it. He looked up at what was still holding the top of the wall in place and went over to the stones on the bottom, wiggling them to see how solid they were there. Then he stepped away, skirting the pile of stones.

"I can fix it, but I will need more help. It is too much of a job for one person."

"I assumed as much. Can you give me an estimation of what you think it will cost to fix everything and repair the chapel wall from the inside as though it were new?"

The mason quoted a sum that caused John's eyes to widen.

No new donations had come to him recently, and the recurring ones were so small as to barely support the orphanage as it was. But this was not something that could wait.

"Find the men you will need and begin on the repairs as soon as you can," he said. "I would like to have the work started as soon as possible so that we suffer no risk of anyone else getting hurt."

John spun possibilities through his mind of how he might handle the budgeting for this. He would have to speak with Mr. Peyton and see if there were funds he was not aware of. It was difficult when he did not have full visibility on the donations coming in. He would manage to find the funds no matter what it took, even if it meant digging into his own savings.

"Very well, sir." The mason looked at Timothy, who was a well-built lad and had shown his curiosity by following the mason around and watching his every movement. "Any interest in learning the trade?"

Timothy looked up at John with an eager light in his eyes, and John nodded his encouragement. "I give you leave to follow the mason while he is here, so you can learn all you can. We will resume your training when it's over. In any case, it will give Gabriel more time to heal, so we don't go too far in the lessons without him."

"Yes, sir!"

"Grab a hold of this line here," the mason said, without wasting any time. Timothy did so and began to help him measure the foundation that was still standing.

John left the mason to it, confident he knew what he was doing. Besides, the groom was there to answer any simple questions that might come, or fetch John to answer the more complex ones. As he exited the stable, a carriage rolled over the cobblestones into the courtyard, the iron gates closing behind it. John recognized the earl's crest. For the first time, a frisson of dread shot through him as he imagined the earl himself stepping out of the carriage and seeing John there.

Fortunately, this did not transpire, and instead he saw the footman helping the delicate Lady Geny to alight. John knew it would be unreasonable to seek a private conversation, especially after what he had said to her in their last meeting when he attempted to put distance between them. He should walk the other way, but he could not help himself.

"How do you do, my lady?" He bowed before her. She turned with surprise at the sound of his voice, a flush of pink touching her cheeks, and a smile coming to her lips.

Another woman might have played games or treated him with coldness after the way he had acted, but Lady Geny was not cast from that mold.

"I am very well, I thank you. Has the mason begun the repairs yet?"

"He is in there now, taking measurements with an eager Timothy at hand to learn what he can of the trade." John smiled, happy to be near her, though reason dictated he should stay away.

A look of satisfaction appeared on Lady Geny's face. "Timothy will excel in whatever he does. He may not be academic, but as I said from the beginning, he is a very clever boy."

John chuckled. "He is indeed clever. And he may even turn out to be more of an academic than either you or I suspected he would. Without Gabriel present for his lessons, he is applying himself most diligently and is learning fast."

"I am glad to hear it," Geny said, a fond look in her eyes. Then she brought those eyes to his.

Their gazes held until John realized that they were in public view and wrenched his eyes away. He could not resist attempting to gain more time in her company, try though as he might.

"Where are you going? I will walk with you, if you wish it."

Her maid had been speaking to the groom, but she now went into the carriage to pull out a wrapped bundle and brought it over to her mistress.

Lady Geny accepted it. "I was planning to bring these curtains to the classroom to see how they will look when hung." She turned to the maid. "Mr. Rowles will accompany me, so you may begin your lesson with the girls." The maid dipped into a curtsy and went off.

John reached over and took the bundle from Geny and began walking toward the entrance.

"A set of curtains will undoubtedly give the classrooms a fresher look. It is a shame the donations have fallen off so greatly that we cannot do some of the most basic repairs. Something like this is bound to help the appearance, at least."

Lady Geny stopped at the doorway and gave him an odd look. "Are there truly no donations?" She corrected herself. "Is it true that the asylum accounts are so tight?"

John held out his hand to help her over the step leading into the entrance hall.

"It is so. To own the truth, I do not know how we are going to pay for the repairs to the wall. There have been no donations coming in apart from the usual ones, but those are only enough to cover the ordinary running of things."

Lady Geny stopped in the middle of the hall as though in surprise, and he drew to a halt beside her, confused. But she only shook her head and moved forward again toward the classroom that lay next to the dining room. John set the bundle on the table and glanced at her again. She had gone curiously silent.

"Mr. Rowles," she said, turning to look at him fully. "Mr. Thompson informed me recently that he gave a donation of five hundred pounds to the asylum. If you have not received any donations, where do you suppose it has gone?"

Surprise gave way to exultation. He had caught the earl at last, for surely it was Lord Goodwin who was pilfering the funds. But then the complexity of proving it dawned on him, and his mood plunged. His next emotion was relief that there would be money to repair the stable wall if only he could get his hands on it. Finally, he chose caution for fear of saying too much to Lady Geny and inadvertently spoiling his plans.

John settled for the truth. "I was not aware of Mr. Thompson's donation, but I shall look into it." She did not look convinced, and he could understand it when he was remaining so vague. "Of that you may be sure. There is no question that the foundation of the asylum must be properly restored."

She nodded reluctantly and began to untie the bundle, pulling out the blue curtains she had made.

"May I hang these for you?" he asked and was rewarded with a warm smile—much more than he deserved.

Chapter Sixteen

Mr. Rowles had had a strange look on his face when Geny brought up Mr. Thompson's contribution, and she could not help but have a seed of doubt that he'd had something to do with its disappearance. It was there and then gone again in a flash. Surely it meant guilt on his part? His back was to her as he studied the window frames.

No, no. Even if he did not give her any reason for why he thought the funds were missing, she had to trust him. The goodness he had displayed in his treatment of Gabriel and Timothy—and of her—could not be conjured up at will. Someone who offered to train orphans with no incentive or prodding was not someone who would willingly steal from them at the same time. And he had shown nothing but tenderness and respect toward her. *And desire,* she thought with a flush.

Mr. Rowles had had rods installed in the windows as promised. She shook out the curtains she had made, and he turned and took them from her—thankfully not glancing at her face at that moment.

"These are very pretty. Did you make them all?" He looked at her now from where he stood on one of the chairs, with one of her curtains in his hands.

She mustered a smile, pleased by his compliment but still troubled by the missing donation and flustered by the way he continually overset her tranquility.

"Yes, I did. I have enough free time on my hands that I am always pleased to have a project like this to keep me occupied."

He removed the rod from where it hung and began feeding it through one end of the curtain before inserting the rod into the bracket on the far side and attaching it to the one closest to him. He hopped down and went over to take the second curtain, pulling a chair up to that window next.

"I saw you at the opera on Saturday." Geny had decided she would bring it up. Of course he must have assumed she would, for it had been evident that they both recognized each other.

She detected a flush of color on his neck as he worked to insert the curtains on the rod, taking a moment before answering.

"I suppose you could not have helped but to notice me, for I was staring at you quite unashamedly."

He looked at her when he said this, but only briefly, and she caught his wry, embarrassed smile. This made her certain he could not be embezzling money from the asylum. No one could be so entirely two people at once—venal and pure, cocksure and bashful.

"Was it your first time at the opera?" she asked him. Somehow, she already knew the answer was no.

Once again, he paused before answering her, focusing his attention on inserting the second rod into the bracket. "I do enjoy the opera, but I have not been lately."

It was cautious in the way of replies but nothing that she could object to. He retrieved the third curtain from her, the last one to hang. "And you, my lady? Did you enjoy it?"

She clasped her hands as she watched him hang the last

curtain, admiring his athletic form in spite of herself. "I enjoyed the music, but perhaps not quite so much the company."

He glanced at her again before returning his gaze back to his task. "There was a gentleman in your box."

How astute you are. But she detected a note of jealousy in his voice and was mollified. He was not indifferent to her.

"He is heir to the Duke of Rigsby. Lord Amherst, who has recently returned to London after overseeing a family plantation in Jamaica. My father wished for us to meet."

He hopped down from the chair and walked over to where she stood. To have him face her directly in such a way caused her breath to evaporate. Every time they were near each other, the air seemed charged.

"I should not ask this. I have no right to do so…" Mr. Rowles's voice was deep as he looked down at her, unsmiling. "But is your father's desire for you to be better acquainted with the marquess what you wish for too, or not?"

His look held a challenge. She knew they had crossed over some invisible line, because in the past he would have excused himself for being too forward. Now he clearly had some proprietary thoughts toward her—in the same way she did toward him.

She lifted her chin. "I do not. My heart is otherwise engaged." She met his stare in a way he could not mistake if he chose to understand. She saw from the flash in his eyes that he did.

"Geny…"

Her name hung in the air between them. He lifted his hand to her face but dropped it before she felt the touch of his fingers on her cheek. The air sizzled and snapped between them. She waited for him to make the first move, her sense of longing only growing. She had already been shockingly forthright.

"I will not pretend to misunderstand your meaning," he said from his close distance. "I am gratified—"

She looked up at him, her brows drawn sharply together revealing the flash of anger that sparked from that word. She did not want his gratitude.

He rectified his words. "No, I will not say what I was going to, for it would be an insult to you."

Geny waited, trying to read the expression in his eyes, to understand what he was attempting to say. The silence grew as he exhaled slowly. And then, almost as an admission—

"I return your feelings. Fully. I believe mine more than likely surpass yours."

She inhaled a dizzying sense of joy, but before she could realize her good fortune he continued.

"But I cannot give full rein to my feelings. I was a coxcomb to have kissed you as I did, for I cannot pursue you as I wish to—and as you deserve after my having taken such liberties. We are not of the same station, and therefore we cannot possibly suit."

Geny blinked, disappointment carving her heart in two. "John, should I not be the judge of that? As your social superior, although I do not make claims to superiority in any other way, is it not for *me* to say what I wish for?"

His gaze held hers for a long moment, and she knew he was tempted. She could see it in his expression and hoped he would capitulate. Then he shook his head slowly.

"Your father would never approve."

"My father has no sway over me in decisions such as these. I wish to be a dutiful daughter, but I cannot be pressed into a marriage that is unpalatable to me, and at the moment that is any marriage where my heart is not engaged."

John had not moved away, for all he professed to be incapable of offering for her. If anything, he had seemed to gravitate toward her as though he could not resist the pull between them any more than she could.

"I understand by your words that you mean as long as your

heart is engaged toward mine, you will not accept any other offer." He bit his lip and looked down. "This is the hardest thing I have ever had to do, but I think you should open up your heart to other offers. I must act in your best interest and not seek that of my own."

"I am the judge of my best interest," she snapped. How *could* he be so stubborn?

"Forgive me for implying anything to the contrary," he said softly.

He held out his hand in invitation to place hers in it. After a reluctant moment, she did. Neither of them wore gloves, and the feel of his hand around hers reminded her of his fingers touching her cheek, her neck, of the intimacy of their kiss. Her breath stuttered.

"If after six months, having grown to know more about me, you still feel the same way," he said, "I will gratefully and fervently lay my heart at your feet." He lifted her hand to his lips and placed a kiss there, his warm lips on her fingers before releasing it from his clasp. He stepped back, and she took in a deep breath, as though coming up for air.

"If you will excuse me, my lady, I have something I must attend to." He had reverted to her formal title. He looked at her and she saw the note of chagrin in his expression that matched her own disappointment, now that there was again distance between them. "If I am to be perfectly honest, I do not trust myself around you, and I want to give you those six months. You deserve them."

"Very well," she murmured, fervently hoping he did not hear the reluctance in her voice. She had some remaining dignity after all.

He bowed and took his leave.

Geny went to the opposite side of the room and sat on the bench by the wall, leaning back. Her limbs were trembling and her heart raw and hopeful all at once. She had laid her soul bare before John. She could not help but do so, for there was too much at stake. Her future *happiness* was at stake. He was rejecting her, but admitted he did not trust himself around her.

She attempted to make sense of his reasoning using cold logic and not the nuanced desires of her heart. It seemed as though he was giving her hope that they would have a future together if only she allowed him time. He wished to give her a way out should she change her mind. Well, Mr. John Rowles would not find her so fickle.

At last, Geny let her eyes focus on the room brightened by the curtains, allowing a smile to touch her lips. It would be useful to have them on the cold winter nights, and it was a great improvement over the bare walls of before.

Geny went to visit baby Ben, who had completely recovered from his cold and was shoving everything he could into his mouth. He even graced her with a smile when she came near. She picked him up, bounced him in her arms a bit, and kissed him on the forehead as she talked to Nurse. Then she reluctantly handed him over and headed toward Gabriel's room on the third floor where he was still recovering from his injury. She knocked on the door and entered, and Gabriel looked up when she walked in. His face was drawn, scarcely brightening at the sight of his visitor.

She pulled the only chair in the room over to the bed and sat at the side of it, sending him a bracing smile. "Have you been keeping yourself busy, Gabriel? You look bored."

"I am a little bored, I suppose. But it is all right. I will not be any trouble." There was a despondent tone to his voice.

"Is your arm still paining you a great deal?" She looked under the covers at the bandaged arm and noted the surgeon's handiwork with satisfaction. The skin near the bandage did not appear red.

"Not so much, especially when I don't move it."

"That is good." She studied him for a moment. "Why should

you worry about being trouble? You have never been in trouble."

Gabriel did not answer right away but furrowed his brow. "I am worried that the person who is sponsoring me will not wish to do so anymore when he finds out I have been injured. Perhaps he will think I was causing trouble near the wall. Or that I am of no use to the orphanage, or to him anymore."

Geny stared at Gabriel with surprise, never having once thought about how he might feel about being one of the sponsored orphans—or about the fears that would accompany such a thing.

"Well, let me reassure you then. I have heard nothing of your sponsorship being withdrawn, and I believe I would be one of the first to know." She patted the blanket near him. "I do not think sponsorship occurs because of the worth that you might bring to the orphanage. It is usually because the person who is sponsoring you feels they have some debt to pay and wishes to see that you are properly taken care of."

"A debt to pay, as in…I am perhaps the bastard son of a man of consequence?" He brought his direct gaze to bear upon her.

She would not hide the answer from him, and replied gently. "Very often that is the case. I cannot say for sure because I do not have access to the records of your past history, but it would be my guess."

She touched him on his uninjured arm. "And that means your being injured doesn't change anything. So I would remove that worry. I am very certain Mr. Rowles will wish you to rejoin his lessons with Timothy soon. He has praised your cleverness."

This seemed to boost his mood, and he smiled more brightly.

"In the meantime, I will see about getting you something to read, even if I have to search through my own library to do so. It can't be good for you to be sitting here doing nothing, hour after hour, while waiting for your convalescence."

"Thank you, my lady." Gabriel looked even more relieved, and it was the first genuine smile she had seen from him that day. She promised to visit him in two days' time but would try to get books sent to him before then.

When she went to the office to review the list of clothing needs, Mr. Dowling appeared in her doorway.

She glanced up from her desk. "Good afternoon, Mr. Dowling."

She did not invite him to enter, hoping he had nothing important to say to her. She had much on her mind, not the least of which was John's declaration of his feelings for her.

I believe mine more than likely surpass yours.

"I was wondering if you needed my assistance for anything, my lady. I fear I have not made myself available to you enough lately." He offered an ingratiating smile.

Geny blinked three times attempting to discern what he might mean by such an offer. "I do not believe so, but I thank you."

Instead of leaving, Mr. Dowling advanced into the room until he was standing in front of her desk. Fortunately, this served as a barrier, for she was beginning to feel as though she needed one. He leaned in.

"Without wishing in any way to go beyond my station, my lady, I hope you will know how much I long to be of assistance to you, even beyond my duties in the orphanage. How ardently I wish to serve you. In fact—"

Geny held up a hand. "Let me stop you right there, for you have indeed gone beyond your station, Mr. Dowling. I think it best to end this conversation here." She stood to make her point, her hands on the desk in front of her until he bowed and took a step back.

"Of course, my lady. It was not my wish to disoblige you."

Geny did not deign to answer but waited until he left the room. Then, she sat back down and pulled the list toward her again, realizing that she was shaking from the encounter. Mr. Dowling was growing bolder.

Her father had once attempted to dissuade her from going to the orphanage with only a maid for chaperone because he did not like for her to be importuned by men of lesser status. She had always shrugged it off, unable to imagine how anyone might do such a thing to her, an earl's daughter. Now she had a taste of what it was like to suffer unwanted advances from a man who was almost repugnant to her. At the same time, she was aware of how disappointed her father would be to learn that she had happily made such allowances for John—a man who could only be repugnant to him. She brought her gaze back to the list and attempted to focus so she could pass it on to Mrs. Harris, whose friends had clothing to donate.

When she arrived at home that afternoon, Matthew was sitting in the drawing room playing a game of marbles on his own. He looked up when she came in but did not jump to his feet in the same eager way he usually did.

"Were you not to go to riding in Hyde Park with Father today?" she asked. His posture reminded her of Gabriel. It was the despondent mood and similar age.

Matthew shrugged. "He said he would not be able to take me today. He had something to attend to."

Geny sighed and went to sit on the sofa beside him. "It must have been a great disappointment for you not to go."

Matthew shrugged but did not return an answer. She recognized in his gesture some of the rejection she often felt from her father, but her own disappointment had been softened by a mother's devotion and love. Matthew did not remember their mother very well.

"Let us take out the backgammon set. Would you like to have a game?"

"I suppose." Matthew's voice could hardly show less enthusiasm.

"I'll ring for tea first so that we may eat, and then we will play."

Geny tugged at the bell pull, and by the time they had finished eating what had been sent up for the tea platter and pulled out the backgammon game, her brother's good nature had returned. They laughed as they argued over the better strategy in play, and she loudly regretted having lost when she had to concede defeat.

"So you will agree that my strategy of making a strong opening is superior."

She threw up her hands. "Why, I must, my lord. After all, you won."

The door opened, interrupting their laughter, and their father walked in. The atmosphere sobered in his presence, although Geny doubted he would have noticed.

"You are both home, are you? Matthew, I received word from your headmaster that there are still cases of contagion, so you will not go back yet this week. He will send me a report in a few days to see when you might return to school."

"Yes, Father." Her brother did not attempt further conversation with their father, nor did the earl apologize for having left him at home.

"Eugenia, it is good you are here. I want you to send an invitation to Lord Amherst's residence, for it must be written in a feminine hand. You will invite him to a small dinner party on Friday. You will need to invite another young lady of your choosing to even the numbers—but not Miss Buxton," he clarified. "Invite Mr. Milton, as well. He is a good friend of the marquess. I will give you a list of the other guests you must include."

When Geny was slow to reply, he looked at her curiously. "Yes, Father. I will do that tonight."

"Very good." Her father walked back to the door. "I will be in my study."

There was silence as the door closed behind him, and as much as Geny wished to continue in the cheerful atmosphere, she could not easily retrieve their former playfulness.

In one day, she had had the only gentleman who mattered express his feelings for her but refuse to act on them because of the difference of their stations. A second one who stepped out of his proper place to express his "ardor" until Geny cut it short. And now, her father was forcing the interest of a third suitor that she would certainly turn away if he attempted to propose. But it would mean a strained relationship with her father beyond what they had experienced to date. It was not an auspicious day.

Chapter Seventeen

Having at last declared his feelings toward Lady Geny, and given her his word that he would seriously pursue her in six months if she still wished for it, a fire now burned inside John to make sure it happened.

He needed to find concrete evidence of the earl's fraud and dishonesty—if there was any, although there could not be any doubt of his perfidy—and he needed to find a way to regain his standing in society. If at all possible, he needed to do it in such a way that would not harm his chances with the only woman he had ever cared for. At the moment, he could not see how all of this might be achieved.

His first step was to confront Lord Hollingsworth with the new piece of evidence, and he went to Blackstone's with that purpose in mind. At the club, he was shown into the drawing room, where he looked around but did not find his target.

He needed luck on his side, for there was much to do. After his conversation with Lady Geny, he was beginning to feel that he had too little time in which to do it. He went into the billiard room next, but there were no players there. Finally, he poked his head into one of the card rooms and was rewarded for his efforts. Lord Hollingsworth was there, playing with another member.

"Good afternoon, my lord. I am loath to disturb you when you are in the middle of a game. I am hoping to have a word with you as soon as you are free."

Lord Hollingsworth responded amiably enough, announcing he was about to relieve Eckert of his purse and would be with John in five minutes. He could wait for the earl in the private room on the first floor that he would find by climbing the stairwell and entering the room directly above this one.

John thanked him and found the room easily enough, taking a seat in one of the leather chairs to wait for Lord Hollingsworth. As the earl had predicted, his game did not take long, and John performed the usual civilities as they ordered something to drink and raised a glass to each other. When this had been done, John laid his business before the earl.

"One of the partially load-bearing walls in the foundling asylum weakened, and the stones crumbled and fell. It laid bare a large hole that now looks into the adjoining chapel. When this occurred, a marble plaque was revealed that appears to have been concealed between the wall and the reredos built around the cross inside the chapel."

"Most interesting," Lord Hollingsworth took a pinch of snuff but said nothing further, as it was clear that John had not reached the point of his visit.

"Your name was etched on the marble plaque, along with other early donors, and I saw the sum of seven hundred and fifty pounds recorded."

Lord Hollingsworth chuckled softly. "Ah, my whimsy comes back to haunt me. Yes, I was inspired to make a donation to the asylum in hopes of showing my abiding affection for Lady Goodwin—and perhaps irking her husband." A reminiscent smile lingered on his face. "Mr. Adam Woode had the marble plaque made and presented it to Goodwin at the opening ceremony."

"How did he know the amounts given for each donor?" John asked, certain it meant that the entries were once recorded in a more faithful manner than they were now.

"They were made public at first, likely in an attempt to encourage more people to donate. It spoke of one's status." Lord Hollingsworth raised his eyes as though thinking back. "There had been a fuss about how the donations would be used, and Mr. Woode loudly championed the earl and had the plaque made as a demonstration of candor. As I did not return to the asylum after its opening, I never knew what became of the plaque."

John nodded. He had no reason not to believe this. "The thing that troubles me, my lord, is that your donation was never recorded in the early books as having been received. However, there is a record of an anonymous donor who gave seven hundred and fifty pounds in sponsorship of an orphan by the name of Gabriel Smith." John stopped, hoping that Lord Hollingsworth would become voluble and fill in the missing pieces.

Hollingsworth was not stupid, and he turned an amused set of eyes John's way. "I suppose that you are implying Gabriel is my baseborn son."

John felt a flush of embarrassment. This was more awkward than he had intended for it to be.

"I will admit that my first thought was that he was yours and Lady Goodwin's—" He stopped when he saw an indignant look flash upon Lord Hollingsworth's face, rushing on to add, "But I quickly deduced that her character would never have allowed for such a thing. However, I could only draw as the most obvious conclusion that you stepped forward to support Gabriel because he was yours."

Hollingsworth sipped his drink and set it down quietly. "Did you never suspect Lord Goodwin?"

This came as a jolt of surprise. Somewhere in his conscience, despite the evidence to the contrary, John had continued to exonerate Lord Goodwin of wrongdoing when it came to immorality.

"I didn't, but perhaps I should have."

"I do not, in general, allow orphans to come under my notice, but I remember the boy because at the opening ceremony, Lady Goodwin pointed him out to me with pride. She said such a bright and handsome boy would represent the asylum in a favorable light, and all of society would see what a good thing they were doing."

He stretched his legs out, although John did not know if he was attempting insouciance, or if he truly felt it. Lord Hollingsworth continued his story in an unhurried manner.

"I didn't think much of it at the time, but I chanced to hear one of the workers saying that he had been brought in from Windsor, where his mother had recently departed this world. I confess that I was intrigued by that little piece of information, for as you likely know, Lord Goodwin's estate is located in Windsor."

John had not known it, although it would have been an easy thing to find out.

"I did a little digging," the earl said, "and it turns out that Gabriel's mother had been the daughter of a blacksmith and a servant on Lord Goodwin's estate. She was turned away from it for her shame and spent the remainder of her short life in a cottage paid for by the earl himself."

Comprehension dawned, and John was staggered by the implications. "So Gabriel is Lord Goodwin's by-blow. The earl did not see fit to use his own money to sponsor the boy and see to his well-being, perhaps for fear of being found out. So he used your donation for the purpose."

"Poetic justice, I suppose," Hollingsworth said.

John puzzled over this for a moment. "Did you inform Lady Goodwin of what you had discovered?"

Hollingsworth met his look with a weary one, as though John were not above average in intelligence.

"I loved Lady Goodwin. I didn't wish to destroy her happiness." He ruminated in silence a time before saying, "But as she died of an infection of the lungs that she had nearly recovered from, I have long wondered whether someone with less scruples apprised her of the fact."

John shook his head, thinking of Lady Geny's loss. "It's unfortunate."

"'Tis. Ah, if only Lady Goodwin could have known all of this before she pledged her troth to Lord Goodwin, her marriage might have been to me instead." Lord Hollingsworth drank the rest of his wine in one gulp.

This was nothing John could respond to. Hollingsworth turned to him. "Do you intend to do anything with your information?"

"I do not know." John still had no evidence that could terribly hurt the earl, even though it was bad *ton* to use another peer's funds to sponsor his own illegitimate child. "Perhaps, but I must think it through. The knowledge will hurt Lady Eugenia."

"The woman you hope to persuade to the altar."

This brought John's gaze back to Lord Hollingsworth. "If there is any way I can do so, yes. Given the fact that I am attempting to expose her father, I find it difficult to imagine how it can be accomplished."

"Well, I wish you luck. I will put off my suit for Lady Eugenia at present, for I have not been entirely persuaded that she can make me happy in the place of her mother."

John offered up a silent prayer of gratitude for that.

"However," the earl continued, "if you do not achieve your objective, I will assume that my way is clear."

The idea that he would lose Geny to *anyone* goaded John beyond measure. "I will find a way."

EARLY THE NEXT MORNING, JOHN DECIDED TO PAY A LONG-overdue visit to Mr. Peyton. It was the next step in his plan to get to the bottom of the missing funds, both the five hundred pounds that Mr. Thompson was purported to have donated, and also the peculiar bookkeeping records that showed no disbursement for Sir Edward Burbank's donation early on, and which let Lord Hollingsworth's go missing. He hoped that Mr. Peyton would be as honest as he had thought him when he first applied for the job. The clerk soon showed him into the agent's office.

"Mr. Rowles, a pleasure. Please come in." Mr. Peyton stood and gestured to the chair across from him. "I would have thought that your work at the foundling asylum must have kept you too busy to come and pay a visit to me."

"It does indeed keep me busy, especially now that the wall has become more damaged than originally thought. I assume you received my letter?"

"Indeed, I did." Mr. Peyton shook his head. "It's a terrible business."

"And that is what brings me to your office." John looked up as a servant came in carrying tea. Mr. Peyton offered him a cup, but he shook his head.

"I am surprised at the lack of newer donors that forces such restrictions on our spending. It is for this reason that I've come to call. To begin with, there were two discrepancies that I could find from the early accounting book."

Mr. Peyton held up a hand. "Perhaps you would care to

explain to me why you are looking into the early accounting books?"

John had expected the question and was prepared for it. "I wanted to research how the spending had been done in the past to make sure I was continuing to disburse the asylum's finances in a similar manner, if not improve it."

"I see. That was a good notion." Mr. Peyton appeared to accept this, but John detected a new reserve in him, as though he were displeased.

"There are entries which I cannot account for, and some of these are recent in the last months. For one thing, some of the entries on the ledger are listed as capital redirected for mill and housing works. May I ask what this is?"

Mr. Peyton sent him a patronizing look. "Mr. Rowles, were you not hired to see to the affairs of the asylum in its present state? I hardly see why you must look into past entries." He settled more comfortably in his chair. "The earl is a charitable man. He is building a mill in Manchester, along with housing for the workers, not that it is any of your concern. In the mill's early stages, the donations were being split between the asylum and the mill as needed."

John absorbed this surprising information. Did Mr. Peyton think him stupid? One did not invest in one venture and accept that the funds would go to another without being notified of it —unless the donors did know of it at the time of their donation. He decided against questioning the agent too closely for fear of drawing suspicion on himself.

"I see. Perhaps you might enlighten me as to Sir Edward Burbank's donation of five hundred pounds in the asylum's early stages? The amount was not redirected, nor was it added to the overall surplus. I did not discover how it was used."

"That I can easily explain," he replied. "Sir Edward donated before we had begun meticulous record-keeping. We used the money in the early setup of the orphanage. There were many expenses at the time, of course."

"I understand." John would let that one pass, as well. There were other, more important issues to address.

"However, when we discovered a marble plaque listing the early donors, I saw that the Earl of Hollingsworth had donated seven hundred and fifty pounds, and yet that figure is nowhere to be found unless it is for the anonymous sponsorship of the orphan, Gabriel Smith."

"*Hmph.*" Mr. Peyton leaned in with a patronizing look. "Had it not occurred to you that perhaps Lord Hollingsworth might have had personal reasons for doing so."

"It did, and so I asked him if Gabriel was his."

Mr. Peyton could not have looked more astonished. "Surely you did not show up at the earl's residence uninvited? How are you connected with Lord Hollingsworth?"

This John had *not* thought through. Of course, it would seem strange that he—a man who supposedly had no connections nor was even gentleman-born—could approach someone of Lord Hollingsworth's caliber.

"It was, I admit, under unusual circumstances that we were presented. However, the opportunity was enough for me to ask him the question and explain the reasons for my curiosity."

Mr. Peyton stared hard at him. "It still seems to me an outrageous thing to do. Are you sure you know your proper position, Mr. Rowles?"

John felt a trickle of sweat roll down his neck. He had to move carefully, for he could not afford to lose his place at the asylum.

"I do know my position. As I said, the circumstances allowed for such frank speech between us. But I do not make it a habit of going about asking members of the peerage if they have any illegitimate children."

Mr. Peyton's posture eased, and John began to suspect he

was hiding something. He still needed to ask about Mr. Thompson's donation.

"There is something else that is curious. Our record books show that we have very little money in the coffers, and I am unsure how we are going to find enough to pay for the structural weakness that has allowed the partial collapse of a wall."

Mr. Peyton lifted his hands in a gesture of helplessness. "Mr. Rowles, I'm sure you will understand that the foundling asylum is not my only concern. I merely distribute the funds as I receive them. I cannot conjure up money where there is none, nor can I tell you how best to use the funds to good purpose. If you feel yourself ill-suited to the position, however—"

"Mr. Mark Thompson has recently made a donation of five hundred pounds. Yet that money has not come to me. I have received nothing more than the usual small donations for the general running of the orphanage."

Mr. Peyton now looked ill at ease. "If Mr. Thompson donated this money as you say, how did you learn of it?"

John was caught between the crosshairs. "Once again, it was an extraordinary circumstance that allowed for this information to come to me. I merely wish to apply to you as the asylum's managing agent to learn if you knew anything of it."

Mr. Peyton was quiet for long enough that John became aware of the ticking clock near the wall.

"I will look into it, but my guess is that this Mr. Thompson, whom I have never heard of, was more likely boasting at having done a good deed in order to impress someone rather than disclosing a donation he truly made. In any case, I have received nothing from a man by his name."

John knew when a battle was over and was wise enough to know that he had lost this one. He got to his feet. "I understand. You must be right. I will make do with what we have then."

Mr. Peyton's features softened slightly, and he accompanied

John to the door. At the last moment, John turned to him, hoping for the element of surprise.

"Would you be able to give me the direction of Mr. Biggs? I would like to get his advice regarding certain aspects of the foundling asylum."

Mr. Peyton looked taken back before he recovered himself. "I do not believe I can, in good conscience, give you the direction of someone who has requested to retire quietly and live a simple life. I am sorry to disoblige you."

John accepted this final defeat. Although he was disappointed, he would find a way.

"I understand. Good day, Mr. Peyton."

When he returned to the office, Timothy was waiting for him and seemed restless and more talkative than usual.

"I have done all of the sums you have set out for me and have found the dis…the dis…"

"The discrepancy," John finished for him.

"The discrepancy in the record books that you hid for me. Do you have any more?"

John looked at him with amusement. "What has happened to you, Timothy? You are asking me for more sums?"

"It is only that I wish to join Mason Cook, for he is to bring the support beams today." He could scarcely stay still in his eagerness.

John laughed. "Now it all makes sense." A small figure appeared in the doorway, and he turned. "Gabriel, are you up at last? I am glad to have you rejoin us."

Gabriel looked pale, but he attempted a smile. "I am afraid I will not be able to write, though, for I have broken my writing hand."

John ushered him to where he usually sat. "Did you know

that it is possible to learn to write with your other hand?" Gabriel looked at him doubtfully, and John held up a pencil to show him. "It won't look as nice as the hand you are accustomed to, but why don't you start practicing?"

Gabriel seemed eager and relieved to have something to do. He took the paper in front of him and attempted writing sums with his other hand.

John turned his attention back to Timothy. "You may go out and join Mason Cook."

"Thank you, sir."

Timothy started toward the doorway, then stopped suddenly as though reminded of something. He turned to walk over to the small corner closet, whose shelves were surprisingly deep.

"I had forgotten. You asked me to arrange the closet. I found these letters, and I thought they might be important." He handed him the stack and was off like a flash.

John brought the bundle over to his desk, animated by nothing more than curiosity. He slipped the cord that tied the papers and flipped through them, finding letters from the curate that mentioned certain orphans to be brought in. It was dated before Mr. Dowling had taken up his position.

As John flipped through the pile, he stopped at one letter in particular, written in a flowing hand and addressed to Mr. Biggs. He opened it and perused the contents, coming to the end where it was signed by a Miss Amelia Biggs, whom he deduced to be the old steward's sister. Her direction was at the top of the letter, and it was just outside of London.

John stood suddenly, newly inspired. He glanced at his pocket watch and saw that it wanted fifteen minutes to three o'clock. He had time if he left now. Perhaps his efforts would still be in vain, for he knew not if these orphanage discrepancies would pin anything on the earl. However, it was all he had to go on.

"Gabriel, I need to go out for the rest of the afternoon. If you wish to remain in the office rather than staying in your room, you are welcome to do so. I will give you the same record-keeping that Timothy has been working on in your absence. See if you can do the sums there, using your left hand."

Gabriel flashed him a smile. "Yes, sir."

John took a hackney to the address indicated on Mr. Biggs's letter and paid the driver. The house appeared to be a comfortable size.

The servant came to the door, and he handed him his card. "I am looking for Miss Biggs. She will not know who I am, but this is my card."

The servant glanced at it. "Miss Biggs is not at home, but Mr. Biggs might be able to receive you. I will ask him if he is free."

It took John all of two seconds to realize that, as this Mr. Biggs could not be Miss Biggs's husband, he must be her brother. His search was at a lucky end. In a few minutes, he was shown into the small sitting room, where Mr. Biggs got to his feet. The old steward was still in the prime of his life, although his hair was graying.

"Mr. Rowles, this is a pleasure. I believe you are my replacement at the foundling asylum."

John was relieved to be so easily recognized. "You are correct. I hope I have not caught you at a bad time."

"Now that I am retired, my time is spent entirely in my garden or in reading the newspaper. I don't think you could come at a bad time."

He smiled pleasantly. John hoped the visit would prove more beneficial than that of Mr. Peyton's. When they were seated and a bottle of cold wine had been brought, John came right to the point.

"Mr. Biggs, I am here because I have discovered discrepancies in some of the ledgers. I did not come to accuse you of anything, but I was wondering if you knew something about it." He was too impatient to word the request more obliquely.

Mr. Biggs sighed. "I had thought it might come to this. You are referring, I assume, to the donations that were never shown as being disbursed. My record-keeping was not as assiduous in the beginning, for I was serving two roles as headmaster and steward."

"I understand that, and as I said, I am not here to criticize. However, as we find ourselves in a difficult situation—"

John realized that Mr. Biggs could not know of the collapsed wall. "A large portion of the stone wall between the stable and chapel fell, and we are attempting to locate funds to repair it. As you probably know, it was a partially load-bearing wall."

Mr. Biggs furrowed his brows and seemed troubled by the news. "No one was hurt, I hope."

"Gabriel, one of the orphans, was. He was standing too close to it when it happened, and he broke his arm when one of the stones fell on it."

"Gabriel Smith?" Mr. Biggs's eyes started. "Does the earl know about this?"

The question was an awkward one. "I have no dealings with the earl, so I cannot tell you. Fortunately, the boy is healing nicely."

When the old steward offered nothing further, John pressed on. "A marble plaque was discovered with the names of certain early donors and the amounts they had given. It was revealed when the wall fell."

Mr. Biggs nodded. "Mr. Woode's gift to the orphanage. His name was at the top of the list."

And contains the largest amount, John thought, wryly.

"What I would like to know is why the plaque had been hidden."

Mr. Biggs shifted in his chair, rubbing his chin before replying. "The earl suggested we place it out of view once the chapel was finished to avoid appearing boastful. It was then decided we would store it behind the reredos. That way it would be kept in pristine condition."

John looked at him with skepticism, which had the result of making Mr. Biggs even more uncomfortable. It was clear that something was hidden, and what was maddening was that he could not get to the source of Lord Goodwin's corruption.

"Were any of the later donors aware that some of their money was being used for another venture entirely? Did they know about the mill in Manchester?" This caused a look of dismay on the old steward's face.

"Mr. Rowles, I understand your concerns. I will not say that there are no discrepancies to look into. I am certain I have made some errors, myself. But there are some that are better left as is. Allow me to hint that there are powerful men behind the money that goes into the foundling asylum. I would advise you not to look too closely into any disparities you might find."

John looked at him steadily. "Is that what you did? Is that why you retired early?"

Mr. Biggs shrugged and rubbed his palms on his breeches.

"I am getting old. It was never my nature to fight against a force too great for me, not even in my youth. I am certainly not equipped to do it now."

Mr. Biggs offered nothing further, and John realized there was no point in attempting to persuade him to give up all he knew. He would not have more help from the old steward. He thanked him for his time and went out to the street to look for a hackney cab, thinking that it would take a miracle to find anything solid enough to expose Lord Goodwin.

For the first time, he was beginning to fear he would never regain his standing in society. What was more, it was even less likely he would win Lady Geny's hand.

Chapter Eighteen

Geny was unable to think of anything but her conversation with John. Had she only imagined it, or had he truly said he would offer for her if she would only wait six months? But why six months? Did he think she would come to her senses and change her mind in that time? He did not know her very well if he thought that.

She had had plenty of opportunities to marry within society if she chose to, but no one had ever inspired her to take that leap. After dissecting every conversation she had shared with John—and reminiscing about the kisses that went with some of them—she was no more enlightened as to his possible meaning and knew she would need to speak to Margery to make sense of it. So when she heard the sounds of her friend's arrival, she sat up, determined to broach the subject.

Margery bustled into the room, her cheerful greeting belying her claim that she was the laziest creature alive.

"Do my eyes deceive me, or are you truly sitting there with nothing to occupy you?" She untied her bonnet and lay it on the sofa next to her, then clasped her hands on her knees and leaned forward. "And my, don't you look fetching today? It is a shame"—she looked behind her and saw that the butler had not quite left the room and waited until he had—"that no one of consequence is here to appreciate it."

Geny smiled and shook her head, comforted by her friend's prattle but consumed by what she considered to be a frustrating, unsolvable problem.

"I requested the servants to bring tea before you arrived, so we need not wait for it. I think you will like the cakes."

"I am not discerning. I always like cake," Margery replied with a fetching smile.

Geny looked at her more closely, at last perceiving how unusually cheerful Margery was, and she began to grow suspicious. "Have you finally opened up to Mr. Thompson's courtship?"

Margery sat back with feigned surprise. "How could you accuse me of such a thing? You know I am never *open* to anyone's courtship. Besides, how did you know he was courting me?"

Geny smiled and gave a small shrug, her own worries temporarily cast aside. "He and I had a little conversation, and he was quite transparent about his admiration for you."

"I hope you did not fan the flames of that admiration," she said severely.

Geny directed her stare at her friend, a smile lurking on her lips. "Would you really object if I had done so?"

Margery sighed loudly and reached for a cake, biting into it. "This is delicious."

"*Hmm.*" Geny would not press her. It was enough that Margery could not contain her happiness over finally returning a gentleman's feelings. Geny knew her well enough to see that, and she would not push for more confidences.

She served the tea and took her own cake, astonished that she was hungry for it. She had been unable to eat of late, and she knew that her loss of appetite was due to her growing feelings for John.

This time, it was Margery who noticed that Geny was being unusually discreet, and she sent her a more searching glance.

"Something is amiss. I hope you will tell me what it is." This was what Geny loved about Margery. She might seem frivolous, but she was a true friend when it mattered most.

Before confiding in her friend, she listened to the sounds outside of the drawing room to see if anyone was on the point of entering. Matthew had finally persuaded their father to take him out riding in his curricle. This was an extraordinary concession on the earl's part, for Geny hardly remembered spending time with him even when her mother was alive, if it was not to go out into society. All was quiet and she decided it would be safe to talk.

"John—Mr. Rowles—and I have kissed." Just uttering the words caused a deep blush to spread throughout her cheeks, and she looked up at Margery then hid her gaze, embarrassed. She mumbled the rest to her lap. "And I have fallen for him."

Margery leaned forward, exclaiming in a whisper, "That is wonderful. Why do you look so miserable, then? I assume he would not be so lost to propriety as to kiss you and then not offer for you." She gasped. "Or is it your father? Has Mr. Rowles approached the earl, and he refused?"

Geny did not have a chance to answer because Margery answered her own question. "Oh, but no, that cannot be, for you are free to marry anyone you like. Unless it is that you seek your father's approval so much that..." She threw up her hands. "Oh, speak. Tell me what happened."

Geny's feelings were too raw to tease her and retort that she had been attempting to do so except she found it difficult to get the opportunity.

She pressed her fingers to her lips for a moment, then said, "He did not offer for me. He thinks it was wrong of him to have kissed me, and that as we are of two different spheres, nothing can come of it. He apologized."

Margery groaned loudly and threw herself back on the sofa in a theatrical gesture then pulled herself back upright. "Oh, men. They haven't a particle of common sense."

Her friend's reaction somehow eased Geny's angst, and she drew a deep breath. "I am ashamed to admit it, but in our last meeting—he came with me to the classroom to help me hang the curtains there." Geny froze for the space of a breath and bit her lip, remembering how fine he looked as he stretched over to insert the rods into the brackets. "I told him that I was the judge of whether or not we might suit when it came to social disparity."

Margery beamed at her. "Well done, you. What then?"

"He relented and admitted he does have feelings for me and finds me tempting enough that he is trying to stay away from me. He requests that I wait six months before he makes me a proper proposal in case I should change my mind."

This piece of news silenced Margery for a pregnant moment, and she stared at Geny with her mouth ajar.

"Six months? What an odd thing to say. Why does he think that would change anything?"

Geny could only shrug. "It is what I have been asking myself. I don't understand why he would not just take his chances if I told him I did not need my father's approval and that I did not consider our social distance to be an issue. To tell the truth, I am utterly at a loss."

Margery sat, her cakes forgotten as she reflected on this. "I do not have an answer for you. There are no possible circumstances which can make me hazard a guess as to why he would propose such a thing. But if the man has any sense, he will take action well before six months have gone by. And if he doesn't"—she lifted an eyebrow—"perhaps he is not the man for you."

Geny was reluctant to agree with her friend, even though

what she had said made perfect sense. It was just difficult to see clearly when love was involved.

"Perhaps." With every ounce of will, she decided to direct the conversation elsewhere. "Now, I hope we can turn to other, more cheerful topics. Tell me what outings Mr. Thompson has escorted you to."

Margery smoothly evaded the question by bringing up all the people she was forced to dance with at last night's rout. With someone else, Geny might feel that the confidences were unbalanced, but she knew that her friend would end up confiding in her. It just took her a little longer to do so.

"Well, Mr. Thompson is coming for dinner tomorrow night, for one thing," Margery finally confessed in the end. "So I shall be obliged to endure his courtship under the gaze of my five siblings and my two parents." She smiled mischievously. "But then, if he is a worthy adversary, he will rise to the challenge."

"Indeed," Geny said laughing as she pictured the scene. Then she sobered and looked at her friend wistfully.

"You are very lucky though. Tomorrow night I shall also have someone over to dine, but it is not a man whose company I enjoy. It is to be none other than Lord Amherst."

At this, Margery picked up another cake from the platter and set it on Geny's plate. "I heartily sympathize with you. You had better take a bite of cake. I think you are going to need some sweetness to offset your bitter trial."

Geny laughed as she obeyed. Bitter trial indeed.

THE NEXT DAY, GENY ARRANGED THE SEATING AT THE TABLE AS her father would expect. She had included Miss Purcell in the party, hoping that somehow Lord Amherst would be attracted to her fortune enough to leave off pursuing Geny. She was thinking of this when Matthew came to see her in the dining room.

"I'm glad I'm not old enough to have to attend the dinner, for I can think of nothing more tiresome than to sit with adults and talk about boring topics."

"You are fortunate to be spared," she agreed. "But remember your words when eventually you must endure one of these dinners. I charge you to carry on an interesting conversation with your female partners on both sides, so they do not regret the dinner or your company."

"I cannot try too hard, or they might fall in love with me. And that would be worse than anything." Matthew went over and twitched the curtain to look out on their narrow garden behind the house. "It is a fine day. Can you sit outside with me for a little while?"

Geny nodded and put down the list of all that needed to be prepared before that evening. Everything at the table was in order, and she knew her brother was lonely. She understood that feeling all too well and, as far as she was able, wished to be there for him.

When they sat on the stone bench that overlooked a fragrant climbing rosebush, Matthew drew circles in the dirt with a stick.

"Mr. Rowles has been teaching Gabriel and Timothy calculations. Gabriel likes it more than Timothy."

She looked at him curiously. "When have you had a chance to speak to them about it?"

"Father took me to the asylum yesterday in his curricle. He said he wished to meet the new steward, but Mr. Rowles was not there. Father also wished to see that Gabriel had recovered. We found him in the steward's office, and he was working at writing a row of sums with his left hand."

Geny's breath hitched when she thought of her father meeting Mr. Rowles. Would he see at first glance how noble, how worthy he was? Of course he would not think of him in any particular way, but only as an inconsequential steward working at a foundling asylum he did not care very much about. But still, the idea that John might meet her father eventually caused her heart rate to speed up.

She also wondered at her father's interest in the orphan, that it was enough to pay him a visit. He could truly be considerate when he chose to. "Is Gabriel doing better, then?"

"Yes, better now that he is out of his bed, I should say. I asked Father if he is going to return to the orphanage so he might meet Mr. Rowles, and he said he supposed so at some point." It did not sound very imminent.

"And you?" she could not help but to ask. "What do you think of Mr. Rowles?" Fortunately, Matthew did not read anything into her question.

"I like him. He seems to be a good steward and handled Gabriel's injury well. Besides, he does not talk up to me as though he were afraid just because I am a peer."

"Yes, he is a fine steward."

This was all she would allow herself to say on the matter to a brother who was only ten. Besides, apart from Margery, she must not lay her heart bare to anyone else when her feelings had not been unequivocally reciprocated by the man himself.

Dinner that night was tolerable, but she quite thought her little brother had the right of it. Her father was a good host and made everyone feel welcome. Geny did her part as the hostess, little though she wished for the post. Of course, Lord Amherst must be seated at her right, but it was not very onerous. For the first three courses, it required little effort to converse with him, as he was principally involved with the fine cuts of meat on his plate.

She listened to Miss Purcell speaking to the marquess's friend, Mr. Milton, although she sent surreptitious glances toward Lord Amherst. Geny could not understand what she saw in him, unless it was the desire to one day become a duchess.

That must be it. Despite being wealthy, Miss Purcell's family had little ties to the peerage, and she likely thought that was the only thing that was missing—even if it meant being tied to a man who did not inspire Geny with any sentiment that was remotely tender.

As the women gathered in the drawing room for tea, allowing the men their port and cigars in the dining room, Miss Purcell took a seat beside her. They were the only two of the same age, so this was natural.

Miss Purcell looked at the four older women, then sent her gaze around the drawing room at large before bringing it to Geny. "I am much obliged to you for the invitation."

"It was my pleasure." She could not expand on that, for it would involve admitting she had few other acquaintances in society, and that Margery had not been welcome.

Geny rarely dwelled on the fact that she had never cultivated deeper friendships with anyone in the *ton*. In the early years, her mother's death had stolen all desire to do so. Later on, when she finally looked to build possible friendships with other women, she discovered no one who shared her interests. After a few attempts, she gave up trying and was content with what she had with Margery. Now, she turned to her guest with a determination to be friendly and sent her a smile. Miss Purcell returned it.

"I was wondering if you would be interested in going with me tomorrow to visit a new haberdasher's shop on St. James's Street. My mother has given me pocket money expressly to purchase some items for the poor orphans."

Geny looked at her in surprise, not having thought that Miss Purcell would in any way be interested in improving the lives of orphans. It made her glad she had invited her.

"I would be delighted to go with you. It was kind of your mother—and yourself—to think of such a thing."

Miss Purcell smiled. "It is settled, then. I will have the carriage sent around tomorrow at two thirty if that suits you. And I will have my maid with me, so you need not bring your chaperone if you do not wish it."

After such a kind overture of friendship, Geny thought that perhaps it was time to dispense with formalities and said so. "If you wish, you may address me as Eugenia."

"I am honored, my—" Miss Purcell stopped herself. "Eugenia. And of course I give you free use of my name."

The servants came in carrying the tea, and Geny gestured to the table on one wall before turning back to Lucy. "I look forward to seeing what we might find for the orphans tomorrow."

GENY CONGRATULATED HERSELF ON HAVING INCLUDED LUCY Purcell as part of the guest list the night before, for it meant that she was spared some of Lord Amherst's focus when the men came in from their port. Lucy sought the marquess's attention naturally, and not even Geny's father appeared to notice her subtle intrusion into the planned courtship the marquess sought to conduct with his daughter.

The carriage arrived in the afternoon as promised, and the footman opened the door for Geny to exit into the outdoors. She looked up at a bright blue sky with white clouds that somehow brought out the vibrancy of spring colors all around her. This sight of renewal gave her hope, especially since she was to spend time with a young lady her father approved of, while also furthering her interests for the orphanage. Such happenstance made it seem as though a happy future would be possible—even one with John. The two notions did not naturally intersect and therefore made no sense, but it was how she felt.

As they rode to St. James's Street, Geny was more voluble than usual and allowed her guard to come down. Their conversation remained impersonal, but she asked questions of Lucy and answered hers in return. Their time together was more agreeable than she would have expected.

Inside the haberdasher's, they purchased needles and thread, along with a quantity of ribbons and buttons, all for a reasonable sum. And as they had spied a milliner's farther down the street, they agreed to stop there afterwards for some shopping of their own.

They exited the milliner's shop with their parcels, and Geny looked up at the budding trees, inhaling contentedly. Lucy was focused on the crowds milling on the street and slipped her arm through Geny's to lean in.

"Do you know that man?"

Geny made the effort to look but could not see around Lucy.

"It is Mr. Aubin," Lucy continued in a quiet voice, although he must have been too far to hear her. "He was shunned from society, and in fact it was at the hands of *your father*, the earl, for Mr. Aubin had made false claims about him."

Before Geny could assimilate that piece of information, Lucy went on. "And he fleeced a man of his entire fortune in one night, so everyone agrees it is better that he has been turned out, for he is not a gentleman that anyone would wish to associate with. I do not know how he dares to show his face on St. James's Street."

Now Geny was even more curious to see who this Mr. Aubin was, having recognized the name. The only new piece of information that Lucy had given her was that it was her own father who had had him shunned from society. She had not known that.

She pulled out of Lucy's grip and stepped back to peer down the street just as the gentleman turned his head. A look of shock, followed by alarm filled his features at the same time that recognition dawned on her.

Good heavens. No...

Not since the physician announced the news of her mother's death did she feel as though the ground had opened up underneath her, pulling her into a black abyss.

Mr. Aubin was indeed none other than John Rowles.

Chapter Nineteen

John entered Blackstone's in a state of shock, scarcely able to return Plockton's greeting. Lady Geny had just learned of his identity. He was nearly certain of it based on her stunned expression, which mirrored his own. That, and the way she turned to step into the carriage without speaking to him. The knowledge that he had lost her good opinion hurt more than he could have imagined. It was only now that he realized just how much he had been fooling himself into thinking he would find a way out of this dilemma without losing Geny. It had been foolish to hope that he would.

John walked numbly in the direction of the drawing room, scarcely heeding anyone around him. Since he had come to the club with no particular purpose that day, he considered going home. Time in solitude was needed to deal with the blow he had just suffered on the street. Strangely enough, though, the undemanding atmosphere of the club soothed the turbulence of his emotions, and he decided to stay. He headed toward the empty chair next to Harry Smart.

"Aubin, this here is Miles Yardley. He's just joined, too. We go two years without any new members, and now we get an assortment at once."

"A pleasure," John said quietly with a polite nod.

Even if he were in the mood to do so, he would not accost the man to learn why he had been blackballed elsewhere as John had been upon his first meeting.

"You will never guess what caused him to be blackballed," Drake said, grinning as he wandered over to them.

"I do not think we need to go into that now," Mr. Yardley said stiffly.

John felt for him and shook his head. "No indeed." Then, in an effort to ease Yardley's discomfort more than anything, he forced himself to make conversation. "Has anyone seen Sir Humphrey?"

"Hasn't been in today," Harry answered. "Why?"

In another world, John would have been more circumspect but given that he had just lost any chance of winning Lady Geny, he threw caution to the wind. "I need to find a way to bring Lord Goodwin to book for what he did, and I realize that I cannot accomplish it alone. I may be losing my access to the foundling asylum soon."

"The foundling asylum? In Bloomsbury?" Mr. Yardley turned to him, an interested light in his eyes. It seemed he recognized it.

"Yes, the very one. Do you have a connection to it?"

Yardley indicated that he did. "As a barrister, I once represented a peer who had made a significant donation to the asylum years ago when it first opened, but he was not confident the money was used for the right purposes. He came to see what might be done."

"Who was your client?" John asked before he thought the better of it. He was unsurprised at Yardley's answer.

"I am afraid I cannot disclose that. Client privilege, you understand."

"Of course." John thought for a minute. Drake had turned away, but Harry was still listening. It didn't matter anymore. He had nothing to lose. "Can you tell me whether you were able to pin anything on him?"

Yardley seemed to feel the information was safe to divulge. "In the end, my client declared himself satisfied. The earl showed him a commemorative tablet that had been engraved with the names of sponsors and amounts, informing him that it would be hung in the chapel. My client thought that if he'd anything to hide he would not publicize the donations that way. Said the early funds had been absorbed in improving the building structure—"

John snorted. When Yardley broke off to stare at him, he explained. "Part of the stable wall crumbled last week."

"Ah. So it was not used to improve the structure." Yardley did not appear to be a man who spoke before he was ready to do so, and he took his time as he mulled over this.

"If you want to expose the earl, you must not attempt to do it yourself, for society will only drag your name through the mud..." He paused as an interested light came to his eye. "Was that it? The reason for your being blackballed?"

John nodded.

"Then I advise you to give any evidence you collect into the hands of a peer and let *him* do the work. My father—"

"His Grace, the Duke of Rigsby."

A voice behind their chairs startled John and caused both him and Yardley to look behind them in an attempt to catch sight of the man who had spoken.

John almost jumped at the ghoulish face that peered back until he recognized it to be a wild boar's head, next to which was Lord Blackstone. A candle lit the viscount's face from underneath, casting black shadows on his features as though he were attempting to frighten them. John suspected this was not the case.

"I beg your pardon?"

"We must approach His Grace. Goodwin has persuaded the duke's son, Lord Amherst, to invest in his textile mill in exchange for his daughter's hand."

"What?"

John leapt to his feet. Such arranged marriages were not uncommon in society, and it mattered little that he could not have her. He would not sit by idly while Lady Geny was bartered off in such a way. "I need Lord Amherst's direction."

He was ready to run off at that very moment in search of him. Lord Blackstone held up a hand and gestured for him to resume his chair, before leaving behind the barred teeth and dim circle of light to take the empty seat next to them. John obeyed, and Lord Blackstone indicated for Yardley to speak.

"Well, Miles? I believe you have something to say?"

Yardley nodded. "Let us have all of the evidence you have currently gathered and see what might hold. You do not even need a court of law to stop the earl. Society's silent rebuke will serve just as well."

John complied, detailing the marble plaque, Gabriel's anonymous sponsorship, the caved-in wall, and missing recorded expenditures, leaving nothing out as Blackstone and Yardley listened. Harry patted his pockets and pulled out his snuffbox, appearing enraptured by the conversation.

At the end of it, Yardley frowned. "I am afraid it is not enough to bring the earl down. It is a lot of circumstantial evidence, but there is nothing solid. You may have to go up north and visit the textile mill yourself to see if you can find any evidence there."

The momentary hope that Yardley would give him the magic solution was dashed. A silence fell that was broken only by some teasing laughter coming from one corner of the room. He glanced over, unsurprised to see Sebastian Drake at the heart of it.

"Get the evidence," Lord Blackstone said. "And I will bring it to the duke's attention. I was able to preserve his favorite spaniel, who now sits happily in his permanent place in the duke's library. His Grace will receive me."

"Thank you," John said. It was the best he could do.

THAT NIGHT, JOHN WRESTLED WITH THE QUESTION OF WHETHER he should bother going to the orphanage the next day or not. The uncertainty of whether Geny had truly learned of his identity, and the fact that he still had work to do there weighed on the side of going. However the apprehension of having her receive him with contempt made it difficult for him to set forth with any confidence.

In the end, it was the thought of Timothy and Gabriel waiting for him that made him go. He could not disappear from their lives without explanation. Even if he was chased out of the asylum, they should know that he had attempted to continue in his role as steward and had not forgotten about them.

He went early and was therefore unsurprised that the carriage bearing the earl's crest was not there. This was a small respite he had depended upon, as it would give him some time to settle into his office and prepare himself for when she did arrive, if indeed she had planned to come today. Perhaps she would avoid him entirely and send word that he should pack his things, never to return.

There was also the risk that Lord Goodwin himself would arrive and throw him out on his ear. The risk had always been there, and he could not blame Lady Geny if—shocked by what she had learned about his identity—she arrived at the orphanage in the company of the earl so he might throw John out.

Although she is perfectly capable of doing the task herself, he thought glumly.

To his surprise Gabriel was already in his office, diligently at work at the small table.

"I hope you do not mind that I came in before you were here, sir. It takes me longer to work on the sums than when I was using my other hand."

John praised him for his diligence, offering an encouraging smile despite how depressed he felt. He looked around the office, conscious that he might be leaving it soon, and removed his hat as Gabriel turned in his chair.

"John Groat delivered the courier. It's on your desk."

"Thank you." John sat and pulled the small pile of letters toward him. In addition to the usual collection of itemized bills, there was a thick letter with many pages, sealed and addressed to the financial steward of the foundling asylum. Without giving another thought, John split the seal and spread open the pages.

Redhill Spinnings & Works
Rochdale Canal
Ancoats, Manchester

Dear Mr. Peyton, the letter began.

John knew he should stop reading at this point since the letter was clearly not addressed to him, but his curiosity got the better of him. This was most likely regarding the earl's mill. Besides, the front of the letter had not listed Mr. Peyton by name, so he had not been wrong in breaking the seal.

We have not received the funds to continue the work on the textile mill and the workers' housing as has been promised many times over in the last months, and I am at a loss for how to understand this. Lord Goodwin came himself and approved the project after having bought the land. We started on those initial proceeds and have met every promised milestone on our side. In the last four months, the money has slowed to a halt until there is not even enough to pay the workers. What am I to do? I have already laid from my own purse a sum to pay the laborers so their families can eat.

Besides that, there are other textile workers who have lingered in the area in the hopes that the mill would be functioning in little time. I can hardly hold my head up in front of them. I demand that you send the money that is owed to me at once. I have attached the invoices with this letter in case you should have misplaced them. And I beg that you will apprise me of whether this project is to go ahead as agreed upon or not. I have my own reputation and livelihood to think of.

Richard Gover

John read the letter over and over again, noting the address and gaining in conviction that this was the proof he needed. He might even be able to hand this to Blackstone without needing to visit the mill in question.

He dropped the papers on his desk and went over to the closet that held the stack of ledgers, flipping through them until he found the one that showed the disbursement entries listed as redirected funds. As irregular as it was to redirect donations from one project to another, if it had truly been what the earl had done, then where had the money gone?

He tucked the papers and book into a bag and set it beside his hat. He would have it ready in case there was a need to leave in a hurry.

With his mind so wholly consumed by the earl's exposure and having achieved the necessary proof at last, it was difficult to spend the morning teaching Gabriel. He hadn't even the heart to go looking for Timothy to see where he had gotten off to. At last, he heard the sounds of the carriage rolling into the courtyard, and he looked out. It was the earl's.

His heart began to race as he waited to see who would alight. Would it be Lady Geny? Had Lord Goodwin accompanied her?

In the end, only Lady Geny and her maid stepped out of it before the groom brought the equipage into the carriage house. She looked up at the window and he thought she saw him, but she gave no sign of recognition, nor did she smile. Instead, her face was solemn as she walked toward the entrance.

His heart sank. He wondered if he had done well to persist in his efforts to bring the earl down. It was by far worse to lose her good opinion. If being shunned by society pricked, then losing Geny cut daggers. If he could give up his place in society forever and thereby gain her back, it would take no time to make his decision. But he had already gone too far. It was too late to pull back.

He heard her coming up the stairs; heard her murmur a greeting to someone in the office, presumably Mrs. Hastings. He waited a little longer, but she did not appear at the doorway.

He could no longer wait to see her and was turning to Gabriel just as Timothy walked through the door.

"Tim, you're getting later and later," Gabriel said in a voice as close to teasing as his sober nature would allow. "I have now caught up to you even using my weak hand."

"I promised Mason Cook I'd clear the floor around the support beams before he arrived. I was busy."

"Good morning, Timothy," John said in reply to the bow his apprentice made him. "Why don't you both go and learn from the mason today? A little sun will do you good, Gabriel. Just take care not to do anything to injure your arm any more."

"Yes, sir." They both bowed and left, with Gabriel moving at a pace that demonstrated the rapid convalescence of youth.

With the boys gone, John waited a few more minutes before drawing the conclusion that Lady Geny was not planning to come to his office. The notion that she might come and *not* throw him out, but simply ignore him, had not occurred to him. He did not know what to make of it, but he could not avoid meeting his fate. It would happen sooner or later.

He walked past Mr. Dowling's office, not bothering to bid him good morning, and went straight to the head mistress's office. It was unfortunate that Mrs. Hastings was there, for he could not simply close the door and lay everything on the table between them.

"Good morning, my lady. Good morning, Mrs. Hastings." He faced Lady Geny. "I was hoping I might speak to you about Gabriel and Timothy's progress since you were so kind as to recommend them to me. Is now a convenient time?"

Lady Geny looked at him for a long moment, before standing.

"I have a few minutes to spare, Mr. Rowles. Let us go to the meeting room." Though the meeting room was directly above the chapel wall, the mason had deemed it safe.

He followed behind her. As they went past Mr. Dowling's office, the headmaster spotted Lady Geny and leapt to his feet. John was determined that Mr. Dowling would not be an audience to whatever it was they had to say to each other, but he did not know exactly how to rebuff him.

Lady Geny paused in her steps and turned to the headmaster as he reached the doorway. "Mr. Dowling, your presence is not needed. I am having a discussion with Mr. Rowles."

She moved forward, and John followed once again through the parlor and into the meeting room, impressed by the efficient way she had disposed of Mr. Dowling. They entered the room, and he waited until she sat before taking the seat across from her.

He moistened his lips; it seemed impossible to begin. He did not know where he should start, and she was not giving him any assistance by opening the conversation for him. He could not blame her.

"I am guessing you have learned that my name is John Aubin."

She returned a slight nod, her regard steady. His eyes drifted to hers, and he wondered if they were red or if he were simply imagining it. Her expression was too aloof to reveal any heightened emotion.

Since she had not said anything further, the onus was on him to elaborate. "I am surprised that you have not exposed my identity in the asylum and chased me off."

"Not yet."

This was not an auspicious beginning, but he deserved it.

"Your father and I are at odds," he said, still struggling to find his way through the most difficult conversation he had ever had in his life.

Lady Geny raised her brow. "Are you indeed? What an odd way to deliver your explanation. I had rather thought you might begin by explaining how you are working in the orphanage under an assumed name. Have you conjured it up out of thin air?"

He knew this was mere quibbling over words, but he could not help but protest. "It *is* my name—or was. Rowles is my birth father's name. Aubin is my stepfather's name. He adopted me."

The news did not seem to relieve any of Geny's ire, and she cocked her head. "So what are you truly doing here in the asylum?"

"I am trying to expose your father's wrongdoings."

That was the worst thing to have said, and in a flash she was on her feet. "Thank you for being so forthright. We clearly have nothing else to discuss." She walked with brisk steps toward the door, but John leapt from his seat and raced toward her, cutting off her path.

"Please, Geny." He held her arm, preventing her from opening the door until he had explained himself. She looked at it pointedly, and he released it.

"Even after everything we have gone through, I did not give you leave to use my Christian name." Lady Geny swallowed, the only sign of a troubled spirit. "And I would thank you for not doing so."

"My apologies." John took a step backwards, yet still partially blocked the entrance, hoping she would allow him to have his say.

"My lady, your father did me an ill turn. I was on my way to my brother's estate in Surrey in November. It was early in the morning, and I had stopped at an inn where I overheard the earl's conversation with a man I now must suppose to be Mr. Peyton. Lord Goodwin had just learned of Parliamentary legislation that would threaten the return on an investment he had made. He instructed his agent to sell off his shares quietly without informing his peers."

She stared at him for a moment before responding. "Impossible. My father would never do such a thing. His reputation is beyond reproach."

"Publicly, perhaps. But there are things you ought to look into." Her expression showed only resistance and disbelief, but he went on. "I tried to expose what he had done to Lord Perkins, and your father had me shunned from White's and Boodle's."

Her eyes narrowed. "If he had been as perfidious as you have accused him of being, everyone would have learned about it when his dealings came to light."

Lady Geny was a clever woman. He had known it would not be easy to persuade her. He could not have loved her as well were she not so discerning.

"Yes, except in the end, the legislature did not pass. And in January, there was a boom on trade so that the other investors lost nothing by it. On the contrary, they gained from the deal. Only your father lost, because he had sold off most of his shares."

"So you maligned my father's reputation for nothing."

She skewered him with her glare, but it was the pain he saw underneath it that destroyed him—pain he had put there. Still, his expulsion from society was unfair, and he did not deserve it. The reminder caused John to grow indignant.

"Not for nothing. A gentleman does not turn on his friends, leaving them with great losses on a bad investment while protecting his own."

"You admit you are a gentleman, then?"

He looked away, desperate for more time with her, while knowing she was rapidly losing what little patience she had. Desperate to be able to tell her everything in hopes that something might redeem him from an impossible plight. He *loved* her. John exhaled silently.

"I am."

"Does a gentleman fleece another man of his entire fortune in a card game?" she asked.

He had no ready answer for that. He had never been able to convince himself in his own mind that he had acted the part of a gentleman in that endeavor. His defense was feeble at best.

"I am a gentleman in every sense of the word. My father was one, but it was my stepfather who had the wealth and connections to bring me into society. It is through him that I have my standing there—although I lost it when your father had me blackballed from the clubs."

"And so you infiltrated a *foundling* asylum to try to get that reputation back." Her voice dripped with disdain, and it seeped into his conscience like poison.

"Yes, I did, but—"

Whatever composure she had held until now suddenly snapped, and she went a fiery red. "You *kissed* me! When you were all the while seeking to expose my father, you traitor. And do you still think you can call yourself a gentleman?"

John stepped back, struck as though he had received a blow

to the chest. *Traitor?* He wanted to defend himself, but he could not. He could not summon a single word.

"I think you should leave," she said after a breath of silence. "Immediately. I will have Mr. Peyton find a new steward to replace you."

She had effectively told him she never wanted to see him again. Although expected, hearing her say it was far worse than he could have imagined, and his hands dropped to his side. Summoning his resolve, he delivered one last argument in rushed words.

"Mr. Peyton denies having received Mr. Thompson's contribution. Six years ago, Lord Hollingsworth's donation was stripped from the ledgers as an expenditure, so no one knew where it went, but there was an anonymous sponsorship in the same amount for Gabriel. And no, Lord Hollingsworth is not his father. I asked. On top of that, I was handed a letter of reproach addressed to both Mr. Peyton and your father for failing to send the promised funds for the mill and worker's housing in Manchester. They have received nothing, and yet there are ledger entries listed as funds being redirected to the mill work."

Speechless with rage, she pointed at the door.

"I will leave as you have asked, but those are things you ought to know. You deserve to know them. Your father has the appearance of goodness. Whether his actions can withstand scrutiny is another matter."

"I said leave," she repeated through gritted teeth.

John opened the door and almost ran into Mr. Dowling, who was standing close enough to have overheard everything. Without thinking twice, he reached back and threw a punch into his jaw that sent Dowling reeling backwards. He crashed against a chair and into the wall, clutching his chin and staring at John with wide eyes.

"I would encourage you," John said, chest heaving, his anger barely contained, "*not* to eavesdrop when a lady and gentleman are speaking of matters that are none of your concern. If I hear of Lady Eugenia's name—*or* that of Lord Goodwin's—being bandied about in any circle, I shall invite you to choose your weapon."

John stormed into his office and grabbed his coat and hat, along with the bag containing the precious evidence. He glanced inside to make sure it was all still there, then hurried down the stairs into the courtyard. He strode toward the gates without saying farewell to Gabriel and Timothy. The iron gates clanged shut behind him, and they rang with the sound of finality.

Chapter Twenty

"Miss, if I may say so, you don't look yourself." Charity paused in uncharacteristic solicitude beside the bed.

"I am a bit tired, that is all." Geny threw off the covers. She could not remain in bed all day no matter how heartsick she felt. "However, it is fortunate it is not my day to go to the orphanage, for I will have some rest."

"Yes, and the young master will be returning to Eton today." Charity pulled out the stool for her to sit in front of the mirror. "Brantley told me."

Geny swiveled to look up at her maid in surprise. "I did not know."

"The earl just gave the orders to Higgins, miss." Charity stopped, and a worried look came upon her face. "But perhaps I've stepped out o' line by telling you."

Geny knew it was more likely that her father had taken a high-handed approach and had ordered his heir's removal without even informing Matthew himself. She could not blame her maid. "It is all right."

Charity began brushing her hair, working in silence, a kindness Geny appreciated. She could not bear any idle conversation at the moment with her heart so sore. The night before had been her second one in tears, with each morning pressing cold metal spoons to her eyelids to remove the swelling before anyone would see her. Tears that should be wasted, given how unworthy Mr. Rowles—Mr. Aubin—had turned out to be.

She had sent her chocolate back to the kitchen, requesting tea instead, and she sipped it now. The hot, perfumed beverage seemed her only solace since she could scarcely manage to choke anything else down.

Yesterday, she had stayed at the orphanage long enough only to see that Mr. Aubin had left the premises. She could not give her heart to the orphans at the moment, not when it was so broken. The rest of the day she had spent at home going over their every encounter and trying to analyze everything he had said to see if she should have guessed.

The decision of whether she should tell her father about his true identity was not an easy one. She had not done so yet and even wondered if the delay was a wise decision. Her father ought to know by all rights, but there was something that stopped her. A misplaced loyalty to Mr. Aubin, most likely. She was a fool.

"Shall I curl the sides of your hair, miss?" Charity asked, taking the tongs from where they had been heating in the fire.

"No. Pull everything back, so that it's neater." Geny watched, her somber expression accentuated by the severe hairstyle, as her maid followed her instructions.

John had fully felt the pain of the consequences of his actions yesterday. She knew he had, for she could see it in his eyes. And he had spoken to her with details about her father's ill dealings that showed he at least had believed himself to be in the right. Her initial reaction had been disbelief, but with the night's reflection, she was no longer quite so sure. Her father had always had an irreproachable reputation, but did this not come from his own assertions rather than an abundance of good deeds? How could she be so sure he was the innocent man he claimed to be, when she scarcely spent enough time in his presence to know for sure?

"Thank you." Geny got to her feet, leaving her food untouched. "You may take that back to the kitchen."

"Yes, miss." Charity began to gather the dishes, and Geny went downstairs in search of Matthew. He was sitting in the library, swinging one foot on the armchair and staring off into space.

"Good morning. I have just learned you are to return to Eton." She sat at his side. "Were you aware of it?"

Matthew turned to look at her, his face inscrutable. "Betty is packing my trunk right now. Father left a message with Higgins to have the carriage hitched, and the footman came to give me the orders. He said Father has gone north for some reason, so he will not be here to see me off."

"Father is gone?"

Geny felt disoriented by all these decisions being made without her knowledge, especially after the upsetting experience at the asylum. Now, even if she wished to tell her father about what happened, she could not do so. If only he communicated with her more, she would not be left in such a state of confusion.

"When do you leave?"

"Within the hour," Matthew said, sighing.

"*Hmm.*" The despondency in her brother's expression made her forget her own troubles in her anxiety to relieve his. "Why don't we play a game of cards to pass the time?"

Although he did not return an enthusiastic reply, he stood and walked over to a side table where a deck of cards was held. She dealt them and searched for something to say, all while looking at him with fondness. He was growing up, but it meant he was not as confiding as he once was.

"They have begun to repair the wall in the orphanage. I think you would have liked to have seen it." She glanced at her cards, then over at him as she lay down a card. "Timothy is following the mason and learning everything he can about the trade. I think I know what future lies ahead of him."

"Lucky him," Matthew said, playing his card and taking the trick.

"Did you wish you could become a mason?" she asked, a hint of a smile on her face.

"No, but I wish I could be as free as those orphans. I could live in the same place without going anywhere and have lots of friends. And I could work at something simple."

Geny knew how futile it was to tell him that it wasn't quite as carefree as he imagined. "I understand."

"And they have Mr. Rowles," he continued, clearly bent on carrying on his diatribe. This time his words inadvertently hit a mark.

Geny took the next trick and asked quietly, "Why do you speak of Mr. Rowles? What is it about him?"

"He seems honorable. I like him better than all my masters combined and wouldn't mind training under him."

His blond hair stood up in front in a stubborn cowlick, and she attempted to pat it in place across from their table. He submitted to it.

"Well, I know this is not what you want to hear, but the wisest course is for you to go to school and do your best there. I promise the future will be brighter than it is now." She attempted to believe her own words.

They played until the footman came in to announce that the carriage was ready. Geny stood and held out her arms and Matthew slipped into them, allowing her to give him a hug. She forced her emotions down so that she did not alarm her brother with her tears. But it was with an overly bright smile that she said, "Farewell. Don't forget to write to me."

"I won't," he said, following the footman out the door. He would forget, of course, but their time together had seemed to exercise a positive effect on him. He was chatting with Brantley as he went to the carriage.

Within minutes following his departure, the house had grown as silent as a tomb, and Geny walked around the library looking at the shelves she knew by heart. There were no books that interested her.

Your father has the appearance of goodness, but whether his actions can stand scrutiny is another matter. John's words came back to her, and she wondered once again if there was any truth to what he said. If only she could know.

An idea then seized her which was so daring it sent her breath out of her lungs in a *whoosh*. If her father had gone north and her brother was no longer home, then *she* was the mistress of the house. Who was there to stop her from going into her father's study? Her decision was made, and with resolute steps she exited into the corridor and walked toward the study. She opened the door and looked around.

The study was her father's domain, and she had not set foot in it above five times in her whole life. It had all the masculine trappings of leather and dark burgundy curtains with lingering cigar smoke. An intimidating room. However, now that she had determined her course, she wasted no time in going over to his desk. If she was to find any clue to what sort of man he was, it would most likely be here. She glanced through the papers on top of the desk and found nothing of note. Then, she began opening the drawers, which somehow seemed like a greater trespass; it made her heart beat painfully fast. Her father would be extremely displeased should he ever find out.

The first drawer held bills and some stationery products, such as fresh wax and pen nibs, and the second drawer was more of the same. It was in the third drawer that she found more sentimental items, and as she sat on his chair, she pulled out the first stack with trembling hands. These were perfumed letters with nothing written on the outside. When she opened the first one, her eyes fell on her mother's familiar handwriting.

Her shoulders slumped in relief. He had kept her mother's letters! This was not the action of an unkind, unscrupulous man—her father was merely being judged for his reserve.

Out of respect for her parents' intimacy, she decided not to read her mother's letters but turned her eyes to the bundle underneath. These were done in a different handwriting and were also perfumed. She gulped, dropping them on the desk as though they were hot and put her fingers over her mouth, staring at them.

No, no. I cannot look at those. I do not want to know. Geny shook her head. *What am I doing?*

She had just decided to stop her investigation when a solitary letter at the bottom of the drawer caught her eye, this time again in her mother's handwriting. The familiar loops unleashed something in her that made her go back on her decision not to read her mother's letters. Just to read one—to hear her mother's voice again through the words written long ago—would fill the aching void inside of her that had become too great.

She seized it and opened it to discover that it was dated only a fortnight before her mother's death. With parted lips, she hurriedly skimmed the lines, desperate to learn the state of her mother's mind before she died.

> *Franklin,*
>
> *I am obliged to write to you in your club, because you have not been home these past five nights, but there is a pressing matter you must be informed of. The blacksmith from Windsor came to the house today asking for you. I received him in the parlor in your absence, and yes—I am sure you have already surmised what I am about to tell you.*
>
> *You will therefore not be surprised to learn the purpose of his visit,*

although it came as a great shock to me. Now that his daughter has died, leaving behind a child whose parentage he said was yours, he has come to request that you continue to send the monthly allowance, so he might raise the orphan. He was referring, of course, to Gabriel Smith, the foundling you had placed in the asylum that I had naively praised as showing such promise.

I suppose a woman of my station must expect infidelity. But I confess that I did not imagine you to be so base as to carry on this liaison whilst I was recovering from the loss of our second child. You told me that important affairs were keeping you away from London, but that was not it, was it? It was to carry on with the blacksmith's daughter. It is the timing of your affair for which I shall not forgive you...

Geny could not keep reading; her eyes were filled with tears at her father's utter betrayal and the gut-wrenching pain her mother had felt which carried through her words. She remembered her mother's convalescence from her lung infection. She had been on the way to recovery before she suddenly took a turn for the worse. It must surely have been this revelation that overset her and caused her to give up her will to live.

Geny laid the bundle of papers on the desk, dropping her face in her hands so that she only heard—and did not see—the door open. She lifted her head in time to see her father on the threshold of his study, looking thunderstruck.

"What in the blazes are you doing here, Eugenia?"

Such a reception would normally cow Geny, but she was too distraught at the information she had just learned to give her father his usual reverence. She lifted the letter her mother had written.

"Is it true? Did you father an illegitimate son—the orphan Gabriel—during the period when Mother was suffering from the loss of her baby?"

Geny remembered that period of mourning well. Her

mother had been several weeks along and had announced to the household that she was expecting a baby, much to the joy of everyone, even—Geny had thought—her father.

She had been looking forward to a younger brother or sister when news of the bleeding spread throughout the household. It had taken her mother many weeks to recover physically from the ordeal and much longer for her emotional pain to disappear. In the years following her mother's loss, Geny had almost forgotten about it, first because Matthew's birth had erased much of that sorrow, and then because the pain of losing her mother had engulfed all else. But now it had all come rushing back.

"How dare you go through my things?" he demanded, moving toward her.

Geny stood her ground. "Answer me, Father. I am hearing all sorts of rumors about misplaced funds in the orphanage, and now this. I could overlook almost anything, but I am convinced that your indiscretion is what caused Mother to deteriorate so rapidly. You are responsible for her death."

The earl snatched the letter out of her hands. "You do not understand the way of the world. You remain purposefully ignorant by burying your nose in the asylum rather than attending to your duties as is befitting the daughter of an earl. How dare you lecture me?"

For the first time in Geny's life, she saw the sign of weakness in him that he attempted to cover with bluster. It was a look of shame that he would conceal at all costs if he could to save face. She stared at him, realization dawning as she saw him clearly for the first time in her life.

"But is it true—"

"I am not obliged to answer any of your questions, and I will thank you to leave this room at once. I had not thought it necessary to lock the door to the study located in my own home. Evidently, I must begin doing so now."

Geny walked to the door, knowing she would have nothing satisfactory from him. No confessions, no apologies.

"I thought you had gone on a sudden trip north," she said dully.

"So that is why you decided to raid my study?" He was stuffing the letters back in the drawer. When she offered no response, he lifted his eyes to hers.

"I was on my way but had forgotten something. I am leaving straight away and will be back in a fortnight. I trust I have made myself clear about going through my things."

"Yes, Father." Geny left the room.

There was no point in attempting a conversation or hoping for any sort of reconciliation with him. This would be the end of the matter. She would be expected to sweep any disagreements under the rug and continue as before. Fine, then. She would do so. But for the moment, she would also keep the news of Mr. Aubin's infiltration of the orphanage to herself.

GENY SAT QUIETLY KNITTING NEW STOCKINGS IF ONLY TO KEEP her hands occupied. It was the only thing she could do to ease her mind, although her thoughts continued to jump erratically from one sorrow to another with no relief in sight. She had heard the sounds of her father's departure earlier, and the gloom of the day oppressed her. Was it possible she could ever feel happy again when she had been betrayed by the man she loved, then again by her father whom she had respected and trusted—after she had just bid farewell to her brother, the only family member for whom she felt true affection?

There was a knock on the front door, and she was about to tell the butler that she was not at home, when she heard the sounds of Margery's voice. It was unexpected at this hour, for Geny had thought she would be preparing for one of her mother's many social engagements. She put down her knitting and stood, waiting for her friend to come into the room. Margery was all smiles until she caught sight of Geny's face.

"What has happened, Geny?"

She waited until the butler left—he would know to send for tea—and allowed Margery to settle down and take off her bonnet. But then, because she didn't know where to begin, she moved over to sit beside her, needing the comfort. Without a word, she rested her head on her friend's shoulder.

Margery put her arm around her. "You are alarming me. Please tell me what has happened."

"Mr. Rowles is indeed Mr. Aubin, as your Mr. Thompson had thought. He kissed me, all while working to expose my father for some corrupt dealing he thought him to have done. I told him to leave the asylum and never to come back."

"Oh." Margery said this on a quiet sigh.

"And before leaving, he accused my father of a litany of scandalous deeds, which I rejected outright," Geny continued.

"Why, there is not a man in London with a more pristine reputation than the earl!" Margery exclaimed, indignant.

"Except that it turns out he was correct, at least in part." Geny could not bear to speak even to her best friend about the things she had learned, but she had to let this truth fall.

After a moment, Margery tightened her embrace. "I am sorry."

"And Matthew has just left."

"So, in other words, a colossally bad day." Margery pulled back to look at Geny, who now sat upright.

"Yes." Her eyes filled with tears despite herself, but she went back to her own seat and lifted up her knitting, although she did not continue her project. She wiped her tears away and met Margery's regard.

A maid entered, carrying the tea tray. She laid everything out and withdrew quietly. Geny stirred in the tea leaves and let them steep as she held out the plate for her friend to take a cake. Margery shook her head.

"You don't have to refuse out of sympathy for me," she said.

Margery smiled in response. "I promise you, I am not."

There was something in her voice, and Geny studied her face more closely. Although she was consumed with her own pain, it was evident that Margery was not acting quite herself. Apart from offering Geny some much-needed consolation, her best friend seemed nervous—and then she had refused the cake.

"Something has happened."

Margery blushed and smiled enigmatically, but shook her head.

With growing conviction, Geny said, "Oh, but it has." Suddenly, everything was clear. "Mr. Thompson has proposed, and you have accepted him."

Margery covered her cheeks. "I did not want to tell you, not with the day you have been having."

Geny looked at her with slight exasperation, despite being touched by her thoughtfulness.

"What do you mean? This news has redeemed the day. I am happy for you. And all this while, you were the one who said you would never marry. Now you are to be married first."

She added silently, *And perhaps will be the only one to do so.*

"It is just that I like him so much. I hadn't the heart to say no when he came to propose to me. He was actually nervous, and I never see him nervous." Her eyes twinkled. "I think that was what made up my mind."

Geny sighed but accompanied it with a smile. At least somebody would have a happy ending. And she would not begrudge such a thing of a friend who had always been there for her. They drank their tea and spoke of wedding plans whenever Geny had her way. Margery, on the other hand, kept directing the conversation away from the subject, and she knew it was for fear of causing her pain.

When at last a silence fell, Margery studied her. "Did Mr. Aubin's explanation enlighten you in the end? Do you think he is innocent of any matter of which he is accused?"

Geny looked down, remembering the conversation, and the pain she saw on his face. She said softly, "I think he was honest at least in his feelings for me."

"Well, there is that at least." Margery folded her hands and made her mouth into a straight line. "For that reason, I will refrain from despising him."

Another silence fell, then Geny laughed suddenly.

"When we left the meeting room—both of us in the height of emotion—who should be standing there but Mr. Dowling, *eavesdropping* on our entire conversation."

Margery's eyes widened as Geny continued, "And John floored him with one punch."

"What?" Margery said, bringing her hand up to cover her laughter.

"He informed Mr. Dowling that should he hear any rumors concerning me or my family being spread about, he would invite Mr. Dowling to choose his weapon."

Margery smiled broadly. "Now *that* is something I would love to have seen. Mr. Aubin may be a rake, but he knows how to be a gentleman."

Chapter Twenty-One

John left London and headed north, leaving instructions for Owen to pack his things and bring them to the estate. As he climbed into his traveling coach for the fifth consecutive day, every miserable word of his conversation with Lady Geny came back to haunt him. The accusation that he had kissed her while he was attempting to expose her father was particularly galling for how true it was. She would have felt that to be the worst betrayal of all.

The pain of having her send him off scorched. It had been so final, mitigated only by his fury against Dowling which he had allowed vent to and which left his knuckles sore for two days. John clicked on the reins urging his rental team to pick up their pace.

There was nothing he could do to salvage his relationship with Lady Geny, and it left him with a raw ache. All that remained to him after that was to leave. London held no interest; the orphanage was off-limits. He no longer even cared all that much about regaining his reputation.

The decision to visit his brother had been a simple one since he could not bear to go to his newly acquired estate and had nowhere else to go. His brother lived in Mossley, West Riding—a trip of six days—and he halted for his last night in Cheshire, at an inn in the town of Cheadle. As he requested a room, John attempted to remember why the name of the town sounded so familiar. He must have come through here before when he visited his brother.

No! The realization of why came to him at once. Cheadle was where Barnsby's estate was located, the man he had ruined. This fact he had learned in the aftermath of his card game when the rumor mills spread about just how much of a fortune John had stripped from the poor fellow. *Well*, John thought as he followed the innkeeper to his room, *that is the nature of a card game. You know going into it that you will either win or lose.*

Despite that resolution, he spent the evening over his solitary supper remembering the card game's evolution. His mind brought forth the desperate look on Barnsby's face when John won the last hand which separated him from the remainder of his fortune. It made him sick to think about it, which was probably why he generally chose not to. But with the other alternative being to think about Lady Geny, he allowed his mind to dwell on the unwisdom of his conduct, replaying the events of the card game over and over. By the time morning arrived, he had reached a decision.

When he went to pay his shot, he decided to try and see what the innkeeper knew.

"I am looking for an estate in Cheadle owned by a man named Barnsby. Do you know of it?" A sudden, desperate hope shot through him that he would not be informed that Barnsby had been forced to sell.

"Ay, that I do. It is not three miles from here. You'll want to take the road past Gatley. Stick to the main road until you cross the Mersey River—there's an old stone bridge—and take the path on your right. The estate's at the end of it."

"I am much obliged." John went outside where a stable hand stood at the head of his lead horse. He climbed in and gave the pair a signal to start forward in the direction the innkeeper had indicated.

John did not know what sort of reception he would receive there, but he had decided on his course. He knew the financials of his estate well and had come to the conclusion that he could return the money to Barnsby without in any way reducing the funds needed for his own estate, although it would require two years of sober living. Given his current situation, that would not be a hardship.

Besides, he had hardly spent any of his winnings from that night, having fallen out of society within weeks of the event. He directed his horse over the stone bridge and followed the shady path on the other side that led to the estate. When he pulled up, a servant came from around the house to hold the reins for him while he went up to the door and knocked. After some time, another servant came to the door and asked him to state his business.

John handed the man his card with the name of Mr. John Rowles. He had had the notion on his ride over that a card bearing the name "Mr. Aubin" would likely have him turned away without being granted an audience.

"Tell him that we met in London."

"Very well, sir. Please wait, and I will see if he will receive you."

The servant went down the large corridor, and John looked at his surroundings. The hall was shabby, but not as decrepit as he might have imagined. In fact, the estate did not seem to be in terrible disrepair, and there were at least two servants. This was a consolation. If he had truly destroyed the man's fortune, such a thing would not be possible. He would still give the money back, but he was relieved that Barnsby had not suffered great want in the months since.

"Follow me, sir."

The servant moved forward, and John fell in behind him until he was shown into a study. Inside, Barnsby was standing next to his desk, and he looked up when John stepped in. His mouth gaped open in shock.

"You!"

John sent an uneasy glance toward the servant, hoping he would not be thrown out before he had a chance to explain.

"The nature of my visit is not an unfriendly one, and I beg you will grant me five minutes of your time. If you are not satisfied, I will leave immediately."

Barnsby looked at him with hard eyes for a long moment, then nodded at his servant who withdrew quietly.

"You may sit," he said, curtly.

John took the seat across from him and swallowed, more nervous than he would like to admit. He had better just plunge right in since he had promised only five minutes.

"I have regretted the effects of our card game last autumn and that I allowed myself to win so much from you. It was beyond what is reasonable between any two gentlemen, especially two who are at least on nodding acquaintance." This statement was met with a fraught silence. And then—

"Go on," Barnsby said, but John heard a softening in his voice.

"I wish to make restitution. I understand that the money I won from you was necessary for the running of your estate, and that it left you in quite a precarious situation. I am prepared to return the sum in full."

A look of incredulity spread across Barnsby's face. "Wait right here." He got up and went to the door and called out for his servant. "Bring us a bottle of Burgundy."

He returned to his seat and clasped his hand around the armrest of his chair, looking John fully in the face.

"Let me understand this correctly. You wish to return the winnings of a game that you won fairly? For I, in any event, do not accuse you of cheating, though I heard rumors afterwards that some of society thought you did."

John gave a shake of his head. "I did not cheat. I was just extraordinarily lucky that night. And yes, I am ready to restore it to you. I am sure that you have heard, but my presence is no longer welcome in London society for other reasons, and I know a little of what it's like to be in a disagreeable position. Let us just say that I've come to my senses."

Barnsby shook his head in disbelief, but there was a gleam of something warm, like approval, in his eyes. And he even smiled when the servant came in bringing a bottle of Burgundy. He poured a glass for each of them, then raised his own.

"I never thought that I would wish to drink to your health, Aubin, but I do so now. It took courage and…nobility of mind to come here to speak with me, and I appreciate it."

Something eased inside of John, a tension he had been carrying for months without allowing himself to realize it was there. Despite the fact that he had lost all chances with Lady Geny—he had no hope that he would be given a second chance in her regard—at least he could make amends in other areas. They each drank, and Barnsby set down his glass.

"However, I will not take your money."

When John looked at him in surprise, Barnsby had a smile on his face that made him wonder why they were not better friends. There was an openness to him that John had not perceived before.

"You did win it fair and square. And Fortune has been kinder to me than I deserved, for a Miss Bradshaw, who is the lovely daughter of a local merchant and who comes with a handsome dowry, has consented to be my wife." His smile turned wry, almost wistful. "I consider the loss of my fortune to be a painful, but fair, price to pay for having learned a very good lesson. I am now ready to care for my wife and the fortune she brings into our marriage without any foolish conduct that might lose her respect."

John took in this most surprising turn of events. Of all the things he had thought might happen, it had not occurred to him that Barnsby would refuse his offer. But perhaps that had been an insult to Barnsby, for he was a gentleman and had lost the game fairly.

John returned his smile. "Well then, allow me to drink to your health—and to that of your future wife."

They drank once again, and he set his glass down. "That will be enough for me. I have been abstaining as of late."

Barnsby laughed. "Funnily enough, so have I. Let us just say that we have both come to our senses? But"—he stopped with a look of confusion—"what are you doing here? Did you come all this way just to see me?"

"I am visiting my brother in Mossley, not far from here." With the novel sensation of relief that came from having unburdened himself on one matter, he decided to invite Barnsby into his confidence on the other. "Had you heard of Lord Goodwin's accusation which eventually had me cut from society?"

"I am sorry to say that I did and was glad of it at the time."

John dipped his chin. He could understand why. "To be perfectly frank, I'm still not satisfied that Lord Goodwin is innocent in his own conduct. Aside from visiting my brother, I have an address for a mill in Ancoats that he is supposedly building with money from investors. I want to see if the mill exists; that is the other purpose of my visit."

Barnsby startled John by laughing at some joke he, alone, seemed privy too.

"Well, isn't this a small world? I am about to do you a good turn, Aubin. Miss Bradshaw's father is in the textile business and has a mill not far from Ancoats. He knows everything that happens in the industry and will surely know everything there is to know about this. If you'd like, I'll give you a letter of introduction from me."

Surprise almost stole John's speech, but he managed a nod. "I would like that very much."

He was still marveling over the amazing stroke of luck as Barnsby went over to his desk to write the letter, then sealed it. John thanked him and took the letter as they both walked over to the door and stood in the entryway.

"I do not know that I will be spending much time in London, but if I do come, let us keep in touch." Barnsby reached out to shake John's hand.

"It would be my honor," he replied, clasping his hand in return. He left the house feeling considerably lighter than when he arrived.

It was only natural that John first go to his brother's house, because it was too late in the day to visit the mill, and his brother was not far. A short while later, he drove up to the house, wondering what his brother's reaction would be. He knocked on the door, and Gregory answered it.

"John!"

Greg immediately threw his arms around him, and John felt an unmanly prick of tears in his eyes at the brotherly welcome. It was precisely what he needed. If his brother saw the tears, he was too kind to mention it, but he smiled and clapped him on the back.

"Anne," he called out. "Have the servants prepare a fine feast. The prodigal son has come home." He laughed at his own joke.

Greg's words, lightly spoken, caused John to be seized again with guilt. "Actually, you are not far from the truth. Perhaps we might have a private conversation after dinner?"

His brother sobered as he studied him, then he nodded. "Yes, we will. But first, let us eat."

Anne came bustling into the room at that moment and

threw her arms around John without ceremony. He had always liked her, although they had not had many chances to know each other.

"Welcome." Her eyes gleamed with kindness. "I will have the best bedchamber prepared for you."

The dinner was a comfortable one, and John's spirits lifted in a way they had not in a long time, surrounded by familial affection. Gregory and Anne spoke to each other in an easy, loving manner, and they made him feel included in the little family unit they had built together. He was fortunate to be surrounded by such warmth—something he knew Lady Geny did not have. This reminder saddened him almost as much as losing her, for it was too late to invite her into his own family circle.

At the end of the meal, Anne smiled at them. "Well, gentlemen, I will leave you to your port."

Gregory glanced at him and said, "What do you say we take tea in the library instead?"

"Much better," John agreed.

They settled in as Anne bustled about to bring the tea herself, then left them alone. The minutes of silence that followed seemed awkward. It was difficult to begin, but John knew it was necessary to have everything out.

"I came to tell you of all the ways I am not worthy to be your brother." He had meant it as something of a joke, but those tears rose again.

"A dramatic opening," his brother replied. "Proceed." His eyes held a glint of his usual humor, but his compassion was unmistakable. He was well-suited for his role as rector.

John proceeded to tell Greg everything—his manner of living with women and drink, the gambling and how he had foolishly spent everything of his mother's inheritance, his guilt over not visiting his stepfather when he was still alive—how unworthy he was to be the one inheriting the Westerly estate. He then went on to recount all that had happened with Lord

Goodwin and how it led to his downfall in society, and then to his eventual position in the asylum with a plan to carry out his revenge.

Greg had listened quietly throughout, but at this he held up a hand. "Revenge is generally a terrible method for anyone attempting to secure his own happiness."

"I believe you are correct, for my plans for a full reckoning came back to bite me."

He explained how he had fallen in love with Lady Geny and how he had destroyed her confidence in him by lying about who he was and his purpose at the asylum. And he sealed his infamy by kissing her when he was not in a position to offer for her. He finished his confession with the argument they had had right before she ordered him to leave the orphanage. When he finished speaking, silence fell once again.

"Do you think you still have a chance with Lady Geny?" his brother asked.

John shook his head. The angry, resolute expression on her face was etched on his mind. He stood no chance of winning her back.

"I am sorry," Greg said. He poured another cup of tea for them both, and they drank it.

"I did come north with another purpose, although it was secondary to visiting you," John said.

"Flatterer."

John returned a weak smile. "I plan to go to Ancoats since it is nearby. I have the directions of the mill the earl is supposedly building with investors' money, even redirecting some of it away from the asylum. However, I received a correspondence that states the contrary—that the money has all but stopped coming in. I want to see it for myself."

"More thoughts of revenge?" Greg asked gently.

At this, John paused to consider his motives first before shaking his head.

"No. I just want to know. I will leave thoughts of revenge to someone else who has actually invested in the earl's project. I do not want Lord Goodwin to fall at my hands. I won't cause Geny that pain."

Greg reached over and patted John on the shoulder. "You are learning, young one."

Chapter Twenty-Two

The next morning, John set out in his brother's curricle, promising to return in time for dinner. He hesitated on what the best course of action should be but ended up deciding to go first to look at the site where the mill was being built and see what he could from the outside. Since he would not likely have a chance to visit the inside, there was not much else he could do there. Then, he would go on to visit Mr. Bradshaw with the letter of introduction that Barnsby had given him.

When he arrived at the site of the mill, he was able to confirm that what the manager had written was true. The foundation was built as far as the ground floor, but nothing further. He could see the empty interior through the windows and had a view of the canal beyond it. He didn't bother to stop to investigate, but rode farther along to where housing was meant to be built for the workers and their families. This was nothing more than a pile of bricks. John clucked his tongue. There was not much he could do with the information, but at least he had confirmed it with his own eyes.

From there, he rode to Mr. Bradshaw's mill where the flurry of activity distinguished it from the ghostlike structure he had just left. He inquired within whether he might see the owner and handed the letter of introduction to the foreman.

A few minutes later, Mr. Bradshaw himself hurried down the stairs with a broad smile and came over to greet him.

"Come with me, Mr. Aubin. You shouldn't be left standing down here with this loud racket."

He had spoken true. The machines made a loud noise, and there were wafts of cotton floating through the air. Mr. Bradshaw led the way upstairs into his office and shut the door, which partially muted the sounds.

"May I offer you something to drink?" he asked, gesturing for John to be seated.

John shook his head. "I do not wish to take up too much of your precious time. I've come to inquire about the mill that is being built in Ancoats near the canal. Would you be willing to tell me what you know of it?"

Mr. Bradshaw leaned back, his expression grim, although John could tell it was not directed toward himself.

"The investor is some earl or other, but I do not know who he is. For some reason, the information has been something of a closely guarded secret. Now I'm beginning to think I know why. There has scarcely been any work done in the last three months, and it makes me wonder where the money is going that was destined for this project."

John nodded, unsurprised. "I am somewhat interested in this venture, but I am reluctant to spread about too broadly why that is. I hope you will forgive my lack of forthrightness. Would you be able to tell me where to find the mill's manager? Or the one handling the construction? I would like to speak to him."

"Of course. If you are able to do something to get this project moving forward, I would be much obliged to you. You may think that we are in competition with one another, but it is actually to my interest that Ancoats has a reputation for stability."

At John's inquisitive look, he explained, "We are more likely to receive and retain the skilled laborers that way. It does nothing for me to have an abandoned project sitting on the edge of town, and a bunch of workers who have grown sick of waiting and seek to move elsewhere."

"I understand," John said.

"You will find Mr. Gover's house by the canal to the left of the mill. It is not far. Follow the path along the canal maybe an eighth of a mile, and you will find it. Although, you might first try looking inside the mill itself by going around it to the back entrance. There is a public path on the other side bordering the canal, and the entrance is open there much of the time. It would not surprise me if Mr. Gover were trying to get something done even without the funds."

"I am much obliged to you for the information." John got to his feet. "And please allow me to congratulate you on your daughter's upcoming marriage. Mr. Barnsby is a fine man. And he considers himself lucky to have secured the hand of Miss Bradshaw."

Mr. Bradshaw beamed with satisfaction. "I could not ask for a better son-in-law myself. Let me show you out, Mr. Aubin."

John turned his brother's curricle back toward the mill, cognizant of how fortunate he was to have been given this introduction to Mr. Bradshaw. He had no possibility of using what he learned against Lord Goodwin, even if that had still been his intention. But he wished to find out just what the earl had done with his supposed investments.

He unhitched his horse and led him around to the canal to allow him to drink, then tied him to the post in front. Instead of following the path toward Mr. Gover's house, he decided to take

Mr. Bradshaw's advice and see if he could be found inside the mill. He wasn't sure exactly what questions he was going to ask the manager, but any information he gleaned might prove helpful. Upon rounding the corner of the mill, he spied a figure that caused him to stop in his tracks. It was the earl.

Lord Goodwin turned at the sound of John's footsteps, and as soon as he saw him, his face flushed in anger.

"Get off of my property, Aubin."

A head popped out of the opening, before the man came fully into view and stepped behind the earl.

"I am on the public path that borders the canal," John said with a confidence he was far from feeling. "I am not on your property."

"What do you think you are doing here?" The earl seemed uncharacteristically nervous, John thought, and was covering it with a sort of bravado.

John took a moment to allow his gaze to roam over the entire structure before answering. "I am not here to expose you, if that is what you are wondering."

"Good. For you would catch cold at it. I am glad to hear you've learned your lesson."

Indignant at the earl's condescension, John brought his gaze back to him. "It is for your daughter's sake that I will not expose you—not for your own."

Lord Goodwin looked startled and paused before asking, "What does my daughter have to do with anything?"

"I love her. I wish to protect her," John said simply. "For that reason, I will not sully your reputation. I came for my own satisfaction—to see if the rumors I had heard were true, and I see that they are."

The earl looked as though he wished to say something about John's mention of Lady Geny, but he refrained, and instead chose a different tactic.

"You know nothing about what I am doing here."

"I know that you have promised to build a mill and housing for workers, and that you have taken investments from peers and other gentlemen of standing to do it. I also know the work is not progressing as it should, and it causes one to wonder what precisely you are doing with the investments."

Lord Goodwin swiveled to stare at the man standing behind him, and he gave a gesture of dismissal. "Leave us, Gover."

The man folded his arms. "If it's all the same to you, I think I will stay right here."

The earl pulled himself into a haughty posture as he turned back to John.

"I am simply increasing the donations I've received, so that they will become more lucrative. They are set to triple what they currently are, and then we will finish the mill and the housing, return the donations to the asylum, and have money left over to encourage the investors to keep giving."

He glanced at the man standing behind him again and then back at John. "By investing in revolutionary bonds, we also open up trade routes to get cotton and dyes that will be used in the mill, which will benefit the laborers, for there will be more work for them. You should steer clear of matters you do not understand."

John listened, astonished at the earl's selfishness. It was evident he thought he was doing a good thing.

"Is that what you did with the foundling asylum? Did you take the donations meant to go there and attempt to increase them by diverting them to other projects? The asylum has not even enough funds to pay for the broken wall in the stable."

At this Lord Goodwin looked self-conscious, John thought, before he deflected. "My investments are none of your business. The other investors have been perfectly happy thus far."

"Maybe it is because they do not know what you are risking with their money," John said looking around critically at the unfinished construction before turning his gaze back to the earl.

Nothing more could be done, and it was time for him to take his leave, but he would have the satisfaction of telling the earl precisely what he thought before he did so.

"As I said, it is not my intention to expose you. But I give leave to tell you that I don't think your method of using investments entrusted to you by peers and friends for purposes other than that which you have indicated is the act of a gentleman. That is all, sir."

Lord Goodwin's eyes flashed as John turned to leave. The earl called out, "Stay away from my daughter."

John kept going as though he had not heard it. He would obey the earl's order, no matter how little he liked it. He would have to, because he was certain Lady Geny would never want to see him again.

He remained two days more at his brother's house, sharing more aspects of his life. It was as though now that he had decided to be open with his brother, he wanted to leave not even the smallest detail hidden. They discussed his plans for the estate, and he asked Greg whether he thought their father would approve of certain changes he planned on making. In an effort to be more communicative, he told his brother he would go back to London to visit his club before likely settling down permanently on the estate.

When it was time to leave, Greg walked outside with him as the groom led his horse and carriage around to the front.

"Feel any better than when you first arrived?"

John considered the question. He did feel better. It had been a relieving thing to express everything he had been holding back—to no longer have secrets he feared would cause his brother to lose his good opinion of him. He had said everything, and his brother loved him the same.

He nodded.

"Good." Greg slapped a hand on his shoulder. "Now use this

reprieve to your advantage and go on acting honorably. Or, as our Lord would say, 'Go forth and sin no more.'"

In the past, John had always derided his brother for his pious words, but this time he felt the truth of them in his core. He did not want to lose the freedom he had been given by having been open and would strive to continue on a more virtuous path.

Chapter Twenty-Three

It was odd, Geny thought, this period of mourning she was in. She knew what grief was, having mourned the loss of her mother for a lengthy stretch of time, longer than any formal observances called for. When one has gone through such a trial, one understood that only time would bring relief. Only the passage of time would allow one to smile again, or to appreciate all of the bright things life had to offer. Things that tempted a person to wish to remain on this side of the living. Now, here she was mourning again, but this time it was grieving the death of a relationship she had hoped to see blossom and flourish, one that would endure for the rest of her life.

The only thing different in this, she noted, was that in mourning the death of a relationship, it was impossible to lay the hope to rest. It added an additional layer of suffering because one could not tamp down the longing for what might have been—the wistfulness. Such a thing was absent in the finality of a physical death, for there, hope and longing were buried along with the loved one. But this purposeful burying of hope by heeding her mind and ignoring her heart was hard to endure. She quite thought its effects would be felt for a long time.

Geny went to the orphanage every day now, explaining to a confused Gabriel and Timothy that the steward had had urgent family business to attend to that would prevent him from returning. She could not bear for John's name to be tainted in their eyes in any way, even though she should not have cared about his good name at all. She wrote to Mr. Peyton to ask that another steward be found, stating the same reasons.

Mr. Dowling's bruise around his eye had begun to heal, and if there was any benefit to all that had happened with John, it was that Mr. Dowling now sought to avoid her at all costs. She was unsurprised when, after a week of his skirting her presence, a letter of resignation was left for her on her desk. Mr. Dowling did not return. Of course that meant there were now two positions to fill, and this gave Geny something to occupy her mind, as she and Mrs. Hastings sought to keep a steady routine in place for the orphans.

Her father came home one day earlier than expected and, rather than waiting until chance put them together, he sent word through the servants that he wished to see her.

It was an odd feeling, for she could no longer idolize her father in the same way she once did. She still loved him, she supposed. After all, he was her father. But she was deeply disappointed and hurt on her mother's behalf; and as far as his worldly reputation was concerned, all respect for who he was had evaporated.

If only he had not set himself up to be so pious, to have her then discover he cheated his friends and cheated on his wife, likely killing her in the process from an overmastering grief. Geny couldn't help but look differently upon Gabriel now, knowing what she knew. But she decided it was not her place to tell him who his father was. She would disclose it to neither Gabriel nor Matthew, but it made her determined to see Gabriel settled and in a good position. He was, after all, her half brother, even though he was not her mother's son.

She appeared in her father's study, from all outward appearances calm and collected. She assumed he wished to speak to her once again about having breached his space. He had been right in his rebuke, but the information that she had learned during her trespass left Geny with an ambivalent attitude. She no longer longed for his approval.

"How do you know Mr. Aubin?" Her father was standing by his desk, his expression unusually severe.

This was the one question she had not expected, and it left her feeling exposed. "Why, I knew Mr. Aubin at the orphanage. He was acting as steward there."

"The steward hired for the foundling asylum was a man by the name of Mr. Rowles. I specifically remember Mr. Peyton informing me of that."

Geny lifted her chin. "That was the name of his birth father. Aubin is the name of his stepfather who adopted him. His purpose there was to look for ways to expose you, Father. He wished to regain the reputation he lost when you had him shunned from society."

"And I suppose you support him in that endeavor?" her father asked severely.

"Of course I do not. He and I are no longer in contact. Once I found out he was there under an assumed name, I told him to leave. However, while he was there, we worked together for the good of the orphans and became friends."

"Friends?" her father said with heavy irony. "He announced that he loves you. You must have been more than friends."

It was as though a sudden roaring in Geny's ears prevented her father's words from reaching her right away. When they did, she felt as though the blood had drained out of her upper body and pooled at her feet, all while her heart soared through her chest. Her words could only come out in a whisper.

"When did he tell you that? When did you see him?"

Her father looked down at his desk and closed the open ledger with an audible *thump*, revealing a glimpse of his anger.

"He had the audacity to come to the mill that I'm building in Manchester. I saw him there. You may be sure that I gave him orders to stay away from you."

"Father, while I do not support his having deceived me, or his efforts to expose you, any decision of whom I see or whom I marry is entirely up to me. I am of age."

"You had better rid yourself of that modern notion," her father snapped, all vestige of control gone. She was seeing him thus for the first time. "You will have nothing from me if you marry him—and what is worse, you will not see Matthew again."

Geny didn't care about her financial prosperity, but she did care about Matthew, and she did not doubt that her father would put his threat into action. Any hope that had arisen in learning that John loved her dissipated with the threat of losing Matthew, and in its place—bleakness. The silence between them grew loud.

Until she rebelled. *No!* She would not allow her father to blackmail her.

"You have deceived my mother and have very likely deceived investors. You have all the appearance of goodness, and yet your actions speak otherwise." Geny paused only to catch her breath. "But even if that is so, I do not believe you would do this to me or to Matthew. I do not believe you would sink so low as to tear apart a brother and sister who share not only blood ties, but also those of affection."

She turned on her heels and left her father's office without waiting for his reply.

Geny and her father did not see each other again that week, except for a brief encounter one morning when they both started toward the breakfast room at the same time. She turned and went back to her room. Charity informed her soon afterward that the earl had gone to his club, taking his valet with him. Despite that the house would once again be silent, it would be better than walking on tenterhooks.

Margery had been coming more often to see how she was faring, even if it meant she had little time to dress for her evenings out with her mother, and now Mr. Thompson. This time she threw down her bonnet and sat beside Geny on the sofa, scarcely waiting until the butler left the room. Her expression was filled with concern.

"I came to find out if you have heard the news. I am afraid you might not have, since you've been keeping to your house."

"What news?" Geny knew Margery enough to know she would not bring her some ordinary gossip, for she understood that Geny was not interested in such things. This must be something else.

"Your father has been ruined by scandal." Margery's eyes were worried. She reached out for Geny's hand. "He is being talked about in all the circles. I am sorry. I only know this because Mr. Thompson told me. He knows how important you are to me, and you may trust that it was with great reluctance that he shared the news with me."

Geny had only thought about her father's iniquity in terms of how it affected their family—her mother. But now, it seemed the whole world must know about it. She sat, frozen in place.

John must have had his way, then. He must have discovered evidence that was damning enough to expose my father. Despite the cold relationship she had had with her father lately, she did not wish him ill. And she wished to break down in tears at the idea that John had been the author of such revenge. He had told her father he loved her, but it must not have meant enough.

"What have you heard? What has transpired?" she asked as soon as she found her voice.

"It was the Duke of Rigsby who exposed him. I don't know

who told him, but he discovered that your father had been encouraging his son to invest in one of his schemes, only to find out that the money had been misappropriated. Mr. Thompson heard that the duke's public rebuke caused the earl to leave White's in a cloud of shame."

"Oh, heavens." Geny sank her face into her hands, a little sorry for her father but trembling with relief that it had not been John who had exposed him. Then she remembered her brother who was his heir and looked up again. "I only hope this does not affect Matthew at school. Boys can be cruel."

"I hope so indeed." Margery was quiet for a moment, then hugged her. "The sins of the father should not be brought upon the son, but sometimes it is unavoidable. And Matthew is such a pure-hearted child, I am sure he will rise above any gossip, especially with a sister who has so much integrity."

Geny did not answer—she could not. It seemed nothing in her life could possibly be any bleaker, and she was grateful to have at least one true friend.

An unusually long silence settled between them—longer than ever occurred when they were together. After a while, Margery started wiggling her foot in its slipper, a sign that she had something else to say.

"What is it?" Geny asked. She needed the distraction, and it surely could not be anything worse than what she had heard so far.

"Mr. Thompson said that Mr. Aubin has returned to London. He ran into him by chance."

Geny looked at her in surprise, irritated at the darts of happiness that poked at her from the news. "Where did they meet?"

"On St. James's Street. Apparently there is a club there by the name of Blackstone's." Margery had a gleam of humor in her eyes, adding, "Mr. Thompson learned that it is a club for members who have been blackballed from the other more prestigious ones."

"Such a club exists?" Geny asked. "I have never heard of it."

"I imagine it is not the sort of thing that its members spread about. Anyway, Mr. Thompson saw him about to enter, and because they recognized each other, they stopped to exchange civilities. I think…I think Mr. Thompson greeted him first, because he knows of his connection with the asylum—and you."

She glanced at Geny as though wishing to reassure her. "Of course he was ever so discreet, so you needn't worry that he would say anything of a confidential nature. Anyway, Mr. Aubin said that he had just returned to London the day before and was renting a room in the club, for he would not be staying in London for long. Then they bid farewell. Mr. Thompson said it was the extent of their conversation."

Geny pondered this for a moment, then slid her hand over to clasp Margery's. "John had traveled north. I know this only because he went to visit the mill that my father is having built, and they met there, also by chance. That is how he learned that Mr. Aubin and I are acquainted." She knew that she was using John's Christian and family name interchangeably, which she did even in her mind, depending on how angry or nostalgic she was feeling. She supposed it revealed like nothing else the changing nature of their relationship.

"And what did your father say of the meeting?" Margery eyed her intently. Geny felt it and lifted her eyes to meet her gaze.

"Father told me that Mr. Aubin said that he loved me."

It seemed impossible to move after confessing out loud the very thing that had spun around in her mind over and over. If she'd had any pride, she should be hurt and disgusted and wish for nothing to do with him—not when he had been deceitful with her. Not when he had kissed her without being in a position to offer for her. Yet the fact that he had boldly declared his feelings to her father seemed to make those earlier sins diminish, as though they were nothing. And she could not deny that she still loved him back. She bit her lip, musing over how hopeless it all was.

Margery drew a deep breath and sat upright. "I fear I am about to be a bit managing and tell you what to do."

Geny looked at her expectantly. For once it would be nice if someone did that—especially if it brought her to a happy ending.

"Mr. Aubin will never seek you out after you have specifically told him that you did not wish to see him again. But I am not so sure you should give up so easily, for I know your heart is already lost to him. What we must do is have my Mr. Thompson send him an invitation requesting that they meet on a matter of importance." She sent Geny a bracing look. "And you must be there when he comes. Then, if your relationship is meant to be, it is meant to be."

Geny felt as though her pride should dictate an absolute refusal. At the very least, she should give it long and hard consideration before capitulating. After all, he had behaved abominably toward her, and she should categorically refuse to see him.

But she could not. Not when she so desperately wanted to see him. Not when it felt a little bit like a resurrection.

Chapter Twenty-Four

John headed back toward his rented room in Blackstone's that afternoon, after having paid a necessary trip to his counting house. He was steps away from it when he felt someone bump into him from behind. He turned, angry at the gesture, only to pull back in surprise. It was Lord Stuart, his friend from those earlier days in society—the one who had been with him when he won the card game against Barnsby.

"Is this where you've been all this time?" Lord Stuart asked, wearing his usual sardonic smile.

John was confused by the greeting and that Stuart was addressing him at all. He responded stiffly, "I am surprised that you stopped to greet me."

"If you are, it shows how little well you know me." At John's baffled expression, the look on Stuart's face grew exasperated. "I go to my hunting box for a few weeks and come back to find you cast out of society, with no one capable of telling me where you went."

It was true John had not divulged, even to his closest friends, that his brother had left an estate to him. He had always remained circumspect about his situation. His friends knew only that he had enough blunt to keep up with them, and that was all they cared about.

"After Theo and Fernsby gave me the cut, I could not help but draw the same conclusion about you."

Stuart lifted his eyes upward. "If all of our years together have not taught you not to lump me in with those fellows, then there is nothing more to be done with you."

He met John's look with a smile, then glanced behind him. "I am not so fickle a friend as to give you the cut direct without at least trying to hear what you have to say to the rumors made against you. I have not moved, so come see me when you have some time, will you?"

John finally emerged from his daze and reached out to shake Stuart's hand, amazed and touched that he, of all people, had remained loyal.

"I will. Thank you."

Stuart lifted a hand and waved as he turned back to where he had come from, and John entered the club with much to think about. He would never again judge a person without giving them a chance.

Blackstone's was bustling with life. It had been surprisingly easy to settle into the rhythm here, and although he had planned to stay for only a couple of days, he found himself in no hurry to rush off again. The room was comfortable, the dinner excellent, and he had even grown accustomed to the beady eyes at every turn from all the animals that had been frozen in time. He greeted two members in the hallway as he headed to the drawing room and there chose an empty seat.

Harry was shuffling a deck of cards, though he was not at a table where a game could be played.

"Aubin, you must be pleased about what happened to Lord Goodwin."

"What's that?" John turned to him in surprise. He hadn't

heard anything regarding the earl. At least nothing that had been reported in *The Gazette* yet. Not even Stuart had said anything, but perhaps he thought John knew.

"His Grace, the Duke of Rigsby let everyone know that the earl's investments for the asylum and for some mill up north were all a scam. Or rather, he said the project had begun, but he was instead pouring the investments into some risky revolutionary bonds in South America."

Harry looked around and saw that he had an audience. "Such a venture might have been lucrative—it has been in the United Provinces—except that the revolutionary army in Brazil suffered a defeat at the hands of the Spanish, which means he lost all of the funds. Everything." He folded his arms as a man satisfied. "Now the *beau monde* is furious, as you might imagine. He won't be able to show his face anywhere. News has it he's gone to his estate in Windsor."

John was silent, too surprised for words by the turn of the events.

"I suppose he'll be blackballed next. Think he'll become a member here?" That humorous remark was from Sebastian Drake.

John tried to follow, but it seemed his mind had turned sluggish. "How did the Duke of Rigsby find out about the bonds?"

Sir Humphrey was seated nearby reading, and he put down the newspaper to look over it. "From Lord Blackstone. I discovered the problem with the mill—as I said, I've been following Goodwin closely. Lord Blackstone learned of the revolutionary bonds, and he was the one who informed the duke of the connection between the two."

"I see."

John was glad of one thing. Other investors would no longer be so easily taken in. It was for this reason that it was best that Lord Goodwin's actions had been made public. But he mourned for Lady Geny. With her father in disgrace, how would she carry on? And what about her brother? John feared she would bury herself in loneliness in her London house, only going out to visit the orphanage. He pictured her growing more and more reclusive until the smile had left her face completely. This dismal image stole any satisfaction he might otherwise feel, and he was powerless to save her from it. Because of his deception, he had lost the right to love and protect her.

"A message has come for you, Aubin." Plockton entered the room carrying a silver platter with a sealed note on it. "'Twas delivered by messenger, and he's waiting for your answer."

John opened the letter and skimmed its contents, lifting a brow in surprise. The note was from Mr. Thompson, requesting John's presence to discuss a matter of some urgency. He was inviting him that very afternoon if he was available. John looked up at Plockton as though he might possess the answer to this mystery. What could be so urgent when they hardly knew each other and had seen each other the day before? He would accept the invitation, of course.

"Inform the messenger that I will be there in an hour or so."

Plockton went off to do his bidding. After a moment's reflection, John decided it must be related to the earl's disgrace, particularly since Mr. Thompson had donated money to the orphanage. Perhaps he wished to ask John how to retrieve his donation, thinking that he might have some advice since he used to work there. John wasn't sure he could satisfy him, but he would do his best.

An hour later, he stood outside a Palladian-style home, admiring how magnificent it was for a merchant who was still living as a bachelor. If he had thought about it at all, he had been expecting something much more modest.

The servant admitted him right away, saying he was expected. Without requiring John to wait, he led him to the drawing room and stepped back to allow John to enter. He did so as Mr. Thompson strode forward to shake his hand.

"Thank you for coming to meet me."

"It is nothing," John replied. He looked around the spacious drawing room with curiosity, noticing how tastefully it was decorated—again for the home of a bachelor. This appreciative regard came to a halt by the sudden appearance of Lady Geny rising from the sofa. The shock of seeing her there stunned him, then angered him. He turned his face to glare at Mr. Thompson before returning his gaze to her.

"My lady, I must ask what you are doing in the home of a man still living as a bachelor?" He couldn't keep the bitterness from his voice. Then the truth fell on him at once, and he took a step back, the air temporarily knocked from his lungs. "You have an understanding? Is that it?"

Movement from the right caught his eye, and he turned to it. Miss Buxton had been standing unnoticed by the window, and she now walked over to where he stood and curtsied.

"This is my home, Mr. Aubin—my parents' home—and you are most welcome to it. You could not know this, since we have not made it public, but Mr. Thompson and I are betrothed." She touched her fiancé on the arm. "And now, he and I have a few things to discuss for our wedding in a couple of months. If we are not needed, we will retire to the library."

Mr. Thompson looked at him ruefully. "Forgive me for the deceit. I trusted my fiancée that this meeting was what you would have wished for. I hope I was not wrong."

He bowed and followed Miss Buxton out of the drawing room, closing the door firmly behind them. John was rooted in place, frozen from what felt like a succession of shocking revelations, but this lasted mere seconds. He forced himself to go to Geny, unwilling to lose his chance to speak to her.

"I hardly know what to say." He allowed his eyes to drink in the sight of her but dared not touch her. "I did not expect to have the fortune of meeting you again."

She looked at him in silence, and he remembered the terrible image of loneliness he had envisioned just hours before of what her future would look like. This propelled him to speak.

"Please tell me. Your father…" He examined her face for signs of tears or pallor. Instead, he found only two bright spots of color on her cheeks. The sight somehow gave him courage. "How are you faring?"

She still did not speak, and her silence now brought John a new and alarming revelation, one he was eager to dispel.

"It was not done by my hand," he explained urgently, lifting both hands as though taking a double oath. "I was not the one to expose your father. I told him I would not do so when we met in Manchester."

"I know, John." Her gentle voice reached him and calmed the worst of his fears, especially when he heard her use his name. "My father informed me of having met you in Ancoats, and he told me that you confessed your feelings for me."

The swift change in topic and—it seemed—his fortunes caused John's throat to constrict, making it hard to bring air in. Dare he hope again?

"I did."

"This is why I wanted to meet. I knew that you would not disregard my order to stay away, so that if I wished to see you again, *I* had to be the one to arrange the meeting. Although"—she lifted her fingers to cool her cheeks—"it is so forward of me that I can scarcely bring myself to look at you."

This broke John out of his stupor.

"I am glad you did." He took the remaining two steps to her and grasped both of her hands. "I was resigning myself to a life of never seeing you again and was trying to learn how to live with it. I must tell you that never in all my days have I contemplated the future with such bleakness as I have in these past two weeks."

She tilted her face upward, her eyes searching his. "Nor I. Everything you said about my father was true. It did not take much to believe you, and once I did, I could not remain angry with you. I...I have missed you."

Though conscious of his unworthiness, John could not refrain from lifting her hands to his lips. He permitted himself this gesture of gratitude, of reverence, before releasing her hands and preparing himself for what he must say next. If he wanted to propose, he was honor bound to lay everything bare before her. Geny must know what bargain she was getting should she agree to become his wife. It was the weight of this confession that made it difficult to fully meet her gaze.

"You need to know what kind of man I am—what kind of man I've been. I spent eight years in London as the worst kind of rake and have nothing to show for my time there." He stopped, forcing air in his lungs, then rushed on before he lost the courage. "I lived a life of pleasure, heedless of anyone but myself. I ruined a man by winning his fortune in a card game—this you know—but in fact, there were many other card games where my own losses were great. I spent my time in the clubs, spending recklessly, drinking, women..."

John stopped, unable to say anything else or even to form a coherent ending to his confession. He burned with shame, waiting to hear what she would say. He waited like a man on the gallows. After a stretch of time that seemed like forever, he heard the question she asked in her quiet voice.

"Are you still that man today?"

"I am not." It required no time for reflection. "That man died with his reputation."

"Good." Her voice was light, and her tone sounded like a smile. It invited him to lift his eyes. "I am glad. For I quite like the man who stands before me now."

Her expression of grace made him want to deserve it. His heart pounded with a new hope.

"I was wrong to deceive you, Geny. I regret it, as I regret the liberties I took while engaged in my deceit. I can hardly believe my good fortune that you are willing to grant me an audience to tell you this, but I promise never to deceive you again, not as long as you will allow me to be a part of your life."

"I believe you," she said softly.

He reached out and gently took her elbow, pulling her closer, his eyes lovingly skimming every detail of her features from her soft blonde hair to her pale brow, her wide eyes to her stubborn dimpled chin, all while breathing in the comfort of her subtle scent... Everything about her left him feeling fresh and hopeful. It always had.

"If I were more of a gentleman"—his voice had gone gruff—"perhaps I would do the honorable thing and insist you forget about me, leaving you free to find a more worthy husband."

Her knit brows caused him to release her hands and lift his knuckles to graze the side of her cheek. "Unfortunately, I am only a man, and I am not strong enough to do that. Will you marry me, Geny?"

She nodded, her eyes bright, her lips pressed together in a smile as though she did not trust her voice to speak.

He could breathe again. John's smile spread. "Forgive me if my ego is too great, but is that a yes? May I hear it from your lips?"

She nodded in broad motions. "Yes," she said, her pressed lips spreading into a grin.

John gave an audible sigh of relief and reached his arms around her to pull her into a tight hug. Then, just as quickly, he pulled away again, dropping his arms to his side in consternation. Too late, he remembered his decision to be virtuous.

Geny looked up at him with bright eyes—trusting eyes—a look which turned to confusion when he continued to stand at a distance. When he saw that look, he wished to take her in his arms again to reassure her of his consuming love for her, but did not dare. She deserved only the best, most honorable treatment from him. The safest way to guarantee it was to keep his distance until they were married. But then, surely, he should act like a man betrothed and not like a mere stranger, shouldn't he?

To his growing dismay, he discovered that any useful skill he might once have possessed in the art of seduction—as well as any talent therein—had fled. Here he was betrothed, with the right at the very least to kiss his fiancée, but he dared not do it. He was not worthy of a woman of her virtue.

"Good," he said stupidly when the silence stretched.

Perhaps if he attempted a reformed lifestyle for a few months first, he might become worthy of being her husband.

Geny took a step back, studying him with surprise bordering on indignation. "Mr. Aubin, after you have shown me what satisfaction it is to be kissed by you, are you now going to deny me this after I have promised to become your wife?"

"No, no," he protested, the ridiculousness of the situation causing him to slap his hand to his head.

"No." He stepped forward again and this time put his arms around her. He looked into her eyes as he pulled her close again. "It is only that you are too good for me, and I didn't dare to take any liberties."

She shook her head at him, her mouth pursed in disapproval. "Do not say that. Our marriage will begin and remain on level ground. I sincerely hope that your stores of goodness will fill out my stores of want, and that my stores of goodness will fill out your stores of want. Is that not what such a sacred union is for?"

John needed only seconds to agree. "Why, so you are right, my sweet."

With such wise words coming from the lips of his betrothed, he was now determined she should not marry a fool. He bent down and kissed her, his lips settling warmly on hers, and his hands pulling her more closely into his embrace. All was just as it should be.

"You wished to be reminded of the satisfaction of being

kissed," he whispered, his lips scarcely leaving hers. "Something like this?"

After a few minutes during which she could only be measuring the level of satisfaction to determine whether she deemed it sufficient, she gave her reply, her lips scarcely leaving his.

"Yes, John. Exactly like this."

Epilogue

The wedding was held a month later in Geny's local parish at St George's, Hanover Square. She had spent three of those weeks at Margery's house, for with Matthew at school and her father at his estate, the pain and emptiness of her home was too great to bear. Naturally, her reputation suffered alongside her father's, but she did not care enough about society to allow this to worry her. Her main concern would continue to be for Matthew when it came time for him to join London society. John assured her that the *ton* would have forgotten all about it by then. There would always be newer, more interesting scandals to focus on.

She read the announcement of Lord Amherst's betrothal to Miss Lucy Purcell and was glad for them both. She even received a nod of acknowledgment when she saw Lucy at the Pantheon Bazaar, which served to raise her in Geny's esteem. As a future marchioness, and one day duchess, Lucy could easily have cut her but chose not to.

As for John, he had been readmitted to White's and Boodle's at the instigation of his friend, Lord Stuart. This development appeared to matter so little to John, she did not even learn of the fact from him but rather from Mr. Thompson, who somehow had no shortage of knowledge about what went on in society, despite not being part of it.

As Geny had only one father, she decided to allow him to continue to be a part of her life—with limits. Lord Goodwin was given a formal invitation to the wedding, although she had not known if he would attend it until he appeared inside the church. To her surprise and relief, he had not only come himself, but had even gone to fetch Matthew out of school so he might attend as well. Perhaps her words that she did not believe her father capable of such baseness as to hinder her relationship with a beloved brother had hit their mark?

In any case, although Geny was not ready to tell him—the occasion of her wedding not being the proper time to do so—she thought she could forgive her father for much, just for this one gesture of bringing Matthew to her.

Her gown was new, designed for the occasion, and it was in a pale rose silk with white flowers embroidered on the bustline and hem, and sewn into the scalloped capped sleeves. Margery had purchased, without her knowledge, a parcel of the white flowers and had waited in her classroom at the orphanage one day, a group of orphan girls gathered behind her. With bashful curtsies, they presented Geny with the string of silk flowers sewn into a ribbon for Charity to weave into her chignon on the occasion of her wedding. She wore it proudly.

John looked dashing in pantaloons, a light olive-green silk embroidered waistcoat, and a darker green coat worn over it. She met his stepbrother and wife after the ceremony, and was instantly drawn to both. This only added to the joy of their union, for she would be joining an affectionate family. She was eager to contribute her part.

Margery and Mr. Thompson were present, of course, and

after the ceremony her friend found a chance to lean in to whisper, "Do you see? You were married first, just as I always said you would be." Her eyes sparkled with humor.

John had told Geny, both the whole of that notorious card game he'd had with Mr. Barnsby, and also of their ensuing meeting. Mr. Barnsby had been invited to the wedding but had written to send his congratulations—and also his regrets. He was to be married on the same day. He invited John and his new wife to visit them in Cheadle anytime they wished.

There had been a brief period when she wished Gabriel could join the wedding, too, and attempted to think how she might do so without anyone perceiving it to be odd. But other than confirming John's suspicions to him that Gabriel was indeed her half brother, she decided that as long as her father was alive, she would leave it up to him to tell Gabriel the truth should he so choose. If he did not, she would tell the foundling herself—and Matthew—after their father was gone.

There were three members of Blackstone's at the ceremony, whose names she learned in a blur, and Lord Stuart had come as well. Mrs. Hastings was invited, along with Geny's quiet companion, Miss Edwards. Margery's parents, Mr. and Mrs. Buxton, completed the wedding party.

Although Geny understood that a large portion of their time must be spent on John's estate, she was touched to learn that he expected them to continue to be involved in the asylum. Her betrothed had also informed her that he had set by a sum to invest in the orphanage, and in particular to make sure the structure was sound and would not crumble in any other place. In time, they would approach the earl about handing the direction of the asylum entirely over to them.

It was John who informed her that the earl was making restitution for the money he'd stolen and was even finishing the construction of the Manchester mill out of his own pocket.

Lord Blackstone had made him privy to this news, since Lord Goodwin had not made it public. This meant that Matthew would have less than he otherwise might in terms of an inheritance, but Geny was relieved her father was doing the right thing before other members of society. This would also help Matthew's entrance into society when the time came.

For many years, her life had seemed to lack color, with everything blending into various shades of gray, although she did not realize it until she knew what a life of color looked like. Now she felt bathed in vibrant hues as one was bathed in sunlight. The clergyman declared them man and wife, and they walked hand in hand out into the world—amid cheers and under the flurry of rose petals that the guests threw.

The wedding breakfast was held at the Buxtons' house in Southwark, and John's carriage waited in the street to take them to it. They would have several hours celebrating with everyone, eating cake, and enjoying the company of those who held a special place in their lives, before they left for their honeymoon. Even her father had gone out of his way to be gracious to everyone present at the ceremony, no matter their station in life. Geny thought that perhaps his exposure and public chastisement had not harmed him, but rather had done him good.

John helped her into the carriage and shut the door behind him giving them a bubble of privacy. As the carriage moved forward, he put his arm around her, turning just enough so that he could see her fully. He looked at her for a long moment.

"How are you feeling, wife?" he asked.

She met his gaze, her heart brimming with every good and perfect thing. "I am not sure it is possible to feel happier than I do right now."

"It is possible," he argued, his smile removing any contention from the words. "Perhaps it won't be this overwhelming sense of happiness squeezed into the space of a couple of hours, but it will be the sort of happiness that fills days and weeks and years until it is so weighty and large it becomes impossible to define. This is the kind of happiness we will have."

"Is it?" she asked, smiling up at him.

"*Mm-hm.*" He leaned down to kiss her, then pulled back just enough to meet her gaze.

"I promise it. Word of a gentleman."

Bachelors of Blackstone's Series

A Bachelor's Lessons in Love by Sally Britton

A Trial of His Affections by Mindy Burbidge Strunk

A Gentleman's Reckoning by Jennie Goutet

To Hunt an Heiress by Martha Keyes

Love is for the Birds by Deborah M. Hathaway

Forever Engaged by Ashtyn Newbold

A Match of Misfortune by Jess Heileman

About the Author

Jennie Goutet is the best-selling author of twelve Regency romances, including the Clavering Chronicles, Memorable Proposals, and Daughters of the Gentry series. Her books have received first place in historical romance for the New England Reader's Choice Awards and have hit the number one spot in Regency Romance on Amazon. They have been featured on BookBub and Hoopla, and are translated into five languages.

Jennie is an American-born Anglophile who lives with her French husband and their three children in a small town outside of Paris. Her imagination resides in Regency England, where her proper Regency romances are set. You can learn more about Jennie's books and sign up for her newsletter on her author website: jenniegoutet.com or purchase her books at jenniegoutetbooks.com.

www.ingramcontent.com/pod-product-compliance
Lightning Source LLC
LaVergne TN
LVHW091146300126
830738LV00025B/244